THE HOUSE ON THE PUMPKIN FARM

Sarah Shadi

Copyright © 2022 Sarah Shadi

All rights reserved. No part of this book may be used or reproduced by any means, graphic, electronic, or mechanical, including photocopying, recording, taping, or by any information storage retrieval system, without the written permission of the publisher except in the case of brief quotations embodied in critical articles and reviews.

Dedicated to my wonderful husband,
my loving parents, and my nephews
Elias and Caspian.

TABLE OF CONTENTS

Chapter 1: Halloween Weekend 1

Chapter 2: The Pumpkin Farm 26

Chapter 3: Halloween Night 46

Chapter 4: Two Invisible Children 68

Chapter 5: The Castle 81

Chapter 6: The Emerald 98

Chapter 7: Falling Leaves 117

Chapter 8: The Forest Owl 135

Chapter 9: The Mission 150

Chapter 10: Surviving 168

Chapter 11: Running Away 185

Chapter 12: Fly, Lily! Fly! 204

Chapter 13: Brave 212

Chapter 14: The Elixir 226

Chapter 15: Falling Asleep 238

Chapter 16: The Note 250

Chapter 17: The Ray of Sunshine 266

Chapter 18: Mirrors 283

Chapter 19: Halloween Tradition 301

Chapter 1

HALLOWEEN WEEKEND

"One hundred pumpkins! I can't believe they've bought a *hundred* pumpkins for Halloween!" my mother said, astonished. "What on earth will they do with all those?"

She was looking out the window at my classmate Alice's mother directing two delivery men. The men's arms were laden with pumpkins which they carried into the house. They made so many trips back and forth, they could wear a groove in the driveway!

"What? *One hundred* pumpkins?" I replied in disbelief.

I stood on tiptoes to have a better view, peering over Mom's head as she peered too.

"Maybe they're having a Halloween party this weekend," my mother said, mumbling as she kept looking at the house opposite. She seemed oddly preoccupied with next door.

"Oh, I don't think Alice will have a party," I said with a hint of certainty that quickly turned into doubt. *Or will she?* I thought. Alice was never nice to me and some others in the school. Neither were her two friends, Juan and Ben. I tried to avoid them all.

"Alice would probably have invited you to her Halloween party if she was having one," my mother said and turned to me with a smile. Well, that showed how little *she* knew!

I doubted Alice would be inviting me anywhere at all unless she was seriously short on numbers for some reason. I smiled back, but slowly, I walked away from the window, leaving Mother to ponder on everything that was going on opposite.

Plus, I had to do some thinking...

I wonder what to do for Halloween? I thought. Staying home alone was depressing.

Alice had three siblings and two pet dogs, whereas I didn't have brothers or sisters, just living with my parents in a small house just opposite Alice's spacious, beautiful home with its immaculately manicured lawns and an array of expensive cars.

I didn't have any pets either as my dad had a severe fur allergy, so obviously, furry critters were a big no-no. No dog, no cat. No anything. Not even a tank of fish.

"Your father might be allergic to the water additives," announced Mom. So that was that.

It left me only with the option of buying some type of reptile or something—an insect, even. One of my schoolfriends had *Sammy the stick insect*. It freaked me out how that thing stared at me with its beady little eyes, spindly and knobby legs waving around. As for slimy and scaly beasts—no thanks. I decided not to have any pets, but still really wanted a dog.

"Have you done your homework, Lily?" my mother asked. Having parents who were both teachers made this sentence more common than I liked to hear. I secretly rolled my eyes.

"Think so," I replied, hoping that my mother would stop there. But I knew she probably wouldn't. That's how she was. A typical teacher, always moaning on.

"You *think so?* Let's try that again. How can you *think so?* You must know whether you've done it or not."

"Yes! Yes, I've done it. I'm sure," I replied.

"Why did you say, 'Think so' in that case?" my mother asked. And she was right.

"I'm *almost* sure," I replied, not knowing what else to say. "I mean, I did some of it. So, it's both yes and no."

"Lily, you need to be more serious about school," my mother explained with a hint of annoyance in her voice.

They often said that I was their miracle child. I still wished that I had at least a sister or a brother so that they could worry about someone else's homework and give me a break.

But once again, Mother was right.

My parents and I loved nature and really wanted to move to a house with a garden and trees. Maybe grow our own vegetables in a small plot. But we could never afford to buy or even rent a house like that. The problem would always be that the garden came with too small a house or the bigger houses with gardens were too expensive for my parents to afford.

Honestly, I felt disappointed not to own a pet or have a garden so I could watch the birds.

The thought of Alice and her mother buying around a hundred pumpkins perished in my mind quite quickly. Instead, I worried about lying to my mother about having done—or not done—my homework. I wasn't the worst student in my class, or the best, just kind of average. But for some strange reason, the teachers always seemed pick on me.

Every time they wanted to make a point, they targeted me yet again.

I didn't understand their need to choose me each time.

That was why I always handed in my homework when it was due. *No, that's not true. I hand it in on time, but always on the last day possible!*

So yes, on time, but only just.

***

I eventually arrived at the school gate about five minutes late, and everyone had already gone into the school. GONE! *Surely, I can't be late*, I thought, but Alice soon confirmed it.

"Lily! Quick! You're late *again!*" she shouted from the half-open classroom window and made the matter worse by notifying everyone in the classroom and beyond.

The kids all turned around and stared at me from the window. I could feel my cheeks turning red, burning, on fire. They'd be all blotchy, I knew it! Miss Eze's big brown eyes stared at me as she shook her head in disappointment. *Thanks, Alice.*

Hopefully, she won't make a big deal when I go in the classroom.

Luckily, I went in and Miss Eze ignored me as she rushed to start the lesson.

Being five minutes late wasn't too bad, I supposed. I had been late for over an hour once in the past. That was probably why Miss Eze didn't want to make a point of my lateness since she was tired of telling me to be punctual almost every week.

But even though I was late, five minutes didn't seem a big deal.

Once the lesson had finished, it was time for lunch.

"Hope we don't get more homework from Miss Eze. Especially not before Halloween," my friend Kate said as we walked down the corridor.

Kate was slightly taller than me, had a round face, dark blond hair, hazel eyes, and wore glasses. We became friends on the first day of school.

"Perhaps you're right, Kate. Maybe we can talk to her and see if we can do our homework next week instead? She might agree, and it's worth trying." I watched Kate looking inside her gray school bag, trying to fish up her lunchbox.

Kate was bothered by the fact that we had more homework despite Halloween coming up. I couldn't blame her. I felt the exact same way.

Alice, Juan and Ben were sitting at the only table in the canteen with two free seats and we didn't have any other choice than to join them. Ben gave us a funny look as soon as he saw us. He was the oldest and tallest of all in our class because he was born in January, and the few months difference was noticeable.

Ben wasn't as talkative as Juan. He had brown hair, blue eyes, and a face full of freckles.

"You're very excited about Halloween, aren't you?" Juan asked Alice as Kate and I sat down at the table. Juan had a long face, dark eyes, and thick, dark hair. Juan was athletic, playing basketball, tennis, and squash.

Alice smiled wide and nodded in response as she took a bite of her hamburger.

"Are you ready for your Halloween party, Alice?" Ben said and continued ignoring Kate and me, just like Alice and Juan had.

Is Alice having a Halloween party? I thought and listened carefully, awaiting Alice's response.

"Yes, I am. We should all be! The 31st of October falls on a Friday, which is the best day of the week, as we have no school the following day!" Alice's voice was full of excitement and pride. She used to always brag about her regular parties. Kate and I looked at each other, but we both remained silent.

We didn't have *any* plans for Halloween.

We had not been invited to any Halloween party, no matter how small.

"Hmm... I forgot to tell you two. We're going to have a Halloween party this year," Alice said and looked at me with a rather mean face.

"We?" I asked with great disappointment.

"I mean, me and... Juan... and Ben. I was going to tell you to join us, but decided not to invite you because we're not friends. I only want my friends to be there," Alice said as quickly as she possibly could.

Juan and Ben burst into laughter.

They must have seen how uncomfortable Kate and I looked.

"Why are you saying this? I mean, why are you telling us about your party, if we aren't invited?" I asked Alice.

Juan and Ben both stopped eating and looked at the two of us as if they were just about to witness a high-profile boxing match.

Juan attempted to smile, but it faded away quickly, and he said, "We weren't even part of the planning. Alice did everything."

Alice's face had turned bright red, not from shame, but fury; she looked at me with her round, piercing eyes.

"Anyway, I don't have time to explain... I'm too busy with my party," Alice said and turned toward Ben and Juan again, explaining how great her party was going to be.

I looked at Kate, and she shrugged before eating her lunch.

***

Right from the moment I sat at my desk, I couldn't wait for that wretched lesson to end!

Fortunately, it was my last class for the day.

"Can you please stop doing that? Lily, please stop tapping your pen on your desk," Miss Chow said while everyone in the classroom looked at me. "It's very distracting for everyone."

"Sorry, miss," I replied.

Miss Chow walked toward me and stopped in front of my desk. She was annoyed.

"Lily, can you explain what I just told you a few seconds ago?" she asked.

"I'm sorry. I don't know. I wasn't listening," I said automatically and continued tapping my pen.

Miss Chow looked surprised, and all my classmates burst into laughter.

I didn't try to upset Miss Chow on purpose, but this was just my honest answer. Didn't everyone always tell us kids to tell the truth?

"Put down your pen, now!" Miss Chow ordered like a seasoned military officer.

She continued looking annoyed, and I didn't know how to get away with what I'd just gotten myself into. I quickly did just as Miss Chow told me. She was not in a good mood and, of course, I hadn't paid any attention in class.

"Lily, please pay more attention next time. You all attend school to learn," Miss Chow said after pausing and taking several deep breaths. She finally walked away from my desk and continued with the lesson.

I needed to pay more attention. I knew that, of course, but paying attention was hard if you found the subjects incredibly dull! But if I didn't focus, I'd only get into trouble again.

The class came to an end a few minutes later, and I was glad it was finally over.

I just wasn't in the mood.

One more day of school, and it's the weekend! I thought.

Then it came back to me. I still didn't have any plans for the Halloween weekend, so what was there to look forward to?

I wasn't going to Alice's party, and didn't have any other invitations!

It was already Thursday; I had only one day left to figure out what to do!

Well, once again, I'd left it to the last minute.

***

Kate was waiting for me outside the school building.

"Hi," she said and walked up to me. But she must have felt the same way as I did, down, because we didn't have any Halloween party to go to.

"Hi, Kate," I replied at the school gate.

"I don't suppose *you* know of any Halloween party we can go to?" she asked.

"No. I don't. I really wish someone would invite me. I mean, *us.*"

"Come on, Lily! Surely there must be one we can attend! This is the first year that my parents have allowed me to go to one on my own, as well," Kate said, and I could hear that she wanted to go. "We should try and find somewhere for both of us."

"Kate, I don't think there *are* any other Halloween parties. Just Alice's. And as we both heard, we aren't invited to that one!" I replied despite hating to rain on Kate's parade. "Besides, let's say we do find one. If they haven't invited *one* of us, they'll hardly want us both, will they?"

She surely wasn't thinking. It was what my mother called *having no common sense.* But I mean, to me, it was obvious! If you want someone at your party, you invite them. If you don't invite them, it's most probably because you don't like them and don't want them!

"What are you going to do on Halloween?" Kate asked.

"Don't know," I said and thought of all the possible things that I could do over the weekend—visiting my grandparents? Walking my mother's friend's dog? Watching a movie with my parents? No. I didn't want to do any of those things, especially on Halloween weekend. Now, I noticed Alice and her friends walking toward us.

"Your Halloween party is going to be amazing, Alice!" Juan said as he passed us by with the rest of them annoyingly. He was definitely speaking extra loud just for our benefit.

Both Kate and I frowned as we stood still to let them pass.

"It's going to be epic! We've ordered so many pumpkins too," Alice said aloud as she turned her head and looked at us before whispering with her two friends.

"That's *so* irritating, Lily," Kate said and continued, "I wish we also had a party of our own, even if it was just a small one!"

"It doesn't matter. Everyone in school's probably going to join Alice's party anyway. No one would bother to come to ours," I replied. "No point inviting people if they won't come."

"Suppose you're right. I'm heading home. See you tomorrow!" Kate said and left.

"See you, Kate," I said and waved goodbye.

Halloween had always been my favorite holiday, and now I'd have to wait yet another year to enjoy one with a party. It didn't seem like it should be too much to ask for an awesome, spooky Halloween weekend! The SCARIEST HALLOWEEN WEEKEND EVER! Full of excitement and surprises!

The big question was, how would it be possible?

When I arrived home, my mother was outside our house, busy fixing her car.

"Hi, darling. How was school?" she said without looking at me. My mother always recognized the sound of my footsteps.

"Hi, Mum, school was OK. But I have to figure out what to do this weekend," I answered and she finally looked up from the hood of the car.

"Why?" she said with great curiosity.

"Because mean Alice planned a Halloween party and for some reason, excluded Kate and me," I said bitterly.

Mother wore her thick glasses and walked toward me with a cloth in her hand, wiping her hands. "Oh, I'm sure she must just have forgotten," she said as she peered through her spectacles with their massive rims. They made her look like an owl, though I never told her.

"No, she actually said we were not invited!" I replied. "Because she doesn't like us. or something like that. Well, because we aren't friends."

"Well, are Ben and Juan going to it?" my mother asked.

"Of course, they are! They're her closest friends," I said as we went into our house. My mother didn't know what to say. Kids and their 'friendship issues' must have seemed like a daunting and complex subject. It seemed she didn't have any advice.

"Aren't you going to fix the car?" I asked because I knew my mother just about never gave up on a project she starts.

"Why do you think I decided to come inside, darling? It's already done," my mother replied and laughed. "Oh well, dear. It's not nice to be excluded, but it's also not a big deal," my mother said as we sat down on the sofa in our living room. "It's their loss, Lily."

I nodded in response. Yes, their loss. Though I wasn't sure what exactly they were losing!

Sure, we were *nice* company but then, Alice knew loads of other kids who were 'nice' too. And they were all going to the Halloween party. But soon, I could put all that to one side because my father arrived home with two big black bags.

"Now then! I bet you can't guess what I've got in here!" he said as he placed the bags down on the long wooden table.

"Hi, Dad. What's in those bags?" I asked. "They look interesting."

"I just asked you to guess! But…" He seemed excited and couldn't wait to tell us anyway. "I was sorting through things in the basement and picked up my old photo albums and some old belongings. I'm going to keep some upstairs in the loft, but I'm going to sell most of it and donate the money to charity," he explained enthusiastically.

"Can I have a look and see if there's anything I'd like to keep?" I asked, knowing Dad had always been adventurous and he'd collected lots of exciting things on his travels.

He'd climbed mountains, gone on safari in Africa, seen the pyramids of Egypt, walked on the Great Wall of China, and been to the Amazon rainforest.

My mother, of course, had also joined him on some of his adventures.

"Yes, you can have a look, but I'm not sure if any of my old stuff will be any use to you," he said with a big smile that revealed his teeth.

"I don't need it to be useful," I enthused. "But I bet there's some fascinating stuff."

My father was almost always optimistic and tended to get excited over the smallest of things. He really appreciated everything he had in life, regardless of value and size. And because of this, it was typical of him to want to put it to use and give his 'earnings' to charity.

"Come on then, Lily! Let's go upstairs and empty the bags. You can see if there's anything you'd like to keep," he said and walked ahead carrying the bags. He was much taller than me and could take bigger steps, so I had to rush behind him to catch up.

We climbed into the loft up the rickety pull-down ladder and my father placed both bags next to the big window. From all the way up there, I could still see Alice's house across the street from our two-floor, garden-less and pet-free home. It looked so... posh!

It must be amazing having a garden like Alice's. She can plant anything she likes and she can have all her birthday parties outside because her birthday's in summer. And I bet her Halloween party will be in that lovely big garden this weekend, I thought.

"Dad, why can't we move to a house with a garden?" I asked, but already knew the answer. My father scratched his head, raised his eyebrows, and looked at me in a way that I knew my question had surprised him.

"Well, the truth is that we can't afford to move to a house with a garden, sweetheart. At least not for a long while. There's a chance that we'll be able to move in a couple of years but not this year," my father replied. "Unless we find something worth a million dollars up here!"

He laughed loudly and I joined in. "If we find anything like that, it's mine!" I said.

But even though my father was laughing and good-humored, I could see I'd asked the wrong question. He looked wistful and sad, and maybe even as though he was letting me down. *Stupid, stupid, stupid Lily. Why ask such a dumb question?* I chastised myself.

I looked down at the floor. I shouldn't have mentioned that I wanted a house with a garden; I already knew that my parents had financial difficulties.

They didn't need any more pressures in their already hard life.

I had a great relationship with both my parents. They had always treated me like an adult and told me the truth about almost everything without sugar-coating it. They did it even to the point of discussing their financial difficulties, and here I was, demanding more.

"OK," I said and unzipped one of the bags. And it really was OK. They tried their very best.

The bag was full. Everything from old books, pictures, and postcards fell out once it was open. One of the postcards caught my attention in particular: two little girls were smiling and looking at the camera as they sat on a massive orange pumpkin, so large that it had room for them both. A big farm was visible in the background, with a house on the top left corner of the postcard. I turned it over and read the handwritten text:

Happy Halloween! With love, Poppy and Charlotte.

"Who are these two little girls?" I asked my father.

He took out his glasses from his pocket and frowned as he tried to look closer. He giggled and replied, "These two girls are Poppy and Charlotte, they are your second cousins. Poppy's on the left and Charlotte on the right. I don't know if you remember, but you met them years ago! This picture is old. Poppy was a toddler here but she must be around twenty-nine now.

"And Charlotte is probably around twenty-eight if I'm right. The last time I saw them, it was... about three years ago. Sadly, both their parents passed away a while ago. I used to take care of them when they were children. They say I'm like their uncle," my father replied.

My mother joined us with a big basket full of red apples.

"Mrs. Ake visited an apple-picking farm today and brought us these. Here, try one."

"Look, Mum! I found an old postcard from Poppy and Charlotte!" I stretched out my hand and gave the postcard to my mother.

"Oh, what a lovely picture. You met them a very long time ago. Can you remember?"

"I really can't, but look, Mum, they're on a farm full of pumpkins! I wish I could spend some time on a farm like that!"

I was nearly squealing in excitement.

My parents must have noticed it.

"Maybe you can visit them? They live in a house on the farm, and I'm sure they still live there. The house and the farm belonged to your great-great-great-grandparents. I visited years ago, and it was an unusual place. It felt almost... magical," my mother said.

My father looked at her. She was now staring into space as she visualized the house and farm. My father didn't look impressed.

"It wasn't as good as you're describing it, Laila. I think you must have put those rose-tinted glasses on again! What I recall was that it was ancient... a muddy farm, they had too many rats in the house, and the road to get there was also very confusing," he quickly said.

"From what I remember, we drove around and around those back lanes for more than an hour and kept ending up back at the same place." He was unimpressed by his memories.

"Well, *I* might like it," I insisted. "And I really want to visit them on the farm! THAT IS THE BEST PLAN!" I said aloud.

Father looked at me perplexed. He pursed his lips but didn't know how to discourage me.

"Can you please ask if I can visit them this weekend? I know it's short notice, but it's going to be amazing if it works out. It would be the perfect Halloween," I said joyfully.

I'd always wanted to visit a farm, and Halloween was certainly the best time to visit a pumpkin farm! My parents looked at each other silently for a moment.

My father took off his glasses and rubbed his eyes as if exhausted by me.

"But aren't you going to spend the weekend with Kate? You enjoy spending time with her, and you always have an amazing time." He tried changing my mind.

"Not this weekend. We don't have any plans," I replied quickly and prepared my arguments in my head to win his vote if he came up with any excuses. "I need to explore and learn new things, and what better than spending time outdoors on a farm?

"Breathing fresh air and being physically active instead of just watching TV."

I knew they'd agree if I used the magical phrases: learning new things, breathing fresh air, and physical activity.

"There are other ways you can be outdoors. We could go to the park downtown together? Have a picnic? We can cycle and play tennis? Or ping pong?" my father suggested.

"Dad, it's *Halloween*." I felt annoyed that my dad downplayed the importance of Halloween. Plus, doing things with Mom and Dad was hardly thrilling.

"She's right, Ted," my mother said. "We can ask them, Lily, but there's a great chance that you're unable to visit this weekend as they may have made other plans already." She turned back to my dad. "Can you please contact them, Ted?"

Yes! My mother was determined, and no one could change her mind when she'd decided something.

Judging from my father's face, he knew he'd already lost the battle.

"OK, I need to call them and ask. Both Poppy and Charlotte live on the farm. That's what they told me when I last spoke to them," my father explained.

"This year's Halloween is going to be a really special one!" I said and jumped up and down, already thinking about the great time I'd have, even though my father hadn't yet called them. Please say it's OK! Please!

"Don't get too excited yet, Lily. I don't want to see you disappointed if it doesn't work out," my father said as he headed toward the stairs.

He turned around. "Bear in mind that having a great weekend is a decision that you make regardless of where you are. You should always strive to make the best of every situation."

"OK. But are you going to call now?" I asked impatiently.

"I need to find my phone first. Lily, go and tidy up your room, please. I noticed that you haven't made your bed for a couple of days. You better tidy up in there as soon as possible if you want to spend

Halloween away this weekend," my father said, disappearing from my sight as he walked out.

I felt a bit nervous, running to my bedroom as quickly as I could, placing my books back on the bookshelf, and making my bed and even adjusting the pillows.

What's more, to impress my parents, I even started doing my homework.

What if I won't be able to visit my second cousins and have to spend the whole weekend sitting in my bedroom completely bored? Is there a chance Kate and I can join Alice's party if the trip to the farm doesn't work out? No, I'm too proud to do that, I thought as I was trying to tidy up. I couldn't wait for my father to come and tell me how the phone call went.

Luckily, someone finally knocked on the door as I placed the last book on the bookshelf.

I hoped it was my father.

"Come in, Dad," I said with a calm voice, hoping he was bringing good news. I'd never been keener for dad to enter my private space; usually, I liked to keep my parents out!

I felt so nervous. My father walked in and looked around to see how much I'd tidied up.

"It's good that you're getting to grips with this mess. I'm impressed. But you have to tidy up some more before your trip to the farm tomorrow! And, if you have any homework, you need to do as much of it as possible before you leave."

My father's serious face suddenly changed, and the biggest smile appeared.

"Yes! Yes! I'm going to the farm! Thanks, Dad!"

I couldn't believe it! I had the perfect plan for weekend!

"Yes, Alice, you didn't invite me to your party, but my Halloween weekend is sorted out," I mumbled. I could tell that my father didn't quite understand what I'd said.

My father let me celebrate for a short time while I made some dance moves and jumped up and down in celebration. Maybe my reaction was a bit over the top, but I really didn't care. I was going to the farm and felt so happy.

"Now, I spoke to Poppy on the telephone, and she said they're more than happy to have you over. She also mentioned that they make specialized organic food that sounds delicious and sell their products in the farmers' market. In fact, Poppy said your mother and I could come too and stay the whole weekend," he said.

My face fell.

"Aww, come on Dad! You're surely not serious? You were just telling me about an hour ago that the house has too many rats, and it sounds as if you don't like that place at all."

My father turned around and left the room as he said, "Honey, I'm just joking. You can spend your weekend away alone for the first time. You will be in safe hands with Poppy and Charlotte, and there'll be so much to do and see there, I'm sure of that. I just hope you'll miss us as much as we'll miss you." He laughed before getting out of my sight.

***

Alice and Juan were standing outside the school gate, and I somehow wanted them to find out all about my weekend plan. They had both, along with Ben, made a point of telling Kate and me that they were all going to attend Alice's party even though we hadn't been invited.

My big smile captured their attention. They both wanted to know the reason behind it. Alice was throwing the year's party after all, and they were the ones who should have been smiling, not me. Or so they thought.

"Hi," Alice said with an annoyed face.

"Why are you smiling? What do you know that we don't?" Juan said impatiently.

"It's Friday and Halloween. That's enough reason to be in a good mood. Plus, I'm staying with my second cousins on their big pumpkin farm this weekend. It looks amazing, and it will be the best Halloween ever," I said proudly, despite hating to talk to them.

Both Alice and Juan stopped and said simultaneously, "Farm? A *pumpkin* farm?"

"Yes, I'm going this evening, and I'll be back on Sunday," I replied, satisfied with my weekend plan announcement. I walked faster to find Kate.

Alice shrugged her shoulders and rolled her eyes to show me that she didn't care, as if she wanted to say "Whatever!"

Everyone took a seat in the classroom, awaiting the lesson to begin.

Biology was the first class of the day.

"Lily, do you think we can skip class today?" Kate whispered as quietly as possible. I looked at Miss Eze and saw her eyes scanning the classroom. It was apparent that she was looking for someone to scold.

"Why would we skip class today?" I replied as quietly as I possibly could, and I wasn't sure my low-pitched voice could be well-comprehended by Kate.

"Because today's class is exceptionally boring, and I'm sure we can leave and do something more fun," Kate said.

"I don't want to get into trouble. Besides, I can't afford to leave school late as I have to go home and prepare for my trip," I said.

Kate took a deep breath to show her dissatisfaction.

She crossed her arms and stopped talking.

"Lily and Kate, what are you whispering about?" Miss Eze said with her back toward the rest of the class and with one hand still on the whiteboard. She turned her head and gave me the coldest look she possibly could.

"Sorry, Miss Eze. We won't disturb the class again," I replied, embarrassed.

Miss Eze didn't give up. She turned promptly around, looked at me again, and replied, "Well, well, well, how come you are so well behaved today, Lily?"

It was too late: Miss Eze had decided to teach us a lesson alongside the one in biology. I didn't know what to say as I didn't want to get Kate into trouble.

"I was saying that we should pay more attention to the lesson," I said automatically, which wasn't a total lie.

Hearing my reluctant sounding reply made Miss Eze believe that I was making fun of her, and she became furious. She was angry; her face got redder than the color of the crab in the picture hanging on the wall behind.

"Lily, when are you going to realize how important it is to pay attention in class? Not only are you not learning the lesson, but you are disturbing others too. You really need to start concentrating, or I shall have to speak to your parents," Miss Eze said.

Should I defend myself? No. I'll get into more trouble, I thought.

Everyone in the classroom began to pay full attention silently, but they'd all been half-asleep until then. Still, they also didn't want to fall victim to Miss Eze's tyranny.

"You are lucky this time. Next time, please be completely quiet during class and try to learn the lesson instead. All you are doing is disrupting the class and spoiling it for the others who want to learn," Miss Eze said and continued teaching.

Kate didn't even dare look in my direction again.

"What a dramatic finish to the week!" Kate said as soon as we left the classroom.

I still felt embarrassed to have been scolded by Miss Eze publicly, especially since I'd done nothing wrong. But I wasn't going to admit to Miss Eze that it was Kate's fault.

"I have to confess I was the one who got you into trouble, Lily," said Kate. "If Miss Eze knew that I was trying to convince you to skip the class, she would have punished me somehow!" I could see fear in her eyes. At least she was honest about what she'd done.

"It's over now. Let's not talk about it. We should learn from our mistakes," I said as I tried to stop thinking about Miss Eze and start thinking about my weekend instead!

MY HALLOWEEN WEEKEND!

"Oh well, enjoy your weekend, Lily. See you next week. Have a good trip," Kate replied and waved goodbye as she headed home.

I was the only one left in the school and as I walked past the school gate, I noticed that the streets had suddenly become empty, a rarity on late Friday afternoons.

Where is everyone? I thought.

It started raining heavily. I took off my jacket, placed it over my head to covered myself, and ran in the direction of home.

"Lily! Lily!" I turned around and saw my mother had stopped her car a few meters behind me. I turned around and ran toward it. What a relief that she had come to pick me up because it was pouring down now! By the time I reached the car, I was drenched.

"Hi, Mum. I didn't know you were coming to pick me up. This is perfect timing!" I said, relieved that I didn't have to walk home in this downpour.

"I saw the weather forecast and knew that it would start raining so decided to pick you up. Oh, and I've packed your bag; it's on the back seat. We can drive to the farm already," my mother said joyfully.

Mum had already planned my trip. She was maybe more excited than I was.

"That sounds good, Mum," I said, suddenly realizing I had no idea where the farm was on the map. How far away from home was I going to be?

"How long does it take to get there?"

"We are going to arrive in two short hours, honey," my mother replied.

I could see raindrops running down the windscreen as we drove through the forest in the rain. I closed my eyes, and all I could hear was the sound of falling raindrops hitting the roof.

"Wake up, Lily," I heard my mother saying with a slightly tired voice. "We've finally arrived."

I opened my eyes and realized I'd fallen asleep for the whole journey.

We'd already completed the two-hour-long trip.

"Thanks, Mum," I said, rubbing my eyes, and slowly looking around. A young woman who looked to be in her twenties was waving at us from the other side of the road, wearing a gray cape coat with golden buttons and long leather boots. She also wore a black hat, and her long brown hair fell freely on her shoulders. Her lips had been painted deep red.

My mother waved back and said, "That must be Poppy. Time flies. I haven't seen her for years. She's a grownup now! But I'm sure that's her."

Luckily, it had stopped raining. Poppy walked toward us as we got out of the car.

"Hi, Laila and Lily. How have you been, Laila? It's great to have you, Lily," Poppy said, giving us both a hug. She had a friendly face with a long bony nose, dark eyes, and glowing sun-kissed skin. Dimples appeared on her cheeks when she smiled.

"I'm good, thank you. It's great to see you, Poppy," my mother said.

"Hi Poppy," I said shyly. Regret filled me, and I asked myself what I'd got myself into. I didn't know them, and what if I disliked them? There was no guarantee that they'd like me either. Maybe I should have welcomed my father's suggestion of having my parents join me. Separation anxiety started kicking in.

Despite my sudden uncertainty, I wasn't going to back off now that I'd finally arrived.

Mum must have noticed I was a bit worried.

Poppy offered to carry my bag, and my mother gave both of us a hug and said, "Have a lovely weekend. I'm sure you're going to have a great Halloween at the farm, Lily."

Poppy smiled at my mother and waved goodbye.

"We surely will have a great Halloween!"

"Bye, Mum! See you on Sunday," I said and watched my mother drive away.

In the middle of the forest, she left me with my second cousin, Poppy, and my Halloween weekend began.

Chapter 2

THE PUMPKIN FARM

I was already impressed by Poppy's sense of direction; she knew the way to the pumpkin farm despite all the confusing crossings along the way. My father was right about the roads leading to the farm. I only hoped he wasn't right about the rats in the house!

"How old are you, Lily?" Poppy asked, and it was obvious she wanted to break the ice.

"I'm twelve," I said and tried to think of what to say next.

Should I ask her about the pumpkin farm? Or should I thank her for having me at the farm this weekend? I couldn't make up my mind.

"Charlotte, my sister, is waiting for us. I'm not sure your parents have told you about us, but before we go to the farm, you should know the farm and the house that you're about to stay at for a couple of days are special," Poppy said, pausing for a short while before continuing. "We're happy you've come to visit us. Charlotte's also very excited about meeting you."

"Well, I'm really excited to be here. I've never been to a farm, and it's so exciting spending Halloween on a *pumpkin farm*. What more could I ask for?"

We were surrounded by thousands of trees as we made our way toward the farm.

The strong wind gently lifted up the red, orange, and yellow leaves on each branch.

"You said the farm is special; in what way?" I asked and noticed that my curiosity had overcome my shyness.

Poppy looked at me, and I could tell from her expression that she hadn't expected that question. "Well, special in the sense that... it's special because we inherited the farm, and the house, of course, from our ancestors. You have to stay there to understand what I mean. You'll have found out by the end of your stay, Lily," Poppy said and laughed.

Poppy's explanation had just raised more questions rather than answering anything.

"Do you work? Or do you study?" I suddenly realized that I was asking too many questions at once, but there was no way I could stop myself.

I was interested and wanted to know more about my cousins.

"Charlotte and I are the only ones living here. We use the pumpkins from the farm and sell pumpkin-based food," Poppy explained, pointing to a house so far away that it resembled a tiny mosquito. "See, that's our house in the distance. Welcome to our Halloween weekend!"

We looked at each other and laughed. *Should I be worried?* I thought but decided to not linger too long on that thought.

Poppy was really friendly, and no doubt Charlotte was the exact same.

After a long walk, we were finally on the farm. I'd quickly forgotten how long it had taken us to get there, but the walk was fascinating.

The farm was full of pumpkins in different shapes and colors. I couldn't believe my eyes! I decided to ask Poppy one last question.

"Poppy, how many pumpkins are there on the farm?" I asked.

Poppy raised her eyebrows, elevated both her arms up in the air, and said, "Thousands? Millions? Maybe you could count them this weekend!"

We both started laughing again. We got along well, and my social anxiety started fading away, making room for new friendships.

Charlotte was waiting for us outside the house as we neared.

Her face wasn't yet visible from a distance. The colorful autumn leaves had decorated both the house and the grounds surrounding it.

"Welcome to our house, Lily," Charlotte said and gave me a hug.

She was wearing a long khaki knitted cardigan. She also had dark brown hair, dark eyes, and a few freckles over her nose and cheeks. She could easily be mistaken for Poppy if her slightly shorter height and slightly rounder face didn't give her away. My social anxiety peaked again. No words came out of my mouth.

We walked inside, and the first thing I noticed was the asymmetrical and bumpy ceiling, then the huge dining table standing in the center of the kitchen.

It soon became clear that the ground floor consisted of just a kitchen with multiple stoves and ovens. There were jars, spices, flour, and pumpkins everywhere I looked.

Charlotte said, "Now, you have to try our signature pumpkin-flavored hot chocolate. Grab a chair and take a seat at the dining table."

I was too busy looking around, trying to wrap my head around what I was seeing. The kitchen was huge, and it was obvious that it was used on a daily basis.

Charlotte placed three big, wooden cups on the table, full of the chocolate delight.

The smell of cocoa powder mixed with pumpkin spice aroma radiated from the cups. Still, there was also an extra layer of smell. Was it from the pumpkin or the cocoa powder?

It was difficult to make out exactly, but it sure was sweet and nice.

The aroma was new to me, mysterious and delicious. It made me think of a remote, peaceful area with strong autumn sunshine.

"Thank you, Charlotte. I've never tried hot chocolate with pumpkin spice before. It smells heavenly!"

I wrapped both hands around one of the cups, the heat soon warming them.

Poppy said, "I'll be back in 2 seconds."

She quickly got up and walked up the stairs leading to the upper floor.

"So, has Poppy told you about our farm and the pumpkin products we make here?" Charlotte asked with a smile.

"Yes, she told me that you produce pumpkin-based products, and sell them at the local markets," I replied.

Charlotte also picked up one of the hot chocolate cups from the table and took a sip.

"I hope you enjoy your stay, Lily. I'll show you around the house later. There's so much to see and so little time."

The old house looked mysterious and seemed full of interesting objects that I badly wanted to explore. However, instead, I resisted my curiosity and sat still politely, enjoying the wonderful hot drink.

"I'd love to go on a house tour," I said with a downplayed excitement.

Charlotte stood and moved toward the stove to stir something, which I guessed was some type of food, bubbling in a large pot.

Poppy soon joined us with a photo album in her hands.

"This is our family photo album. I thought it might be interesting for you to have a look. You'll find pictures of your grandparents and our common great-grandparents in it," Poppy said and handed the thick volume over to me.

I took the book in my hands. It was old and much heavier than I expected, and I almost dropped it on the floor. Luckily, the dining table in front supported my full, heavy hands, and the album flipped right open with the hit.

"Wow, this is such an old album!" I said as I touched the damaged cover with my fingertips and felt the smooth damaged patches under my fingers.

Time seems to always hurt even the toughest things.

"Yes, it's antique. It's over 100 years old," Poppy declared proudly.

There was a noticeable difference in Poppy and Charlotte's characters despite their extremely similar appearances.

Poppy seemed more interested in talking about history and the past.

On the other hand, Charlotte appeared more obsessed with cooking, and she somehow looked a bit annoyed when Poppy brought out the photo album.

"Poppy, I'm not sure Lily wants to see those old pictures," Charlotte said as she added what seemed to be exotic spices to the food in the pot. "You're boring her."

But she wasn't! In fact, quite the opposite! I could've sat all day looking at them.

"It's always interesting to see pictures of your ancestors. Lily, do you really want to look at the album? Don't feel pressured if you'd rather have a house tour," Poppy said, trying to dismiss Charlotte's statement.

"Actually, I'd love to see the photo album if you don't mind. I've never seen pictures of my great-grandparents," I said and looked down at the already open card pages.

The first picture was of the house we were in now. The place looked exactly the same in the picture, but it was hard to tell what color it had been when it was taken due to the old, almost faded, black and white photograph.

"This must be the oldest picture!" I said.

Poppy and Charlotte burst into laughter from my enthusiasm.

"*It is* the oldest picture in this photo album. This is the only picture we have from the year the house was built, since taking pictures wasn't as widely accessible at that time as it is nowadays," Poppy explained. "My grandfather once told me that the photographer initially refused to take a picture of the house. Who on earth would come and spend money—when cameras were scarce—to take a picture of a very ordinary farmhouse?

"So, our great-great-grandfather offered to pay extra to have the picture taken. For this reason, there's no family picture from that year because the house picture was prioritized instead. And here it is after all those years."

Poppy took a sip from her now cold pumpkin chocolate and continued.

"See the damage on the edges? It's due to a massive water leak from the ceiling years ago, and unfortunately, some of the pictures got spoiled."

The photo album was so fascinating that I looked at every detail with full attention and great curiosity to find out all about the house's history.

Turning the page, there was a photo of a couple standing next to one another with serious looks. They gazed straight into the camera. The woman was wearing a stunning dress. Her long dark curly hair fell elegantly on one shoulder. She must have been in her thirties.

The man in the picture was tall, had a long face with a beard, and wore a shirt, dark pants, and a coat. He must have been around the same age.

"These are our great-great-grandparents. They lived on the farm and inherited it from our great-great-grandmother's parents. No one really knows how old the farm is or who owned it first. We do know it's been in our family for at least seven generations," Poppy said, confirming my assumption about her history-loving personality.

"My parents never told me about the farm or about our great-great-grandparents. Even my grandparents passed away when I was a baby," I said, with a sense of betrayal.

How come they never told me about the farm?

Charlotte got up from her chair in a manner that signaled she'd already had enough of the topic. She took away the photo album and said, "Oh come on, you two. That's enough with old pictures and history; it's so boring. Let's go on the house and farm tour! Follow me, Lily. There's so much to see." Charlotte turned, heading toward the wooden staircase behind.

It must have been decades old.

Charlotte's first step on the aged piece of wood made a loud cracking sound, indicating the wood's old age. At least fifteen stairs formed a spiral up to the first floor.

"The architecture's amazing. How can such a tiny house have a ceiling so high?" I asked.

Charlotte laughed and continued walking. The corridor was also so long, it was difficult to see where it ended. It seemed to go on forever and appeared totally out of place, especially as the ceiling looked at least fourteen feet high.

When did my vision get so bad? I thought in disbelief.

Dozens of doors were either side of the corridor, and a bright red carpet covered the floor. Candles were lit on our way as we walked down the hall.

Where should I look? There's so much to take in!

"What do you use all these rooms for? How many bedrooms are there?" I asked as I caught my breath.

"I've never counted," Charlotte mumbled. "Let me show you your bedroom first, and after that, you can see the main parts of the house."

Charlotte stopped in front of a mighty white double door with gold-colored doorknobs.

The room was fabulous, with a wide window opening out to the farm just opposite the doorway. A bed dominated the center of the room, and two bedside tables hugged the bed at each side. A colorful but faded carpet was the humble crown of the room, covering the very center of the floor.

A large, dark-brown, wooden wardrobe covered the wall on the right-hand side of the bed.

"Such a lovely room," I said, continuously observing every detail.

Never could I have guessed that the house had such a vast first floor.

Are we still in the same house? The tiny old house on the pumpkin farm?

"We can bring up your bag once we've shown you the house and farm," Charlotte said. "Let's go see the library."

We walked further down the corridor, skipped several doors on both sides, and stopped when we reached a dark-green double doorway. With both hands, Charlotte opened it. Bright daylight shone on us, and I fought hard to keep my eyes open.

The intensity of the light blinded me for a moment, but I gradually reopened my eyes.

What a beautiful view: a library full of books!

The whole wall in front of us was made of glass hence the light flooding in.

Had I seen the library's glass wall from outside? I was sure I hadn't.

On each side of the library were shelf after shelf full of books.

There must have been millions!

"This is my absolute favorite part of the house," Charlotte declared and walked in through the double door. She stood in awe at the sight before us, still amazed by the number of books despite living here all her life.

My eyes caught a tiny, furry, moving object on top of one of the bookshelves.

A living being was in the library! I could hear it scurrying about and moved toward the tiny object as if in a trance. Meanwhile, Charlotte walked toward one of the bookshelves on the other side, picked up a book, and started reading.

My curiosity for the tiny furry thing prevented me from exploring. The small creature was moving, so were the third, sixth, and ninth books on the left, on the fourth bookshelf. I got closer and closer, the fear growing inside me, but my nosiness was growing even more.

I lifted up one of the moving books. The furry object was hiding just behind it!

"Ahhhhhhh," I shouted out, so loud I even scared myself. The brown, furry critter ran toward Charlotte and disappeared up her sleeve, hiding.

Charlotte laughed, amused by my reaction. She spoke as soon as she was done laughing. "It's nothing to be scared of, Lily. This is Mr. T."

Charlotte shook her sleeve and out fell the furry thing, and she grabbed it by what seemed to be the joint between a round head and a round body. Was that a neck?

Barely, I'd say. And there it was! The mysterious furry object! A brown longhaired hamster appeared in Charlotte's palm, covering his two tiny eyes with his paws.

Mr. T cautiously uncovered one eye when he noticed that he wasn't in imminent danger.

"Come on, Mr. T! There's nothing to be scared of! This lovely girl here is Lily, my second cousin. She's going to stay with us this weekend. Make sure to treat her well now, won't you? And don't you go stealing her food," Charlotte told Mr. T softly.

Mr. T observed me for a few seconds and slowly uncovered his other eye. He wiggled his legs rapidly in the air in an attempt to escape from Charlotte's grip.

Charlotte released Mr. T's neck, and he landed freely on the floor. He then quickly approached me and climbed up my left leg and trunk. I stretched out my arm and Mr. T continued climbing until he reached the palm of my hand.

He looked at me as he rubbed his chubby cheeks. A peanut dropped out of his mouth. Mr. T took the peanut in his tiny paws and held it in front of me proudly, ready to give it to me.

"He wants to be friends with you! Usually, he doesn't warm up to people that quickly," Charlotte explained joyfully. I looked at Mr. T. His round black eyes were looking at me.

"Thank you, Mr. T!" I took the peanut from him and placed it in my pocket.

"Mr. T is the guardian of the library. He's lived here for so long. Mr. T, come over here," Charlotte said. Mr. T jumped down immediately, rushed toward Charlotte, and stood by her feet. "Where's the book that I read last night?"

Mr. T rushed high up on one of the bookshelves, found the book, and gently carried it down. Charlotte observed him as if about to hurry and grab the book any second.

"Thank you, Mr. T!" She walked out of the library with the book held tightly. As much as I loved staying and exploring the library, I knew our house tour wasn't over yet. I walked behind Charlotte faster than usual as she moved speedily.

"Let me show you the greenhouse," Charlotte said, turned right, and continued walking down the seemingly never-ending corridor.

Will I ever get to see the end of this corridor? I thought.

It seemed eternal, revealing many doors along our way.

"There are so many doors in this house. It's much bigger than I expected. It looks tiny from outside," I said, hoping Charlotte would explain the reason for it.

"We're only touring the relevant rooms because you're only staying for a few days," Charlotte said without stopping or looking at me.

We finally reached a few steps and entered what I expected to be the greenhouse. I could barely see Charlotte now, lush greenery covering almost everything there.

There were a lot of exotic plants which I'd never seen before in my life.

Some were so exotic that I hadn't even known such plants existed.

Poppy walked in behind me and said, "You can find plants from all over the world here. Some of these plants can't be found anywhere else as they're almost extinct. For this reason, the door to the greenhouse is always kept closed."

I swallowed hard as I noticed that I hadn't closed the door behind me.

"Some of these plants are also extremely sensitive to the environment, and any minor change can destroy them," Poppy continued. "Within a few minutes, the change of atmosphere can make them curl up their leaves and die."

Charlotte's head appeared above one of the gigantic plants, and she said, "All you need to know is to never, ever leave the door open."

"Sure, I'll always keep it closed," I said and quickly walked back and closed it.

I was hoping that Charlotte hadn't noticed.

One of the trees had small pink flowers covering its bark. Red, round, small fruit were hanging from its branches.

"Also, don't eat any fruits in here, especially not from the sakura memory tree," Poppy warned as she quietly entered the greenhouse.

"Is it the name of this tree?" I asked.

"It is," Poppy answered and put her arm around me. "Let's see the farm now. There's someone I want you to meet."

Poppy and I walked out of the greenhouse, and Charlotte shouted from behind the plants. "Don't leave me behind. We're not done with the house tour yet." Defeated, she finally agreed. "Fine, Poppy. Go ahead with the farm tour!"

Poppy turned around and replied, "Thanks, Charlotte!"

We walked down the corridor without saying a word. Everything seemed unreal, as if I was sitting in the classroom daydreaming during a boring class. I had so much to process.

"You should know certain things. Don't enter any room you haven't been shown. I don't even think you need to go to the greenhouse or the library. You can always let us know if there's anything you need. Let's go and see the farm. I think you'll enjoy spending time outdoors. You don't have a garden at home, right?" Poppy looked at me.

It was apparent that she already knew the answer.

I briefly answered, "Yes."

Poppy could tell from my disappointed face that I wanted to explore the house further and wasn't that keen to see the farm yet.

"Right, and you should also never leave your room at night," Poppy explained.

"Why?" I was surprised by her strict and unexpected command.

"Hmm, it's because your parents don't want you up late at night," Poppy answered, but I could tell she was struggling to come up with a convincing response.

We walked down the stairs and got back to the kitchen. The space was full of the aroma of cinnamon, and the big pot was still on the stove.

There must have been more to it, I suspected.

"We're making our special pumpkin and cinnamon soup," Poppy said.

We walked out of the house. The sky was clear now, with only a few patches of white clouds resembling flying candy floss. The fields were covered with yellow hay, and I could make out the vast number of pumpkins spread across the farm.

"We're lucky! The weather is wonderful again!" Poppy smiled. "The boy you see over there is Tom. Let me introduce you to him."

A boy around my age was standing over one of the pumpkins.

He hadn't noticed us as he bent down and peered at it closer.

"Hi, Tom!" Poppy shouted to gain Tom's attention. "I'd like you to meet, Lily. She's our second cousin. She's going to stay with us over the weekend," Poppy said.

"Hi," Tom replied and stood up straight.

He looked at me before quickly looking away shyly.

"Hi Tom," I said and could also feel my cheeks turning red from the awkwardness.

"Tom comes to the farm often to grow pumpkins, and he's very interested in farming too," Poppy said.

Tom was just a bit taller than me, with dark hair and dark almond-shaped eyes.

"Tom can show you the pumpkin farm if you want? Do you mind, Tom?"

"No, I don't mind at all," Tom replied and laughed nervously.

"Well, I'll leave you in that case. We'll have the pumpkin and cinnamon soup later. I'll let you know when the food's ready." Poppy walked back to the house, leaving us on our own.

"How old are you, Lily? Same as me?" Tom asked as he tried to break the ice.

"I'm twelve. And you?" I said, relieved that we had something to talk about.

"I'm thirteen. You're one year younger," Tom said somewhat obviously. But he wore a bright and warm smile.

"Let's go and explore the farm," we both said at the same time and laughed. I knew immediately my adventures had started.

"I discovered the pumpkin farm by accident, one day after school. I was always fascinated by pumpkins and how they grew and decided to ask if I could come to the farm. Luckily, Poppy and Charlotte agreed. I've been coming here almost every week since I discovered this place," Tom said, trying to fill the silence between us.

We continued walking through the vast farm.

I was somehow hypnotized by the atmosphere, and by the orange, yellow, and red colors surrounding us as well as by the chilly air and the slightly eerie melody of the wind.

"So many unique pumpkins! Tom, I've never seen such a vast pumpkin variety," I said.

They even had different shapes; some were long, others rectangular, but most were round.

The color variations between them were also huge. Pumpkins from all the rainbow's color shades, from purple to green, could be found in their plump and shiny skins. Looking beyond, the pumpkin field started glimmering like a field of gold in the sunset.

"Are you sure they're all pumpkins?" I asked Tom and hoped that he wouldn't find my question silly.

"Of course! They're all pumpkins, just different species. Some even have thorns. Look, like this one," Tom said, taking a few steps and bending over the pumpkin he was referring to. It was red, round, and had many green patches.

Tom was right. I could just about see thorns sticking out from the top of the pumpkin, and its skin looked rougher than the type I was familiar with.

"It looks like a toad," I said and gently touched it. I could feel its small rough thorns under my fingertips. "Ouch! You're right. This pumpkin has so many spiky bits! They hurt!"

I realized a little bit too late that I shouldn't have touched it; it stung slightly.

"Let's go and see the rest," Tom said, and we continued walking.

"Where does the farm end? It seems to go on forever," I asked.

"Well, I never manage to reach the end. It's like an adventure, and I always discover new pumpkin species. One of the most interesting I've ever seen was burgundy, with a really smooth surface and shone as if it was a precious ruby reflecting light," Tom said excitedly.

"Was it really a pumpkin, Tom? Maybe you found something else?" I asked.

"No, I'm sure I found a special pumpkin. I could even smell it. Let's see if we can find it again," Tom said.

"What did it smell of?" I asked.

"It smelled like a... freshly baked cake," Tom replied.

"That sounds delicious! What did you do with it?" Perhaps I was asking too many questions at once. *What if he's lying?*

I'd just met him after all, and maybe he was joking about the pumpkins on the farm.

I decided to keep asking questions regardless and judge everything based on what I heard, saw, and felt. Any information would be helpful, even if I detected a lie.

"It was so special that I wasn't sure if I wanted it," Tom answered and was silent for a long while after. "Frankly, I was scared. It was such an overwhelming experience that I didn't know... if I deserved it. I was also scared that the moment would cease. I wanted to hold onto the feeling it gave me, forever," Tom said truthfully.

"What if we never do find it again?" I couldn't stop being so negative about finding that great pumpkin. *How would I react if I were Tom?* I thought.

Tom was friendly, somewhat insecure, and seemed way too anxious. I'd always worried about all my own anxieties, but against Tom, I seemed quite chilled out!

"If we keep searching for it, we'll eventually find it! We shouldn't give up," Tom said.

He looked across the pumpkin field, determined to find that unusual ruby pumpkin.

"When did you see it?" I asked, sincerely hoping that it wouldn't be impossible to find.

"I can't remember exactly, but it was weeks ago," Tom mumbled.

We reached a part of the farm with almost interconnected pumpkins. An unusual blue one immediately caught my attention.

"Wow! Look at that pumpkin!" I bent down immediately to reach for the blue ball.

Suddenly, everything became blurry. Was it fog?

Where did Tom go? He can't be far away.

In a flash, I tripped and fell.

Once I opened my eyes again, all I could see were red ladybugs. The sea of ladybugs flew in the same direction as if someone was orchestrating their perfect movement.

Or maybe they were dancing in the wind? I looked up and could only see the clear sky.

Where are all these ladybugs coming from?

The yellow hay field was now covered in green grass and flowers.

Some flowers were red, others white or yellow. A maze made of ladybugs surrounded me, appearing from one direction after another.

The sea of ladybugs didn't cause any harm, but I had to focus to break free from the cage created by them. The wall of the ladybug maze turned right, left, behind, and in front of me.

They suddenly flew upward, disappearing into an even bluer sky, setting me free.

A beautiful flower field was now the only thing that seemed to exist in the universe. This was a glorious, wonderful place, a place that warmed my heart.

But in a split second, that peaceful feeling quickly vanished when a rhythmic and unsettling noise penetrated the air. Two enormous snakes had appeared far behind me.

Each was so enormous that I could even see the patterns on their rough skin. The one to the left was white with yellow stripes, the one to the right black with had blue lines.

They started to slither toward me! I ran in the opposite direction, but the snakes moved extremely fast! Much faster than I could go.

I ran and ran until I reached a forest full of willow trees. The ladybugs must have led me away from the snakes!

"Tom! Tom!" I shouted, hoping that Tom would rescue me or at least call my name so that I could find my way back.

I ran between the willow trees, but there was no farm in sight.

I stopped once again to think of my next move, but a willow tree branch swept around me, lifting me off the ground, higher and higher in the air.

"Lily! Lily! Open your eyes!" a familiar female voice said. It was Charlotte. I opened my eyes and saw Charlotte and Tom. They looked horrified.

"She's awake now. We should get her back to the house immediately," Charlotte said.

"OK," Tom replied anxiously.

"Are you OK, Lily?" he asked as he helped me get up on my feet.

What happened? Where did I suddenly go? I wanted to ask.

But I couldn't say a single word.

"I think she needs some time to recover," Charlotte said and walked me to the house.

Chapter 3

HALLOWEEN NIGHT

"Have a rest before dinner if you like?" Poppy said.

"No, I'm feeling fine now, but thanks," I replied.

Tom kept looking around.

"It's my first time in the house," Tom said quietly as he noticed that I was observing him.

"I see," I said and leaned toward him. "How long are you going to stay?" I asked.

"Hmm, I don't know," Tom replied.

He seemed uncomfortable because he'd never been inside the house before.

"Stay for dinner, Tom. You two get along very well. I'm sure your mother wouldn't mind if you ask her?" Charlotte said as she placed several plates on the table.

Poppy looked at her, and so did Tom. Neither of them said anything at first, but Tom broke the silence after a while.

"My mother's hospitalized," Tom said. His eyes shone a little extra, his smooth forehead wrinkled, and the corners of his mouth sank down. Tom was sad.

"Oh, I'm sorry to hear that, Tom. I didn't know. Do you have any other family members we can contact instead?" Charlotte said.

"I can call Tom's uncle, one of our regular customers. We know him well," Poppy said.

Charlotte looked relieved. "Poppy can ask your uncle if you can stay for dinner."

"Yes, alright, thank you," Tom said.

"So good you're staying, Tom," I said with a smile.

Tom smiled back. "The food smells delicious. What are we having again?" he asked.

"Pumpkin and cinnamon soup," Charlotte said.

"Do either of you have any food allergies?" Poppy asked.

"No," I replied. Tom shook his head in response.

"Good. Well, let me go and call your uncle," Poppy said and went upstairs.

Why doesn't she want to speak to him in front of the rest of us? I thought.

Charlotte placed several pumpkins on the table.

"We're going to use pumpkin shells instead of bowls, and we'll eat once Poppy's back. It shouldn't take too long," Charlotte explained, placing wooden utensils and cups on the table.

"I like your eco-friendly lifestyle," I said, realizing the reason Poppy and Charlotte had so many wooden objects.

"We need to be kind to Mother Nature," Charlotte said.

The wooden kitchen table was also cozy with all its layers and imperfect edges.

"This table must be old," I said.

"Yes, it is. It was made from a fallen oak tree as a result of a storm over a hundred years ago. It's also been kept on the same spot for years," Charlotte explained.

"Wow! A hundred years!? That was a very long time ago," Tom said, astonished.

Poppy walked down the stairs and joined us.

"Your uncle agreed with you staying overnight!" Poppy said with a smile and took a seat next to me at the table.

"I can stay?" Tom looked happy but concerned as if Poppy was hiding something from him. "Maybe I should call and speak to him too," Tom said.

"Of course, you can. Let's first have dinner before the food gets cold," Poppy replied.

We waited patiently before Charlotte put out two bowls of the steaming soup.

"This is the most delicious soup I've ever tasted!" Tom commented.

"Same here!" I said, too busy eating the soup to say anything further.

The taste was unreal!

"Did you add anything extra to this? It tastes so different," Tom said.

"No, Tom. All the ingredients are organic and freshly picked from the farm. They taste so much better, so that's probably the reason why it tastes so good," Charlotte said with a laugh.

"Tom, the main reason it tastes so good is that I cooked it!" Poppy said.

We all laughed.

"No way, Poppy! *I* did!" Charlotte said from the other end of the table. "You only picked the ingredients from the farm and added some spice!" Charlotte continued.

We all laughed again.

Poppy and Charlotte's sibling rivalry was prominent, even if they were just joking.

The soup was delicious, and it didn't take long for us all to finish.

Tom immediately went to phone his uncle.

"That was fabulous, thank you," I said honestly and saw Tom enter the kitchen again.

"I called my uncle, but he didn't answer." He looked worried.

"Maybe he was busy doing something, or he may just have missed your call. I spoke to him earlier. There's nothing to worry about, Tom," Poppy said, reassuring him.

Charlotte cleaned up after the feast, but it didn't take her too long.

"I'm glad you enjoyed the soup and your day. I'm going to be upstairs if you need me. Goodnight, and sleep well!" she said, and walked up the stairs.

"Sure, goodnight, Charlotte!" Tom said as he washed his hands.

"Lily, would you mind showing Tom his room, later? It's directly opposite yours. Thank you," Poppy asked.

"OK, I'm sure we'll find it," Tom replied.

Looking down, I suddenly noticed that my sleeve was ripped.

"I'm going to get changed. I'll be back soon," I said.

"Fine," Tom replied without looking up as he was busy with the recipe preparations.

I walked down the seemingly never-ending corridor again. *Maybe I should use a bicycle next time,* I thought and laughed.

I finally arrived at my bedroom door, and once inside, grabbed a jumper from my bag as the temperature had dropped, cold autumn breezes blowing periodically through the old wooden doors and windows. I could hear a voice vaguely in the corridor. Poppy.

"Well, he had to visit Tom's mother today as she's had emergency surgery..."

I took several slow steps toward the door to try and hear more clearly.

"Poor Tom. We shouldn't worry about him. Probably the right thing to do is to not say anything and leave it to his uncle. It's really good that Lily's also here and that they can spend time together as they're around the same age," Charlotte answered.

Tom's mother must have been very ill, and he didn't know she was having surgery. Charlotte was right that he shouldn't find out just yet.

"Hopefully, he'll be OK staying here tonight," Poppy said. The sound of her footsteps slowly faded as she must have entered one of the rooms.

Slowly but cautiously, I moved toward the bedroom door and continued to walk toward the staircase that felt as though it was miles away.

"Lily, are you coming?" Tom said from the kitchen downstairs.

"Yes," I answered and carried on walking down the stairs speedily.

"I couldn't reach my uncle on the phone," Tom said.

"Try again tomorrow, maybe?" I asked.

"Yes, it's getting too late," Tom replied. "I'll call again in the morning."

Poppy also joined us in the kitchen. "You should both go to bed soon. I have to work on a project upstairs. Let Charlotte know if you need anything as I won't be able to hear you when I wear my headphones."

"Sure," we both replied, but Poppy was already gone before we could say anything else.

Tom and I sat down at the kitchen table.

"I don't want to go to bed yet," I said.

"What do you want to do?" Tom asked.

"Why don't we bake or cook something?" I replied.

Tom scratched his head and said aloud, "Where do we start?"

I looked across the room. Poppy had placed the pumpkin soup recipe on the dining table.

"We can work through this recipe," I said and picked it up. It was written on a ripped piece of a paper, with neat handwriting. The required ingredients were pumpkin, cinnamon, pumpkin seeds, lentils, water, salt & pepper.

"Should we go through it together?" Tom asked.

The best idea suddenly crossed my mind. "We don't have to follow the same recipe. We already know what to expect, and why make the same dinner we just had? Let's look for a cookbook in the library and cook something else!" I said.

"A library?" Tom repeated, surprised that the seemingly small house even had one.

"Yes, a library. There's a library in this house with *thousands* of books," I replied, absolutely thrilled.

Tom looked a bit worried but remained silent. He eventually spoke his mind. "I'm not sure that's a good idea, Lily. We shouldn't go there..."

He was worried, worried about the unknown in the house. Did he also feel its spooky air? I looked at Tom, smiled, and knew we'd follow my adventurous plan.

I had to persist.

"Charlotte told me that I'm allowed in the library. You don't want to miss it, Tom! There are thousands, or perhaps millions of books in there! You should also meet Mr. T, the cutest hamster ever!" I said, trying my best to convince Tom.

He slowly appeared slightly more relaxed.

Tom generally came across as a person who worried excessively.

"A hamster lives in the library? Who on earth would leave a hamster there?" Tom asked, concerned. "Surely, it must nibble all the books!"

"I don't think so; in fact, he's some sort of curator, believe it or not! And one thing I know for sure is that a lot of things are... *different* here, in this house and on the farm."

We remained silent for a while. Even I started having goosebumps.

Finally, I broke the silence hanging in the air between us as I overcame my fear.

"It is Halloween night, Tom! Let's explore the house and have a good time. We're not going to do anything bad, just some cooking, baking, and going to the library," I said, adding, "It's nothing that can get us arrested.

Now, he looked more anxious than ever. "You think we could get arrested?"

His eyes went wide.

"No, no, no. I said the opposite..."

"But even so," he said nervously, looking around us as of the police were about to take over the place and drag us out in handcuffs.

"Tom," I said firmly. "It was just a joke."

Talk about having a sense of humor failure!

I got up from my chair, determined to go to the library and get what I wanted.

"Fine." Tom finally agreed and got up from his seat. "I've never been in this house. You have to lead the way... but it's better if we stick together. And no pranks."

I couldn't tell if Tom was still scared or knew something I didn't.

"I only went to the library once, but think I know the way," I said.

Tom looked at me with raised eyebrows. "You *think* you know? How big is this house that you 'think' you know where the library is?" Tom asked impatiently.

"This place is much bigger than you could ever imagine. Even the corridor seems to extend endlessly, but maybe it's just in my head," I said and walked toward the staircase.

It already felt as if I'd known Tom for a long time. My shyness had vanished completely. I walked up the stairs and could hear Tom following behind.

"This place is so creepy. Especially at night," Tom said with a taut voice.

He was right. I also felt that the house was horrifying, but tried to ignore it.

"It *is* Halloween. We naturally both feel scared, but that adds to the excitement," I said trying to convince Tom and myself.

"No, it's the whole place. There's something about it... it's creepy! I've felt this way ever since I stepped inside the house." Tom had lowered the volume of his voice as we approached the upper floor.

"Wow!" Tom said loudly.

Is he surprised to be on the first floor? I thought and turned toward him.

All I could see was a big orange balloon.

It came down from above and bounced between us. Was it a pumpkin? But how could such a heavy pumpkin jump and fly up in the air like a feather?

Gravity would surely pull it right down again.

"Fooollooow meeeee," the giant pumpkin said as it turned, revealing two hollow eyes and a big smile appearing on the previously clear pumpkin skin. "Fooollooow meeeee."

I wanted to scream but knew I should keep quiet.

Tom's jaw dropped as he stared at the pumpkin, completely frozen.

"Let's run downstairs?" I said, but it was too late. The pumpkin laughed and continued further down the corridor. We both turned around and saw that the staircase had disappeared! There were no stairs or any sign of a route leading back to the kitchen.

"Fooollooow meeeee," the pumpkin repeatedly said and had almost disappeared from our sight. I grabbed Tom by his sleeve and dragged him down the corridor, doing just as the bouncing pumpkin told us to do. The staircase had disappeared in the thin air.

Our only option was to follow the pumpkin.

The pumpkin seemed harmless, and it appeared safe to follow. Tom finally ran faster as he regained control, but the pumpkin was far ahead of us, turned right through double doors and left them wide open. WE WERE BACK IN THE LIBRARY!

Mr. T appeared in front of my feet, rubbed his eyes, and looked me up and down.

We had woken him up from sleep.

"Hi, Mr. T," I said as calmly as I possibly could, but my eyes secretly searched for the bouncing pumpkin.

"Gooooood. Gooooood," the pumpkin said over and over.

It flew up to the ceiling and bounced back and forth between the walls, the roof, and the floor. Tom and I took several steps back, afraid the bouncing pumpkin would accidentally hit us. Mr. T stood next to us, observing the pumpkin, clearly quite unimpressed.

He held his two stubby front legs in the air as if preparing to catch the pumpkin that was at least one thousand times bigger than his small, chubby hamster trunk.

Suddenly, the bouncing pumpkin stopped at one of the top bookshelves close to the ceiling then bounced at the bookshelf, sending a book crashing to the floor.

Mr. T ran rapidly toward where the book landed and stood still with his paws in the air.

He grabbed the pumpkin and re-directed it toward the door. The pumpkin bounced out of the library as it said, "Goodbyeeeee, Goodbyeeeee."

Tom and I looked at each other. We were both in shock, unable to process anything we had just witnessed.

"What book is that?" I said once I was able to catch my breath and speak.

"Maybe it's a good idea if we go back downstairs and stay there," Tom said, shaken by the event.

"No! We can't go downstairs. We wanted to get there! Remember?" I said, doing my best to convince him, but Tom had made up his mind as he walked toward the door to make his way back to the kitchen.

I ignored him and walked toward the book on the floor to pick it up instead. Mr. T ran in front of me and tried to block my way as he kept shaking his head.

"I want to take the book, Mr. T. Surely Charlotte and Poppy won't mind. Move aside, please," I said, but Mr. T persisted in his resistance. I bent down and gently pushed Mr. T to one side with two fingers and picked up the book anyway. I turned around and walked out of the library. Mr. T made sounds indicating that he was unhappy with what I'd done.

All I needed to do was hold onto the book tight and go downstairs to the kitchen where Tom was. I ran down the corridor and saw Tom ahead, ready to walk down the now existing staircase. Was its disappearance just an illusion?

"Tom, wait! I'm coming with you," I shouted after him.

"Fine," Tom said in a way that gave away he was annoyed at me. He rushed toward the kitchen, and wasn't even turning around to look at me.

"I'm so glad to be back downstairs," Tom said and took a deep breath.

"Me too, but nothing bad happened," I said reassuringly and looked at the book I was holding in my hands for the first time. It was heavy and seemed ancient.

The cover was gray and bore some watermarks. *Spice and pumpkin* were the cover's title, and the author's name was missing. Who was the author, and when had it been written?

Tom finally surrendered as curiosity won over his annoyance.

He came over and stood next to me, looking at the book.

"What kind of book is it?" he asked, excited. My focus was on the book, and no word made its way out of my somewhat talkative mouth.

I flipped the book open and could see that, over the many years, the pages had already turned yellow. Some were ripped, while others were covered in faded handwritten text, the casualty of the passage of time.

Pumpkin Ginger Balls was written on top of the page, followed by what appeared to be a recipe. I flipped the page and found another recipe.

Pumpkin, sea salt, eggs, ginger, and water were all required to make the dish.

"A cookbook! Just what I wanted," I said and turned the page. *Bean, pumpkin & lentil stew* was the second recipe in the cookbook.

All the recipes had one ingredient in common: pumpkin, of course!

"The author of this book must have lived on the farm at some point. All the recipes contain pumpkins," I said as I explored the book.

"Most likely," Tom replied.

"Let's make one," I said and looked for a dish to prepare together.

"Shouldn't we just go to bed?" Tom said with an anxious voice.

His face matched his tone.

"The night has just begun!" I said, despite knowing that Tom was clearly worried. "We'll have so much fun!"

"Hmmm... Ok... Let's see what we can make," Tom said, now knowing I was determined to stay up.

"That's the spirit! Can we make the first recipe, 'Pumpkin Ginger Balls?'" I asked joyfully.

"Pick whichever you want," Tom replied.

We both got up and started the preparations. "I'm going to wash my hands. Why don't you read the recipe?" Tom said and walked toward the kitchen sink.

"The first step is to prepare all necessary ingredients. We need a pumpkin, sea salt, pepper, ginger, and water. Let's look for ginger. They may not have it," I said.

"Or... maybe we can find it. There's so much room in here. I'd be surprised if we don't find any ginger!" Tom said as he dried his hands.

"Maybe. Let's look in the cupboards," I said and started searching.

Moments later, "I found it. I found ginger!" I said as soon as I spotted it in one of the cupboards.

"Great! We also have pumpkin over there," Tom said, pointing behind me.

I turned around and saw a small slice of pumpkin on the table.

"Hmm... I don't think it's enough. Should we go out to the farm and bring more? They'd be fresher too!" I suggested.

"Well, I guess we'll have to because the one pumpkin slice isn't enough," Tom replied.

We walked toward the door and quietly stepped outside into the farm.

The sky was full of shining stars as if glitter had been poured all over it.

The moon radiated its light generously and equally on everything on the ground. As a result, the farm and the pumpkins were visible, making our search easier.

A mild breeze stroked my face. I took several further steps forward and heard the sound of my footsteps against the uneven earth. Tom walked next to me, and we continued further into the farm on the pleasantly cold October night.

"How many do we need?" Tom asked.

"Maybe four," I said and approached a shining, bright, purple pumpkin.

The light from it was so intense that it could easily replace a lamp bulb. I observed it for a moment before deciding to pick it. *Why not?* I thought, lifting it. My eyes were attracted to the cloudless sky, and to the seven moons lining up within it.

Did Tom see the seven moons too? I turned around and looked at him.

He stared at the sky and said, "Can you also see this, Lily?"

Tom also saw the seven moons! It wasn't a fantasy!

"Aha," I replied quietly and with great effort.

We both stood still and watched the seven moons. The big clock hanging on the kitchen wall was clearly visible through the window, indicating it was almost midnight.

We stood there on a breezy Halloween night, in the middle of what seemed a somewhat mysterious place. Neither of us was scared this time.

Tom looked more relaxed than before.

"Let's put the pumpkins in a corner and run across the fields as fast as we can!" he said with an excited laugh.

We quickly placed down the pumpkins we'd picked and ran as fast as possible. We ran so far away from the house it was now barely visible to the naked eye.

"This is such an amazing place!" I said as we approached a patch of small golden pumpkins. "Let's pick some of these," I said, and we both picked as many as we could carry.

"I think we should head back now because there's no way we can carry any more," I said.

Slowly and carefully, we managed to bring back all the small golden pumpkins, the purple pumpkin, and two red pumpkins that Tom had discovered.

Back at the house, we carefully rolled the colorful pumpkins onto the kitchen table.

"Look at all these amazing colors," I said as we rinsed off the mud from our haul.

The seven moons were still visible from the kitchen window.

"This experience feels like a dream," I whispered as I had my eyes still on the seven moons in the night sky.

"It does feel like a dream. Should we get started?" Tom said, less enchanted than me and more excited about the pumpkins.

"It does. OK, let's make a start. I'm really excited," I replied, and Tom started cutting and chopping the pumpkins.

We began following the recipe cooking instructions. I filled a pot with water while Tom cut the golden pumpkins into small pieces. Once everything was ready, we added all the remaining ingredients to the pot. The seemingly old stove slowly heated up the pot.

"It's easy to follow the recipe," I said. Tom nodded in response. His excited facial expression gave away his feelings despite not saying a single word.

"I will find some bowls and spoons for us," he finally said as he searched through the cupboards. "I've found them. These coconut bowls and wooden spoons are great," he added as he'd found what he'd been searching for.

"It's amazing that everything in the house is eco-friendly. Seems like there are no plastic objects in here! Everything appears to be made from nature," I said proudly.

"Yes, we should all take care of nature," Tom replied.

"Agreed, everyone on the planet should. I think the food's ready, so let's eat. I hope it will taste good," I said and picked up a big wooden spoon, tasting the dish we'd just cooked.

A sweet taste filled my mouth. I couldn't recall adding honey!

Where was the sweetness from?

"Mmmm. This is so delicious! You'll love it," I said. Tom nodded with a smile and grabbed a spoon.

"It's as sweet as honey or caramel!" Tom said and quickly ate the sweet-tasting delight. Once he had finished, he placed the two coconut bowls next to the stove and added food to both. "The sweetness must be from the golden pumpkins," Tom said after a second spoonful.

"How did anyone grow such delicious pumpkins?" I asked, despite knowing there was no way Tom would know the answer to my question.

"This place is magical, Lily. I sensed it from the second I discovered the pumpkin farm. Luckily, Poppy and Charlotte have always welcomed me with open arms," Tom said.

"Why did you want to come in the first place?" I asked, taking a break from eating.

Tom looked down quietly for a while before eventually saying, "I don't really want to talk about it, but my mother's poorly. There's nothing she likes more than a delicious pumpkin pie." Tom got up to wash his hands after he'd spilled some food on his left hand.

I decided to remain quiet and continue eating.

"Lily!" he called.

I dropped my spoon, turned around, and saw Tom floating in the air!

He was flying! His head almost touched the ceiling.

"Oh, Tom!" I got up from my seat to help him down.

But something strange happened to my body. It felt as if I was spinning! I was flying too! "We're flying! We're flying!" I cried out. The objects in the kitchen seemed so much smaller from above. The dining table, chairs, and stove were below us.

"This is amaaaazing!" Tom said. He moved his four limbs and floated around the kitchen.

Tom and I held hands as we started spinning in the air, faster and faster.

Tom suddenly hit his head against the ceiling.

"Lily? Tom?" That was definitely Charlotte's voice!

We both let go of each other's hands and dived as fast as we could, grabbing the side of the cabinet, keeping ourselves on the ground.

I found a cloth and quickly threw it over the pumpkins we'd picked.

Charlotte entered the kitchen and said, "Are you all right? I heard a sound like someone or something hitting the ceiling."

Tom and I both tried to look as surprised as possible.

"What sound? *Someone* or something hit the ceiling? That's odd," I replied, feeding Charlotte's words back to her to sound more surprised.

"We're cleaning up and will head to bed shortly," Tom said with a forced smile.

"Is there something you want to tell me?" Charlotte asked suspiciously, arms folded.

"No, no, no," I said, hoping Charlotte would leave.

Our night would be ruined if she found out what we were up to!

"Place your hands in front of you," Charlotte ordered like an experienced ship's captain.

I placed one hand forward, and Tom did the same. "No, place *both* your hands in front of you!" Charlotte said, slightly irritated.

Tom and I brought one hand forward each, with our palms facing up, and we pressed them together.

"Don't be silly! Both of you have to place *both* your hands in front of you! Not one hand each!" She was now extremely irritated.

Tom and I looked at each other, released our hands, and launched immediately upwards in the air. Just like two small human rockets.

"What have you both done!" Charlotte shouted.

She hurriedly poured some water into a glass and splashed some on Tom.

He landed immediately on the floor in a fraction of a second. She then sprinkled some droplets on me too. I, too, fell straight down on the floor.

"What did you make?" Charlotte asked with a harsh voice and peeked inside the food pot on the stove. She smelled the food for a while, then walked over to the bin and emptied the pot without saying a word.

"Where did you find the recipe?" Charlotte asked and looked around for a hint.

"We just made it up," I said with an unconvincing tone, afraid that Charlotte would take the recipe book from us. Charlotte didn't seem to believe my explanation.

She kept looking around.

"We'll go to bed soon," I said, trying my luck to see if Charlotte would finally give up and leave.

Charlotte looked at us and said, "You better go to bed. Otherwise, you'll get yourselves into big, big trouble."

She walked toward the staircase, turned around, and added, "And by that, I don't mean trouble caused by Poppy and me."

Charlotte was more serious than I expected. Poppy was the one who looked strict, not Charlotte. Tom and I saw Charlotte disappear up the stairs into the dark.

Once I was sure she was gone, I turned to Tom and whispered, "Where did you place the recipe book?" He responded with a smile.

"Here," he replied, stretched out his arm, and reached for the book on top of the fridge.

"When did you put it there?" I asked. I couldn't believe Tom had acted so quickly. "I'm sure Charlotte would have taken it," I said.

"Well, that's exactly why I hid it," Tom said as we both giggled.

"When we fly, does it mean that touching water makes it stop?" I asked, despite knowing the answer.

"Yeah, I can't fly again. Look," Tom said and spread out his arms in the air, but nothing happened. I smiled and said, "We aren't going to bed yet, are we? Let's make another recipe. It's Halloween night! We should have fun!"

I grabbed the recipe book from Tom, searching out another recipe.

"We should make one or two before going to bed. It won't harm anyone. We'll be finished and gone before Charlotte or Poppy check up on us again," Tom said.

We were on the same page. Tom was also excited about our new discovery!

"Will we be able to fly with the other recipes too?" I wondered.

"We'll only know if we try. Let's use another pumpkin this time. Chocolate pumpkin cake sounds good. What do you think?" Tom said.

I nodded in response and glanced at the menu that Tom had chosen.

In merely a fraction of a second, we both started looking for all the tools we needed.

"I found a round baking tray! Just what we need," I said and held up the baking tray for Tom to see. Once all mixing and blending was done, Tom placed the tray in the center of the oven. Shortly after that, the smell of chocolate pumpkin cake filled the kitchen.

"I'm excited to taste the cake! I've never tried pumpkin cake before," I said after sitting and waiting for over half an hour.

"Really? My mother loves baking pumpkin cake. It's delicious!" Tom replied and took out the steaming chocolate pumpkin cake from the oven.

"I wonder if anything magical will happen to us if we eat it... hmm?" I said and took the first bite to see. The cake was so delicious that I indulged in more than half of the cake in just a few minutes. I'd stopped noticing Tom altogether, but was sure he enjoyed the cake as much as I did. I devoured the final bite and took my eyes off the cake, but Tom wasn't there. Where was he? He'd been sitting across the table.

Panicking, I got up and ran around it.

But suddenly, something caught my foot, and I fell.

"Ouch!" Tom cried, but I still couldn't see him.

"Where are you, Tom?" My right elbow was hurting, but I didn't care. I had to find him.

"You just fell over me!" Tom said, annoyed.

I felt Tom's arm under my leg, but there was no sign of Tom.

"I'm just next to you, I think... hmm... I think I know what's happened. Let's go in front of the mirror," Tom said. I finally realized too.

I walked over to the mirror, but neither of us was visible in it!

"We're invisible, Lily!" Tom declared, horrified.

Chapter 4

TWO INVISIBLE CHILDREN

"We're invisible and won't be seen! Let's go upstairs! Poppy and Charlotte will think that we already went to bed!" I said.

"Sure, but we need to be extremely quiet, " Tom said.

"How are we going to know where the other one is? We'll end up colliding, just the way we did a few moments ago," I said.

"I have an idea. Let's both tape a leaf to our right feet. That way, we'll be able to locate each other," Tom replied.

"Sounds good. Let's get two leaves from the farm," I said. In just a minute, we had brought in two leaves. Mine was red, Tom's yellow.

"We just need to find some tape," I said and began rummaging inside the cupboards.

"Here you go," Tom said as a tape roll floated in the air. We quickly attached the leaves to our shoes. I could see Tom walking ahead of me; the yellow leaf was moving forwards on the floor as if blown by the wind. Slowly, step by step, we walked up the stairs, and only the faint sound of our footsteps gave us away.

"Let's walk cautiously," I whispered, but Tom didn't reply. "Tom?" I whispered again impatiently. He must have been there since I saw the yellow leaf ahead. "Tom?" I whispered again, but this time slightly louder. The yellow leaf was entirely motionless now. He must have been standing still. Why didn't he say something?

Maybe he was seeing something I didn't?

Suddenly, something grabbed my left wrist and pulled me. What was it? *Who* was it?

Thankfully, it was Tom.

"Lily? Tom?" Charlotte said, coming from the other end of the corridor.

I could feel my heart beating in my chest, fluttering like a trapped butterfly as I knew we'd be in big trouble if she detected us.

Maybe I'd even be sent home first thing in the morning.

"Let's hide in your room," Tom finally whispered. I could see the yellow leaf moving forward and followed it toward my bedroom.

Charlotte headed toward it too, but she was still far away in the endless corridor.

"Lily?" Charlotte called out again as she walked faster. I entered the bedroom, jumped in bed, and covered myself with the blanket, making sure that every inch of my body was hidden. She was now outside my door and I heard her walking into the bedroom.

"Lily? Are you awake?" Charlotte asked with a soft voice. I had to make some noise so that she would leave. But instead, the sound of her footsteps grew louder as she came closer. I closed my eyes tightly under the blanket and hoped she'd somehow turn around and leave.

Something cold suddenly touched my left index finger.

Charlotte lifted up the blanket! *Oh nooooo!*

"Lily, I'm really sorry to wake you up. I just wanted to check to see if you were OK."

I opened my eyes and looked up. Charlotte looked straight at me! But how?

"I'm going to get back to bed. Let me know if you need anything. Sorry again," Charlotte said and left before I could say anything.

How come I became visible again? I thought. I got up from the bed and walked toward the window; sure enough, I could see my own reflection in the glass.

"I placed your finger in water," Tom whispered over my left shoulder. He was still invisible, but the yellow leaf indicated he was standing a few steps away.

Tom had saved me from being sent home!

"That was close! She must have suspected that we'd become invisible. Where did you get the water from?" I asked.

"From the bathroom next to your room," Tom said. The leaf on the floor continued toward the door as he added, "Let's go. We need to make you invisible again."

I followed Tom carefully as I no longer was invisible. We headed back to the kitchen.

Eagerly, I walked toward the table and looked at the empty baking tray.

"There's no cake left, and I can't turn myself invisible," I said.

We had forgotten that we'd just finished the whole cake that had made us disappear. The water tap started running, and now I could see Tom as he'd touched water too.

"Let's go to bed," Tom suggested.

I wanted to be up the whole night since, sure we'd have other experiences if we continued cooking with the pumpkins, but Tom was right.

"Let's quickly clean up. Poppy and Charlotte probably don't want us to leave the kitchen in a mess," I said and started cleaning.

Tom looked at the recipe book and said, "Should we make one of the drinks? I'm really thirsty." *A drink can't hurt*, I thought.

Tom flicked through the pages of the menu book.

"Ah, here's one. Looks like an easy drink recipe. All we need to do is to mix pumpkin slices and orange slices in water." Tom walked over to the cabinet and looked for a jug.

It didn't take long before he found one. Tom then sliced the purple pumpkin and the oranges. He then added water to the jar before blending in the pumpkin and orange slices.

The drink was ready!

"I want to try it as well, please," I said.

Tom poured an equal measure, and we both drank a glass each.

"Is anything extraordinary going to happen now?" Tom asked.

What would happen now we'd had the drink? I moved around to check for any magical property but didn't notice any difference. Tom flapped his arms but remained on the floor.

"I guess the pumpkin in the drink wasn't magical. What a wonderful night! I've had so much fun, but want to go to bed now," I said, walking to the kitchen sink to wash my glass.

"Me too," Tom said.

From the kitchen window, I glanced up at the sky which had turned gray with no stars.

Thunderstorms started unexpectedly, the house shook, and the strong wind blew into the house through all the small openings. There was a sound... Did someone knock on the entrance door? It sure sounded like they did.

"No one's knocking. It's just the wind blowing," I said, but knew that didn't sound very convincing. The knocking on the door became louder.

We both looked in the direction of it.

"Oh, what a thunderstorm!" Tom was worried and turned around to walk up the staircase. The knocking grew louder and louder, and the raindrops hit the window stronger and stronger. "How come the weather changed so quickly? The sky was clear just before," I said.

I had a bad feeling in my gut. Tom also appeared anxious. "It's nothing major. Just a simple thunderstorm," I said, trying hard to reassure myself and Tom.

The knocking on the door became more intense as we ignored it, as if someone was behind the door, waiting for us to open it. It couldn't have been the wind.

Did Charlotte know something we didn't? She had insisted that we go to bed.

It now felt as if several monsters were shaking the house! I took a step closer toward the window and could make out several moving objects... they looked like... scarecrows! Something moved far away on the farm.

Tom froze. The scarecrows were now getting very close to the house.

I looked out of the window on my left-hand side.

One of the scarecrows was trying to open the window!

It was around six feet tall, with slim hands and hollow gaps where its eyes should have been. The door handle was shaking too; those wretched scarecrows were trying to break in!

More than a dozen were surrounding us, and I quickly grabbed Tom's wrist and ran upstairs, pulling him along. We got to the first floor, and Tom finally started running without my aid. He hurtled ahead until he reached his bedroom. I followed.

We both knew where we should hide without even talking to each other.

Under the bed! That was the best hiding place. Many movies showed that people hid under their beds so it seemed the best idea. Tom and I rolled under there.

It took some time for me to catch my breath.

We're safe now, I thought. *There's no way the scarecrows have watched the same movies as us.* All I could hear was the sound of my breaths echoing in my head.

Where was Charlotte? I wished she would walk in any minute now to save us! We hadn't even bothered to listen to Charlotte when she'd told us to go to bed.

It was all our own fault, and I was willing to go home as soon as I woke in the morning.

"The drink caused the scarecrows to hunt us! We should have gone to bed!" Tom whispered with a shaky voice.

No words came out of my mouth as I was too afraid to speak. The rain became heavier, and the sound of thunder louder and louder, lightning strikes lighting up the room.

A strong wind blew in; the window was now fully open!

I looked over my left shoulder and saw two hollow black eyes staring at me. One of the scarecrows had bent down and found me! It stretched its slim, wooden hand and tried to grab my arm. I shouted so loud that my eardrums were hurting.

Tom realized what had happened. He quickly rolled the opposite way and got out from underneath the bed. It was too late for me to follow and escape from the other side.

The scarecrow grabbed my arm and pulled me in closer.

"Tom! Tom!" I shouted as I could see that he was running out of the room. "Please help!" I cried out as something tugged me from underneath the bed. Tom was already gone.

Another scarecrow was climbing into the room from the open window. It was almost identical to the first: tall and slim with hollow eyes.

The scarecrow lifted me up from the floor and turned me toward its big face.

No eyes were visible, just two dark holes for eye sockets. It had an emotionless face made of hay, a black hat, and a deep brown coat.

I fought back by kicking the scarecrow's trunk, but it felt as if I was kicking a pillow.

It seemed immortal!

My legs went numb, and my vision became blurry. The scarecrow suddenly started to loosen its grip and fell forward. A shadow appeared behind it now.

Tom! He was standing behind the scarecrow, holding a chair in his hands. He had broken both of the scarecrow's legs! "Quick! Run!" he instructed bravely.

He ran out of the room in a fraction of a second, like a world-class runner.

A third scarecrow entered the room, racing toward me.

Tom could not help me a second time, and I had to run for my life!

Running out didn't mute the loud sound of the scarecrow's footsteps following me.

I knew immediately that I had to run faster, much faster than I'd already run. Tom was running far ahead of me, looking back with a horrified look.

My horror prevented me from turning back to see how far back the scarecrow was.

Soon, we reached another corridor. The long corridor led to another similar one, just like a labyrinth. The only difference between the two was the mirrors hanging from the walls of the second. The noises from the scarecrow behind became more intense.

We had to hide somewhere, but where? Nowhere felt safe as the scarecrows constantly found a way to reach us.

Tom was out of my sight. Maybe they'd already caught him?

There was a mirror similar to the others on the wall in front of me. The only difference was it was hanging on the wall at the very end of the corridor, blocking my way.

It prevented me from escaping from the monsters chasing me.

My eyes couldn't escape the reflections; dozens of scarecrows were just a few steps behind, all looking equally horrifying.

Horror filled my mind and intensified the longer I saw the reflection of myself and the scarecrows in the last mirror. My eyes closed automatically, and I couldn't register the details of the moment that followed.

Something hit me hard in the face and trunk.

Somehow, I'd walked into the mirror blocking my way. It was the one hanging on the very last wall of the corridor; it fell and broke into a thousand pieces. *Where's Tom!*

Tom was standing in the corner next to a door, holding several keys in his hands. With one at a time, he fumbled, attempting to unlock the door.

Would Tom finally succeed in opening the wooden door that seemed firmer than a hundred steel ones in that situation? The scarecrows were getting closer!

This was our last chance! *Come on Tom!*

"Please hurry up!" With my last fading optimistic thought, I hoped the door would eventually unlock before the scarecrows were upon us.

The experience I was having was much worse than a nightmare. The scarecrows were incredibly close, and my nightmares were blurry, missing fine sound details, smell, and taste.

The scarecrows' hay-feet made a loud cracking sound, the spicy flavor of the pumpkin drink filling my mouth, and the smell of wet hay from the scarecrows permeating the air.

This was real. We had to find a solution.

I picked up the only weapon available: pieces of broken glass.

Firmly, I aimed at the scarecrows and threw one piece of broken glass after another. Some of the scarecrows stopped moving for a short while when the glass pieces hit them, but they shrugged it off and quickly continued ambling toward us.

"Come on, Lily! Quick! The door is open!" Tom had unlocked it.

We both rushed in and slammed the door behind us.

I locked the door as soon as I possibly could. The scarecrows were knocking on the door and trying to break in simultaneously.

Where are Charlotte and Poppy?

Where are they now that we need them the most? I thought.

We were in a room full of glass bottles. Everywhere I looked, there were bottles of different colors, sizes and shapes.

"Is there another way out of here?" Tom asked.

"There's a window over there," I said and pointed to the only small window in the room.

"What if there are other scarecrows outside *that* window?" Tom said, and I realized the likely possibility of his assumption. They were finally going to break in any minute as they kept banging on the door harder and harder.

We couldn't take any risks, but at the same time, didn't have any other choice.

"Maybe we can fight them back with the bottles," I said, lifting up one and examining it. There was some sort of solution inside, but I couldn't identify it.

"What is this fluid in the bottle?" I asked aloud.

The solution turned into powder as soon as I shook the bottle. "I don't think we should touch the bottles," I said and placed it back on the shelf.

"But we need to figure a way out. There are far too many of them for us to fight, and the door will break soon!" Tom shouted, and I could tell he was nervous.

The door opened up slightly with every hit, all four walls shaking.

The door banging grew louder, and the bottles started vibrating vigorously.

Tom and I were both frightened and stood far from the door.

Suddenly, a strong and forceful bang on the door resulted in two bottles falling back and exploding! Smoked quickly filled the room and eventually, our lungs too.

I opened my eyes and spotted a scarecrow walking in.

It was holding something… a sharp wooden stick! And aiming it at us! I turned around and discovered an opening in the wall where the explosion had occurred.

"Look at that!" I said, and before thinking any further, I escaped through it to wherever it might lead. But my feet did not touch the ground.

Instead, they floated freely in the air. Tom followed not far behind.

The scarecrows looked down through the opening, and the one with the sharp wooden stick aimed and released it in our direction.

The stick hit the side of my left arm, a sharp pain radiating through.

We spun around multiple times as we kept falling to the ground.

Around us, I could only see books.

We were in the library! I immediately recognized the black and white tiles on the floor.

This is going to hurt! I thought.

"Aaaaaaaaaaah," I screamed and waved my arms as if that would help me to fly somehow. I couldn't see Tom anymore as the gravity seemed to pull me down faster.

I saw the solid ground inches from my face, shutting my eyes tightly, hoping it would soften the blow of hitting the floor. Maybe it was an automatic reaction.

Three... two... one.

Unexpectedly, I hit a soft surface, rolled to one side, and opened my eyes.

Why had I counted in my mind?

Apart from me, who did that when they were about to hit the ground?

A bouncing pumpkin had saved me! It then quickly moved into position to save Tom as he was about to land. Tom also had a soft landing and rolled aside similarly.

About a handful of scarecrows had gone through the opening and were falling down toward us. "Run!" I shouted.

Too late. The scarecrows landed on the ground one by one and were completely unhurt. Their soft hay bodies could land on any hard surface without causing them the slightest harm. The scarecrows then got up like zombies and walked toward us.

We ran in the direction of the library entrance door, but I was hesitant that we'd manage to get away.

I was right: two other scarecrows walked through the entrance door. Tom and I were surrounded without any route to escape!

A noise came from above, perhaps from one of the many bookshelves.

It was Mr. T! He held his tiny, furry paws in the air and ran back and forth in panic.

The scarecrows encircled us and moved closer with each step. Tom and I stood back-to-back, looking at the scarecrows in great horror.

"Charlotte! Poppy! Help!" I shouted loudly. They were our last hope of survival, but to my great disappointment, no one came. Mr. T held up a book in his tiny claws. The book was at least five times his size. He opened it and threw it down on the scarecrows.

"Seriously? A book used as a fatal weapon?" I asked.

Mr. T seemed to wrongly aim at us. The angle was a bit off too.

"No! Mr. T, aim further to the left!" Tom shouted. Mr. T shook his head and continued aiming at us as he threw it down. Tom tried to prevent the book from falling on us by stretching his hand over our heads. His attempt failed, and the book fell over us and hit my head. An excruciating pain started in my temples. I opened my eyes and saw a big gray castle in front of me... and no scarecrows in sight!

Chapter 5

THE CASTLE

The castle looked ancient, at least several hundred years old, surrounded by a green forest.

"I must be dreaming," I said despite knowing I wasn't.

"You aren't dreaming! We can't possibly dream the same thing..." Tom said.

He was standing right next to me.

We were both mesmerized by the castle and couldn't take our eyes off it.

"We were in the library just a moment ago. We got chased. The last thing I remember is... Mr. T throwing a book down on us." I tried to recap everything that had happened.

"Yes," was Tom's only reply. I wished he could say more than just 'yes', but he didn't know any more than I did. The gloomy sky had dark gray patches of cloud. The ice-cold wind blew against my warm cheeks.

We were alone in front of an ancient, gray, stone castle in the middle of a forest somewhere unknown.

"What do we do now?" Tom asked as he looked around trying to find something familiar.

"I don't know. I'm still processing all the events," I replied.

"Let's ask someone how to get back to the house," Tom suggested.

"Getting back where? To the house with all the scarecrows?" I asked without really meaning to ask. "You're not getting me to go back there!"

"Well, I wouldn't have anywhere else to go," Tom said, looking at me with his sad eyes. It suddenly hit me; that was true, Tom *didn't* have any alternative place to go other than going back to that scary house full of scarecrows. Unlike me, he had no home to get back to while his mother was sick and in the hospital.

"No matter what happens next, we'll stick together," I said, and a raindrop fell on my face. Then another. We sought shelter under the trees in the forest, moving further away from the castle.

"Shall we walk deeper into the forest?" I asked.

"No, we'd probably get lost. It's safer to stay here," Tom replied sensibly.

"But we can't just stand here. We'll get into big trouble if we don't find our way back soon," I said.

I looked around and could only see the gray castle and the forest's green trees surrounding us. The trees were bearing fruit! I spotted an apple tree, but its apples were still unripe.

"Have you noticed? It's not autumn here. It's spring," I said, but Tom was silent as he kept observing the surroundings. He appeared completely captivated—or confused.

We were somewhere far, far away from the house on the pumpkin farm. A sound came from the other side. I took several steps toward the sound, and Tom followed.

"Look, there's a group of people over there. They are wearing... strange clothes," Tom said.

A group of men, women, and children stood a distance away from us, and they seemed to avoid getting too close to the castle. Everyone in the group wore old-fashioned clothes as if they were backstage in a theater, preparing to finally act in the play.

They looked awfully drab to me, their clothes mainly gray, black, and white. The women had their hair covered in a white cloth while the men wore black hats and dark brown pants.

Three toddlers were in the group, attired in brown vests and black shorts.

"Oh! We must have traveled back in time!" Tom said.

I suspected the same: We had traveled back in time and were in another location, seemingly far away from the house on the pumpkin farm!

"Let's come up with a plan for what to do," Tom said.

How could we possibly come up with a plan when we were stuck in an unknown place and had traveled back in time?

"I agree, but where can we go?" I asked. Tom didn't reply.

The group turned toward the castle and observed it with great fear in their eyes.

A little boy in the group ran toward the castle. Still, a woman, perhaps his mother, pulled him away, and the group continued walking along the muddy road.

Tom turned to me and said, "We have three options: following the muddy path, going into the forest, or entering the castle. Let's not decide yet. First, let's find out where we are." I nodded and knew that Tom's suggestion was reasonable.

We strolled along the tall gray castle walls.

It was almost hushed. Only the sound of the wind echoed in the breezy air.

"How can we get back to the pumpkin house? We shouldn't be too far from it," I said.

"Anything's possible," Tom replied. "I didn't think eating pumpkins could make us fly or become invisible. I didn't think having a pumpkin drink could turn into a living nightmare with walking scarecrows and bouncing pumpkins. It still happened, so what is *im*possible? I'd suggest there's no such thing, only what the mind tells you."

Tom was right.

The grass under our feet was thick, green, and uneven. We walked along the castle wall, but no entrance door was in sight.

"Look, ripe apples are hanging from the tree over there," Tom said, pointing to a tree close by.

"Let's pick some apples. I'm starving," I said.

We walked toward the tall apple tree, and Tom picked a rosy fruit and took a big bite. It made an almighty crunch that reverberated around the trees.

He reached for another and gave it to me.

"It's sweet," Tom said, but he abruptly threw it to the ground.

"What's wrong?" I asked.

"There was a worm in the apple," he replied.

Hearing that, I dropped mine too.

A burst of laughter echoed in the forest, that of an old woman. The source could not be identified. Who was it? Where was it coming from?

I could begin to see a wooden walking stick coming into view from behind a tree, and the laughter came from the same direction. An old woman with long, thick, curly, red hair and freckles on her face came forward. She wore a long dark cape over her extremely hunched back. She was petite. Her eyes were sunken as though she kept no fat on her face.

The old woman was still laughing when she approached.

"Hello," I said.

"Hello," she replied and observed us for a while before saying, "Welcome! You must be new here."

"How do you know?" Tom asked, surprised.

"I just do," the old woman replied. "Be mindful of what you do here. Your actions have consequences." She laughed some more, turned around, and disappeared into the forest before either of us could do a thing.

Tom and I looked at each other, not knowing what to say.

"It's probably best if we just continue walking along the castle walls and find the entrance," Tom said.

"The castle seems a safer place than the forest," I agreed.

We continued walking and searching for an entrance to the castle.

A young woman with long blond hair, wearing a long white dress, appeared from nowhere. "I don't suppose you're lost?" she asked. "Everyone gets horribly lose here!"

Her makeup was classic. Her skin was pale, she had blue eyes, and she wore small round golden earrings. Tom and I both froze on the spot, not saying a word. The young woman was beautiful and must have been the same age as Charlotte and Poppy.

Slowly, she came closer. Her face was smile-free and emotionless. I glanced down to look at her feet, but her dress covered both.

We... we... we're not lost," Tom said finally.

The lady's eye makeup ran down her cheeks.

Was she crying? Was it because of the wind? Or did she have an allergic reaction? I couldn't tell.

The young lady turned around and said, "Follow me."

Tom and I looked at each other, nodding before following the stranger.

"I'm Betty," the young woman said, becoming less of a stranger.

Tom and I did as we were told without thinking twice.

We followed Betty toward what I guessed was an entrance door to the castle. Finally, she stopped in front of a little, hidden, imperfect rocky staircase leading to a wooden door.

Betty placed her pale hand on the rusted metal door handle, and the door unlocked immediately. Darkness filled the space.

Where are we? I thought.

I ran my hand along the wall and realized that were in a dark, narrow corridor in the castle. The young woman lit a small old-fashioned lamp, the type I'd only seen in movies.

My gut feeling told me that we shouldn't have followed Betty. We didn't know her after all, but at least we were now in the castle.

It was too late to return to the forest.

Even if we got to the woods, we still had to figure out how to get back to the house.

I turned around and saw Tom's frightened face just before we looked back simultaneously to see if it was possible to run all the way back. It didn't seem possible. We'd probably just hit a wall and collapse accidentally without the light from the lamp.

"We shouldn't have followed," I whispered quietly.

But my voice echoed in the rocky corridor.

"Maybe not, but what other choice did we have?" Tom whispered back when he probably should have remained silent. His voice echoed in the corridor too, and Betty could hear our conversation clearly.

"Don't be afraid. You know my name, but what are yours?" Betty asked without stopping to walk or look at us.

"I'm Tom, and this is Lily," Tom said as quickly as he could. It was evident that he was nervous. I wasn't sure that giving away our real names was a good idea.

"It won't take much longer before we reach the main hall. You can have food and drinks once we get there," Betty said, trying to reassure us.

Instead, her emotionless voice made me more alarmed.

It seemed more likely that we were the food! But surely, stories like that were only fairytales. *I have nothing to be scared of,* I thought silently.

The old-fashioned lamp Betty held in her hand lit up merely a small part of the corridor at a time. Betty turned right and then left. We couldn't see what was ahead of us as she blocked our view.

How can she remember the way? Of course, she does! She lives here! I thought.

"Is this your castle?" I asked before I could stop myself.

"Could be," Betty answered coldly.

What did she mean by that? It was hard to know from her monotonous voice. Was she living here on her own? After a few minutes that felt like a lifetime, a door eventually appeared ahead of us. Betty opened the second door with a key.

Rays of light penetrated the no longer dark corridor, and we walked in through the open door. We were inside the gray castle! We entered a large hall with several doors opening into it. The windows were large with maroon velvet curtains while the castle walls and floor were made of gray rock. A huge metal chandelier hung from the ceiling with tens of candles all around. The roof was high, and the air was cold, only slightly warmer than that outside.

The candles lit up the room with dim light, but it wasn't enough to brighten the space due to the size of the great hall.

"Welcome!" Betty said.

Two women entered the hall, each from a different door. They seemed to have been expecting us. One wore a long red corset dress. Her dark brown hair was made into a bun. The other wore a navy-colored corset dress and had black hair, dark skin, and green eyes.

Both stared at us with a smile as they entered the hall, resembling two prowling lionesses. All twelve chairs around the enormous table were empty.

"Well, well, well, looks like our guests have finally arrived! I'm Isabel," said the lady in the red corset dress.

"And I'm Danielle," said the lady in the navy-colored corset dress.

They both sat down at the table.

"Both of you, take a seat," Betty said as an order, almost automatic. Tom and I walked over to the table and sat down next to each other.

"No. Don't sit next to each other, sit *opposite* each other," Isabel said. The two women laughed; Betty didn't.

Isabel signaled me to the other side of the table.

Tom was asked to stay seated on the same spot by Danielle. They behaved oddly.

Isabel snapped her fingers and all doors opened instantly.

Food appeared, carried on platters by small creatures with blue, rough crocodile-like skin, small dark eyes, beak-like noses, round stomachs, short limbs, red hair, small horns, and tails.

They moved very fast despite their short legs.

The blue creatures carried the trays of food on the tops of their heads. One of the creatures approached me, placed a laden tray in front of me, turned around, and left.

The table was full of trays of food before we knew it.

Chicken, beef, potatoes, gravy, tomatoes, olives, nuts, oranges, apples, milk, fish, eggs, cucumber, and much more.

"Eat, children!" Isabel ordered. "Eat as much as you can," Isabel added. The three women kept circulating around the table.

The blue creatures disappeared again and left us alone with the three women.

Confused and scared, Tom and I looked at one another and at the food on the table.

It was basic, just as I imagined medieval food.

Judging from the castle and the way the three women were dressed, I suspected that we had traveled back in time, as well as to a new place.

Luckily, we were still ourselves.

I wanted to get up and leave but felt as if I was stuck in my chair.

"Music, please!" Danielle shouted. Music started playing soon after.

All three women surrounded me, waiting impatiently for me to take my first bite.

"Have your food," one of the young ladies ordered. I couldn't tell which one it was as I tried to wrap my head around all the events taking place at once.

"Fine," was the only word I managed to say.

Isabel and Danielle smiled when they saw me cut into the potatoes on my plate. I looked at Tom. He was utterly still, staring at me from the other side of the table. Slowly, he shook his head. I could read his lips. He said, "No." I knew what I had to do.

Finally, I got up from my seat and picked food from every tray on the table.

"Can I please get another plate?" I asked as I tried to waste time.

Tom did the same thing. He got up and took as much food as possible.

This way, we knew we didn't have to eat because we were worried about getting poisoned. All we wanted to do was win time to figure out how to escape from the castle.

We had to return to the house despite all the scary scarecrows in there. In the process of escaping them, Tom and I had reached an even scarier place, BACK IN TIME!

The castle gave me chills. Tom appeared to share the same feeling.

My gut feeling was warning me that something terrible would happen and that we had to leave before it was too late. Isabel didn't hesitate and quickly handed me another plate. Soon, even my second plate was full.

"It's time to eat now. You can have more food later," Isabel said with a confusing smile. Her smile didn't indicate friendliness, nor did it show any cruel intentions.

"Don't bother our guests too much," said a man's deep voice unexpectedly. I almost dropped my plate.

A very tall man wearing all black had entered the hall without us noticing. His facial features weren't visible, but his long face became apparent when he moved closer.

His face was visible in the dim light; shining on his pale face, it shone similarly on the other pale faces across the hall.

The man looked at me straight in the eye without even blinking.

I could not bear his gaze for so long and looked down to break his intense eyes.

I felt hypnotized despite looking away for a short while. The man's dark eyes and hair became clearly visible when he stood directly under the chandelier. He was smiling at me.

"I am Duke Lukas. Welcome to my castle. Who are you?" he asked with a soft voice.

"Lily," I replied, in short, but on point.

"It's good to have you here with us, Lily. Who is your friend over there?" he asked.

"That's Tom," I answered.

Duke Lukas walked over to Lily and said, "You have met Isabel, Danielle, and Betty, old friends of mine. They all live in the castle. I hope they have treated you well so far."

"Duke Lukas, where are we?" Tom asked after gathering all his courage.

"In my castle," Duke Lukas replied with a laugh.

Everyone except me, Tom, and Betty laughed.

"I can see that you haven't eaten much. Let's all have dinner," Duke Lukas said and took a seat at the dining table. Tom was done taking food and sat down again.

"We're awaiting another guest to join us tonight," Duke Lukas said.

His eyes pierced through mine as if wanting me to finish my food immediately. I had no choice but to do so. Everyone except Betty was eating.

My first bite reminded me of how hungry I was; I ate much faster than I should have.

"Drinks! Cherry juice for the children," Duke Lukas roared and clapped his hands. The small blue creatures came in again, pouring a deep red drink for us.

"Thank you," I said to the creature, but it didn't reply and walked away as soon as it was done with the task. I took a sip of the drink. It was delicious!

"Hmm! Such a lovely drink!" I said as I couldn't resist expressing myself.

Maybe being in the castle isn't that bad after all? I thought.

Duke Lukas spoke after clearing his throat, "The cherries were picked from the forest today. The juice is as fresh as it can get." He, too, took a sip from his drink.

Danielle, Isabel, and Betty were all still, observing Duke Lukas as if waiting for something to happen.

"The food is tasty as well," Tom said.

"They were so shy initially. The children wouldn't eat anything," Danielle said as she wiggled her right index and middle fingers at the two of us.

"Luckily, I saw them outside and brought them to the castle. Imagine if these poor children had been left out in the cold late at night," Betty said. Her tone of voice lacked the excitement of her words.

Duke Lukas looked at Betty and nodded.

"Oh, our friend is late," Isabel said.

"Don't worry. He is a beast!" Duke Lukas said and threw an apple up in the air before catching it. Both Tom and I stopped eating and looked at Duke Lukas, hoping that he'd say that he was joking, but he didn't.

"A beast?" I asked, seeking clarification.

"No, no, no! I didn't mean a literal beast," Duke Lukas replied quickly, perhaps trying to reassure me. Hearing that made me slightly less worried.

Can we trust Duke Lukas?

When did this nightmare start, and when will it end? I thought.

"Entertainment now!" Duke Lukas shouted and clapped his hands twice. The blue creatures rushed out from every corner, dancing in circles, forming rings by holding each other's arms. They looked cute rather than scary. Their tiny legs supported round bellies as they jumped up and down, dancing as fast as their short legs allowed.

Isabel and Danielle also clapped their hands with massive smiles on their lips.

The music stopped suddenly, and apart from one, all the candles in the chandelier were blown out one by one. The creatures stopped dancing abruptly, trembling in a way that showed they were frightened.

A thunderstorm started, shaking the walls of the rocky castle.

No one made a sound. The storm found its way into the castle as the wind blew in.

And not a soul moved, not even Duke Lukas.

One of the doors opened, and someone entered the room. It would have been pitch black if only the single candle would allow darkness to take over. The face of the person who had just arrived in the room wasn't clearly visible in the dim light.

"Welcome, my friend. We have been waiting for you." Duke Lukas stood up. The newly arrived one moved closer to the table. It seemed to be a man with a round face and round eyeglasses, though in the dullness, it was hard to be sure.

"How are you doing, old friends?" the man replied with a soft tone of voice.

"Good evening!" Danielle replied.

"Dr. Herbert, it is a pleasure having you with us tonight. You rarely grace us with your presence for dinner," Isabel replied, giggling.

"It's good to see you," Betty said with her characteristic emotionless voice.

Her statement was not too convincing.

"Two guests have joined us in the castle! Let me introduce them to you," Duke Lukas said. "Lights on!" He clapped his hands twice.

It didn't take long before four blue creatures came in again, each holding two candles, lighting up the space.

Dr. Herbert's face became clearly visible: he did indeed possess a round face, big round nose, bald head, and blue eyes. He wore a pair of huge circular eyeglasses that magnified his eyes, making me feel I'd been placed under a magnifying glass whenever he looked at me.

"This is Lily," Duke Lukas said. "And the boy sitting over there is Tom," he added as he pointed at Tom.

"Hello, Lily and Tom. It's a pleasure meeting you both," Dr. Herbert said with what I imagined was a perfect example of an evil smile.

"It's a pleasure meeting you too," I replied, knowing for sure that I didn't mean the words automatically tripping out of my mouth. Still, it was possibly the politest way to respond.

"Should I ask for more food for you, Dr. Herbert?" Duke Lukas asked.

"No, thank you. I don't have any appetite," Dr. Herbert said and tapped his round protruding abdomen.

"Oh well," Duke Lukas said and shrugged his shoulders. He turned to Betty. "Betty, show the children their room, please. It's bedtime."

"Follow me," Betty said as she led us away from the table.

Only the three of us left the hall. We walked through the dark and quiet room before Betty opened a double door leading to a slightly bigger space.

Mirror after mirror after mirror hung on the walls, barely an inch of space free.

All the mirrors looked ancient as expected, given that we were in an old castle. They were all of different sizes, their shapes varying from circular to rectangular to square.

"This is the Mirror Hall," Betty explained.

Obviously! What else would they name the room full of mirrors? I thought as we continued walking through the Mirror Hall.

We exited through a door at the other end, reaching a broad staircase with hundreds of stairs covered in an old red carpet. The walls appeared dull.

We walked down the stairs until we reached an open area with a fireplace and two armchairs. Betty didn't stop. She took us to a narrow corridor.

"That's your room," Betty said and pointed at a door. Tom and I moved slowly and hesitantly toward the room.

Should we be cautious? I thought.

Tom opened the door and entered the room ahead of me.

My heart was racing in my chest.

What if they imprison us? I thought.

There was one thing I knew for sure: we had to escape the castle as soon as possible!

I stepped inside and looked around to see if there was a window from which we could escape. All I could see were two single beds, but on the far wall...yes! A window!

We had to assess if we could get down to the ground safely. What was the distance between the window and the ground? I didn't want to check yet as Betty was still around. Instead, I turned around and said, "This is such a lovely room!"

Betty stood at the door without saying anything, but she finally said, "Go to bed, children. It's late." She then left swiftly. The door was left half-open.

Tom and I looked at Betty from the small opening. She walked strangely, something that was more prominent from afar. She was almost sliding. I tried to look at Betty's feet, but couldn't see them even though her dress was several inches above the floor.

She reached the staircase, but instead of turning right to head up the stairs, she moved straight through the wall! I couldn't believe my eyes! Betty passed straight through the wall!

That meant that she was a... ghost!

Chapter 6

THE EMERALD

"Tom, we need to leave as soon as possible," I whispered from my bed.

I knew he was still awake. How could we sleep despite everything that had taken place?

"I know, but how?" Tom whispered back.

I could see his eyes shimmering in the dark.

"Let's look out the window and see if we can get out somehow," I said. But only the dark forest was visible.

"Lily, it's far too dark outside. We don't even know the area around the castle. What if we get ourselves into even bigger trouble?" Tom explained. I knew he was right, again.

We were both quiet, as if thinking about a way to escape.

"Betty's a ghost. Does that mean they're *all* ghosts?" I asked.

"I think so," Tom replied and paused before saying, "No, they can't all be ghosts." He got up from his bed, standing up straight, as he continued, "Betty was the only one at the table who didn't have any food. She's unable to eat food since she's a ghost. Duke Lucas had food... Danielle had food too," Tom continued, trying to identify anyone who hadn't eaten.

"Isabel, she also had food," I said.

"That's why Betty's the only one who has an emotionless face and a monotonous voice," Tom said as he scratched his head.

"She's the only ghost... But wait a minute, what about Dr. Herbert? Is he a ghost? He didn't have any food either!" I said, proud of my discovery.

"Maybe. I noticed that the blue creatures were scared of him," Tom said. The blue creatures looked terrified by Dr. Herbert's arrival.

"We have to figure a way out of here soon. We don't know exactly how to return to the house on the pumpkin farm. Poppy and Charlotte must wonder where we are. We don't know anything about the people in the castle other than the fact that Betty's a ghost and Dr. Herbert is a terrifying person," I said with a worried voice.

Tom looked at me. "Are you thinking what I'm thinking?" he asked.

"Yes," I replied quickly.

It didn't take long before we were outside the bedroom.

We continued toward the hall with the fireplace and staircase.

Ghosts like Betty could walk straight through walls, but not us humans. We had to walk up the stairs—boring but true.

We took each step as quietly as we possibly could, but we couldn't move fast as we had to walk on tiptoes. All lights were off, but the moonlight made it possible to make our way. There was no sound other than our footsteps.

Suddenly, I felt something flying over my head. It was a black bird. It was, in fact, a crow, passing with such incredible speed that I couldn't even see where it had disappeared to!

"Oh!" I shouted. Tom immediately covered my mouth, afraid we'd be detected.

What if Betty or someone else comes to check on us? I thought but hoped they wouldn't. We walked up the stairs, and luckily, no one did come.

A ray of light beamed out of a slightly open door close to the staircase in the corridor. Odd! I hadn't noticed that door when we'd walked past with Betty earlier.

Tom and I looked at each other, communicating by hand gestures to not make a sound. We decided to peek inside the room.

We positioned ourselves behind the door, listening to see if anyone was inside. It was quiet initially. Then someone started speaking. It was Duke Lukas!

"Dr. Herbert, the timing is just perfect. When was the last time you experimented?"

"You should know, Lukas! The last time was... today," Dr. Herbert replied.

I suddenly felt a cold hand on my left shoulder. I turned around and saw Isabel standing right behind me. Her eyes had turned red, and her skin was much paler than I remembered it.

She was towering over the two of us, and I couldn't help but jump up and scream.

"Who's there?" Duke Lukas asked aloud, taking several heavy steps toward us.

"Those naughty children have been walking around when they should be asleep!" Isabel barked. She wrapped her arms around our shoulders with a firm grip and brought us back to the bedroom before we knew it. "Now you stay here! Don't come out again until I say so!" She shut the door behind her before leaving.

"Oh... we were *so* unlucky," I said in shock.

Tom just nodded as he took a deep breath and sat on his bed.

"Lily, what do you think they were talking about?" Tom asked once he caught his breath.

"I don't know, but apparently, Dr. Herbert's doing experiments. What sort of *experiments*, I don't know. I dread to think..." I asked.

"We need to find out tomorrow. We shouldn't leave the room again tonight because Isabel and the rest know we want to leave, so they'll monitor us extra carefully now," Tom said.

"I agree. Let's try and find out more in the morning," I said.

We both went to bed, resigned.

I shut my eyes. No way would sleep come when there was so much whirring in my head. Were we ever going to succeed in returning to the house on the pumpkin farm?

We shouldn't—couldn't and mustn't—give up.

The question was: how on earth were we going to get back?

"Do you think we'll be able to return?" I whispered.

Tom opened his eyes and replied, "I don't know. I hope so."

"Do you think Poppy and Charlotte have noticed we've disappeared?" I asked Tom again despite having decided to not speak for the rest of the night.

Tom didn't say a word as he'd already drifted into dreamland.

We needed to rest because the next day would welcome us with new challenges.

I decided to go to sleep too as we had to do everything in our power to return to the house the next day. I missed my parents and my friends. Plus, I didn't want anyone to start worrying. What if Mom and Dad tried to get hold of me on Poppy's house phone?

They'd have no idea where I was. They only knew I was spending time on the pumpkin farm with Poppy and Charlotte. They had no idea that my short trip could be forever.

Something soft touched my face, tickling my skin.

I opened my eyes and saw the face of one of the blue creatures.

The blue creature was standing on my bed, holding a long white feather touching my face, tickling me. It giggled as it did that.

I sat up in my bed.

The blue creature jumped onto Tom's bed and did the same.

Tom opened his eyes, stood up, and stared at the blue creature as if ready to defend himself like a medieval soldier.

The poor blue creature fell on the ground and rolled several times before hitting the wall. It then ran toward the bedroom door.

Isabel was standing at the door. The blue creature passed her and left as fast as it could.

"Good morning!" Isabel said and smiled. "Time for you to get up. We have a long day ahead of us."

Tom and I jumped up immediately. We were both scared of her, especially as she'd caught us being *naughty* during the night.

Isabel, friendlier than the night before, turned and said, "Let's have breakfast."

She walked up the stairs and we had to almost run to keep up with her.

How come she's so much friendlier than yesterday? I thought. *She's just so... weird!*

Her looks had also changed; she didn't appear scary at all now!

She seemed more like a friendly *clone* of the mean Isabel.

We entered the same dining room as the night before. Several small, blue creatures were present there, awaiting us.

The fresh bread, pancakes, jam, and butter smelled delicious!

"Where are the others?" Tom asked.

"Hmm... they aren't here, but you don't worry about them. Have your breakfast." Isabel smiled, but it seemed as if she was hiding something by the look in her eyes.

We sat down at the dining table. Isabel was observing us, but didn't sit.

She walked back and forth. The sound of her heels echoed, *click-clack, clickety-clack.*

The sun's rays penetrated the windows, and it felt as if we were in another castle.

Where was Duke Lukas? Danielle? Betty? And Dr. Herbert? Why were they not joining us for breakfast?

"Are you not having any breakfast?" I asked Isabel.

Isabel suddenly started grinding her teeth and erupted like a volcano as she shouted, "EAT YOUR FOOD! AND SHUT UP!"

Wow! Goodness me! I jumped sky high—what a transformation in her!

Isabel quickly calmed herself down and said, "Eat," with a smile on her lips, again.

I slowly started eating the food that the blue creatures had prepared.

Tom was also quietly eating his breakfast.

The blue creatures gave us more food as soon as we emptied our plates.

Everything they'd given us was absolutely delicious. The butter was creamy, and the jam sweet and flavorful. I don't know how long we kept eating.

"I'm full. Thank you for the food. It was delicious," I said as my stomach was hurting from overeating.

Tom also stopped eating and took a deep breath. Obviously, he was also full.

"Thanks for the food," Tom said.

Isabel smiled and clapped her hands as she said, "Well done! Well done, both!"

I didn't know how to react. No one had ever clapped for me after eating food or said well done for eating breakfast. Isabel certainly was full of surprises.

"Come on. Let's go!" Isabel said now, walking out of the nearest door while Tom and I were still in our seats.

We followed her until we reached a vast empty basement. Here, the floor was just mud.

Not knowing what would happen next, Tom and I looked around for a cue.

Isabel saw our confused faces and explained, "It's good that you had plenty of food. You need high energy levels to dig the ground and to find a green, shining emerald!" Isabel looked in the empty air as though imagining the emerald in her head.

"Start immediately! Don't stop! You have until midnight to find it. Otherwise, you'll be stuck in the castle basement forever!" Isabel said and locked the door behind her.

"Oh, Tom! This is a nightmare! I want someone to wake me up from this." I sat down on the muddy ground, holding my head between my hands. Tears were forming. I thought I could cry so many that soon, this mud would become pools of slimy, slippery water.

"It doesn't help to be upset. We should think hard instead of becoming hopeless. What can we do to improve things?" Tom said and sat down next to me. I knew he was right. I closed my eyes and took several deep breaths, glad of his wise words.

"We only have until midnight. We should start digging immediately. I don't want to be stuck here forever!" I got up, looking around for digging tools but couldn't find any.

"Come on, Tom. We better start immediately!"

My bare hands clawed at the rough cold earth, but it didn't take long before I had bleeding blisters on both of them, and my knees and back were sore from kneeling.

Then I had an idea: we could use our shoes to dig! I took off one and started pushing down. It worked!

"That makes digging easier," Tom said and followed my example. I didn't know how long we were digging for, but we didn't talk, didn't look around, didn't stop; all we did was keep digging, digging, digging... to eventually find that emerald.

I stopped for a moment to catch my breath and saw we were in a deep hole now—literally! My hands were aching, my legs were cramping, and my back had a nagging pain. I wiped the sweat off my forehead with the back of my forearm.

How long have we been digging? I thought.

Looking up, I realized that we were at least two meters underground.

"What makes Isabel believe that the emerald's here somewhere? It could be anywhere," I said and sat down. The earlier sense of defeat was back.

Tom was too busy digging to pay any attention to me. My eyes were tired, and the darkness made it hard for me to keep them open.

Several ladybirds started flying around in the dark hole.

Where have all these ladybirds come from? I thought, following the direction of the ladybirds. They flew the same way toward a spot on the muddy wall before me until a circle was formed. *Maybe it's a sign,* I thought.

I got up and started digging the spot the ladybirds had surrounded. I was now searching the wall of the hole instead.

A bright light shone through the mud where I was digging.

I dug as fast as I could, using both my hands. The daylight became stronger and stronger as the ladybirds flocked toward the light, creating a red cloud.

The hole became bigger and bigger as I removed more mud.

Tom had stopped digging. He was standing behind me, looking at the light penetrating the deep hole wall. The only sound echoing in the room was that of our hands removing more and more mud, moving toward the light and hopefully, our release.

Had we just found the emerald? Were we that lucky?

The intense light made it hard to see anything other than flying ladybirds.

My eyes hurt from its brightness. I shut them tight before slowly trying to see again. A familiar laugh broke the silence.

It was the laughter of the old lady we had met in the forest before getting to the castle! She stood in front of me in a forest.

"Well, well, well, you found the way," the old lady said. What was she talking about?

"Found the way? The way leading to the emerald?" I asked.

The old lady laughed again. "Maybe I can help you find what you seek. You'll otherwise be stuck in the castle forever."

The trip to the farm had been a terrible idea. Great horror filled me when the thought of never being able to leave came to my mind. I didn't want to be stuck in that place forever just because I'd gone for a trip on Halloween weekend.

Trusting the old lady was the only option we had.

Time was ticking, and we had only until midnight to find the emerald.

It felt as if the old lady could read my mind. She looked at me and nodded calmly.

"Don't be afraid. Trust your instincts. Always do the right thing, and you'll reach your goal," the lady said. The ladybirds flew around in the wind once again.

I shut my eyes, and once I'd opened them again, she was already gone.

The opening in the mud had led to a green forest, vibrant sunshine penetrating through the small gaps between overlapping tree leaves.

"What we thought would lead to the emerald maybe isn't just about digging. It's more complicated than that," I said and felt Tom's presence next to me. "It's about all sorts of stuff! Tests. Probably lots of little ones, one after another."

"Yeah," he answered quietly. "Guess so."

He was awfully quiet at times, as if he'd handed the whole job over to me!

Well, thanks, Tom. Thanks a bunch. Great to have all your help.

Fresh air filled my lungs as we made our way through the tunnel of green trees.

The way ahead was divided into two, one path continuing to the right-hand side and the other to the left-hand side. We had to make a choice.

Everything seemed to be *about* choices, in fact.

Somehow, both Tom and I simultaneously took the road to the left.

We rushed as we didn't have any time to waste.

Hours passed digging the hole, and we had to locate the emerald before midnight.

The old lady had told me to follow my instinct, so I did. Nothing was different on the new path compared to the last. The trees were similarly forming a tree tunnel too, again just like the previous path. There was an unusual noise... of a bird.

Sure enough, I saw a white bird on the ground, injured, with bloodstains on its white feathers. I instantly felt so sorry for it, wanting to fix it, heal it, save it.

But how could I?

Plus, the danger for the bird still persisted.

On top of a nearby tree, a black cat slowly crept toward several chicks in a nest.

The next turn ahead was just a short distance away. We therefore quickly walked by the injured bird to see if we'd finally get hold of the emerald. But that sad little bird never left my mind. I was determined to do whatever we had to right now, then see if I could help the bird.

I also wasn't sure... maybe if we did locate the emerald, the poor bird's wing would be fixed magically too. Who knew what magic could do? It was worth a go before I picked up the bird as lifting it could even make whatever injuries it had worse still.

I knew the other path could be checked if we were unsuccessful in finding the emerald.

All we had to do was to quickly run back.

What if we reach a dead end? Should we keep walking forward or turning around? Time kept moving, fleeing from us. Yet we were the ones who sometimes moved slowly or stopped altogether. Seconds ran out of our day like sand corns flitting through a tiny opening in an hourglass. We rushed toward the precious emerald.

But the noise from the birds became louder, as if the white bird knew that it was too weak and helpless to fight the black cat. The chicks too were shrieking, in danger.

Could we resist the temptation of walking faster on the path we believed led to the emerald and our release from the castle?

Something inside me urged me to stop and walk back to the tree with the nest and chicks.

At the foot of the tree, I saw that the black cat had almost reached the chicks. There was a small rock on the ground that I could throw at the cat and make it run away.

What if I injure the cat? I thought. *So, I save the chicks but kill the cat? It's only nature that makes it hunt prey. It's not the cat's fault. But... well, it won't get much food from tiny chicks or one injured little bird. The cat won't even gain anything!*

My mind was made up.

"Tom, help me climb up the tree. I need to save the chicks," I said. "You stay near the hurt momma bird. The cat won't go near you. We're too big for it. Make a lot of noise if she doesn't run away when I get her down. Cats are like big bullies. They scare easily."

Tom locked his hands together; I stepped on them and stretched out my left arm out as much as I could. My fingertips almost touched the cat's tail.

"Please push me up higher," I said. Tom took a deep breath and lifted me again.

"Be quick! I can't hold you for much longer," he replied, breathless.

"I'm doing my best," I replied.

Fortunately, I managed to grab the body of the cat and dropped it onto the ground.

"Go away!" I shouted behind the running cat. "Shoo!"

Tom couldn't hold my weight any longer and prematurely let go of his locked hands. We both fell to the ground in a heap. The cat had fled.

Once I stood, I took the injured bird in my hand and examined it.

Its abdomen had a puncture wound from the cat's teeth. I placed the bird on my lap, took up a broad tree leaf, and wrapped the leaf around the tiny hole, tucking it into itself securely around the back. It would heal in no time.

"It needs to be back in the nest with its chicks," I said.

"Let me try this time," Tom said.

It didn't take long before Tom had climbed the tree.

I elevated the bird in the air, placing it in Tom's outstretched hand. He put the bird next to the chicks, and the white bird started singing, fluffing up her plumage, joyful.

The chicks cried out in glee too—the terrified shrieks had all stopped.

It was so beautiful, so heartwarming!

"Who cares about some stupid emerald, Tom?" I asked. "What we did was a miracle for the bird. I could just sit here and enjoy watching her with her babies. I feel so happy!"

Tom gave me a black look. What some would call a *filthy* look!

Tom, come on... Give me a break.

"We *have to* move. We *have to* find the emerald. Don't be so silly! I wouldn't have come up this stupid tree if I'd known you'd be like that!"

I came back down to earth with a bump. *Well, thanks, Tom.*

But he was right, of course. I sighed, long and deep.

We rushed on the path to find the emerald as soon as Tom had jumped down.

It was getting dark. We had to hurry up. *Where is the emerald?* I thought.

A new bent road led us to three paths. Should we continue forward, turn right or take the path to the left?

We continued walking straight ahead and noticed that the leaves fell from the trees as the wind blew strongly. They didn't fall far but danced freely in the air, skipping and whirling.

The air was as cold as ice. The trees around us shook as if they were rootless.

Did we take the wrong path? But something deep inside told me to continue forward.

A small pond appeared unexpectedly in the middle of the muddy path.

I looked closer at the imperfect reflection of my face on the surface of the water. The image faded the closer I looked, and instead, a hand with long, black fingernails appeared in the muddy pool. I jumped back, horrified. My heart was beating out of my ribcage!

My knees straightened automatically as I flew up from the earth to straighten myself, pulling my hands back from the dry, earthy ground at the pool's sides.

The hand moved slowly toward me as if it aimed to grab and pull me underwater. I pulled away, but the hand moved faster.

What I did instead was to stay still without escaping. Not hiding. Just facing the unknown. In my case, the *unknown* I encountered was a free-floating hand in the water.

My eyes were wide open. I stood as straight as possible and took a step forward toward the pond with the hand within. Looking closer inside the pond, not only was the same hand with long black nails visible now, but also a body with green algae growing on it!

Tom had momentarily disappeared from my reality.

Two shining blue eyes... and the next thing I saw was the dragon-like face.

The creature moved toward the water's surface, but I was there at the edge of the pond. Something seemed to have passed over me, a calming sensation. I was not afraid anymore.

The ugly, disgusting creature moved closer and closer. Yet I'd never felt such calmness inside me before. The dragon-like face caused ripples on the pool's surface as it emerged, rising, second by second a fraction of its revolting skin rising from the little pool.

The face stopped by mine; it was several times larger than an average-sized human face.

Its body was enormous too, and I could hear Tom as he returned to my reality, yelling from behind me. "Run, Lily!"

But I didn't.

There, in front of me, was the dragon-like creature. The calmness within me was more powerful than all the noises outside.

The creature made some strange noises too, breathing heavily as if preparing to fight. I waited for the attack. It was so close to me that I could see every tiny detail: blue eyes, pale skin, and algae covering its body. The face resembled some sort of human and dragon hybrid. *Is this a dead monster coming back to life?*

We looked eye to eye for a moment before the creature returned slowly to the water. I knelt and looked into the pool. As if it gone into thin air—or stagnant water in this case—the only thing visible in the pond was the reflection of my own face.

"What was that?" Tom asked, horrified.

"We need to continue our search," I said, mindful of time. We both walked around the pond and continued on the path without saying anything.

The path became narrow and covered in thick ice.

Were we now walking on the frozen pond?

I tried walking fast but almost lost my balance, so we walked slowly.

"Let's lock arms to balance each other," Tom said.

We took several careful steps as our shoes were not suitable for walking on ice, now being so badly damaged from the process of digging the ground in the basement.

"Walking carefully wastes our time," I whispered as if my voice could crack the ice.

"Then let's try to walk carefully but fast," Tom said.

"Fine," I said. We took quick steps, but it felt as if the faster we moved our legs, the slipperier the ice got, and I fell backward, pulling Tom with me.

"Rushing won't help," Tom said as we both tried recovering from the pain. "But we shouldn't stop," he added and got up.

Tom stretched his hand and helped me up on my feet.

This time, we walked much slower than before.

A cracking sound echoed in the air, but the only option we had was to move forward regardless. I looked down to make sure that the ice wasn't cracking.

The ice layer was thick, and I was almost sure that the cracking sound hadn't come from the ice underneath our feet. It was intact, and I felt relieved.

Or maybe that was what I wanted to believe.

A loud siren started from nowhere, and I had to cover my ears. The sound penetrated the air, vibrating my eardrums. I shut my eyes from the intense pain of the loud noise.

What noise was it?

A purple creature was a distance away from us on one side of the ice.

We hadn't noticed its presence, focusing way too hard on taking careful steps.

The creature was enormous and had a round body, seal head, and flippers, but it wasn't a seal because it also had some human features such as a long human nose and a big mouth.

The high-pitched noise ended abruptly.

A crack was now visible in the ice underneath the seal monster.

"Where are you going?" it asked in a deep, loud voice. It then hit the ice with its flipper, and it cracked even more. "Where are you going?" it repeated.

The painfully high-pitched siren started again.

The seal monster's noise triggered a headache I'd never experienced before. "Are you looking for the emerald?" the seal monster asked.

Despite my fear that the beast wouldn't let us continue our path, I replied, "Yes. We are!"

The seal monster made noise again for a prolonged period before jumping up and down in a way that made its body shake.

The block of ice cracked into smithereens, and we fell into the ice-cold water.

Chapter 7

FALLING LEAVES

Something grabbed my feet and dragged me deep underwater.

What was it? The seal monster!

Tom was being dragged along as well.

A gigantic human hand was sticking out from the side of the seal monster's body, clutching my foot. The seal monster's other hand had grabbed one of Tom's feet.

Where were we heading?

It was dragging us all the way to the bottom of the water and releasing us on the sand. Then, the hideous seal monster disappeared into the dark.

The smooth sand touched my skin as I was about to push myself upwards. A small solid object was underneath my hand. It was a key!

I grabbed it, pushing myself up quickly.

The ice was still intact when I'd reached the water's surface.

There was no way out.

Follow your instincts! Follow your instincts, I kept repeating in my head while I focused on finding a solution.

I swam in the same direction in which the seal monster had disappeared. I turned around and saw Tom trying to break the ice a short distance away.

I moved closer to Tom, touching his arm to get his attention.

He looked at me as I made a hand gesture, indicating for him to follow me.

My head was spinning. Oxygen. I needed oxygen, running out of air.

The seal monster reappeared from nowhere and blew a giant air bubble and enclosed us in it. What a gift it was to be able to breathe in air.

Finally, we could speak.

"Oh... finally... air," Tom said breathlessly.

I was so breathless that I couldn't talk, even now.

"Are you all right, Lily?" Tom asked.

"Yes," I answered between heavy breaths.

"The air bubble is shrinking. We need to find a solution as soon as possible," Tom said.

We were using up the oxygen in the air bubble, and the bubble itself was getting smaller with each breath. We were soon going to struggle without air underwater again.

How could we get out?

"Let's find a solution," I said as if it'd be as easy as that.

In silence, we looked around to find a hint of a solution.

"I've already lost track of time. Hope it's not past midnight," I said. Time was running out, and so was the oxygen in the shrinking bubble. We needed to think and quickly.

"Look, there's an opening in the ice over there." Tom pointed to what seemed to be a small patch on the water's surface without any ice.

"But how do we move the air bubble?"

I tried to take my hand through the edge of the bubble to see if I could push the air bubble along, but my hand just got wet. The bubble didn't move.

"Let's blow the air bubble!" Tom said. "We'll consume more oxygen in the process, but the air bubble will hopefully move." It seemed an excellent idea!

We blew at the edge of the air bubble. It worked! We were moving! It took several minutes before we reached our goal. Almost nothing remained of our air bubble.

"Let's swim toward the surface. It doesn't matter if we leave the air bubble if we manage to get out of the water soon," I said.

Tom was the first to leave, and I quickly followed.

Maybe it was just an illusion or perhaps we'd keep slipping into the water and not be able to get out due to the slippery ice. But Tom got out easily using the gray rocky edge.

A smile appeared on my lips. I also got myself out.

Tom stood still with his back against me, blocking my view. I was eager to see where we were... We were in a small cave that didn't lead anywhere, a dead-end!

"This is it. We're stuck. The opening's led us to a small cave with no way out, other than getting back into the water," Tom said.

I didn't say anything and scanned the cave. The gray cave walls were shining from the reflection of light. I took several steps and placed my hands on the uneven wall.

"What are you looking for?" Tom asked. I was too focused on my task to answer.

Finally, a small keyhole appeared on the uneven wall. I placed the key that I'd found at the bottom of the water in the keyhole, turning it. The secret door had opened!

I took a step, feeling soft grass under my right foot. Hot air radiated on my skin.

The temperature was so high that I could hear the ice melting and cracking. I quickly walked in through the opening.

Tom was behind me, and his left foot was still on the ice... when it cracked completely. Tom quickly found his balance to avoid falling into the water.

He jumped out of the cave as fast as he could.

We could continue our search for the emerald! A brand-new path had appeared, covered in yellow, orange, and red leaves this time.

The surrounding nature and warmer air indicated that it was autumn.

Tom and I continued walking side by side but without looking at each other.

I could tell there was a smile on Tom's lips despite only looking at the path ahead. I just felt it, his smile and happiness radiating. I guessed he could sense mine just the same.

Leaves fell gently, and I could hear the sound of a piano, its melodies floating in the air.

The warmer temperature heated up my body slowly. The seal monster and our experience of being trapped under the ice were already erased from my memory.

We could see a black piano from afar, under one of the trees. I could also see two legs, but the bulky piano was covering the face of the musician.

"Isn't it beautiful?" I asked Tom.

"Yes... it is," Tom replied.

Tom had his eyes fixed on the piano, bewitched. We got closer and closer to it.

"Tom?" I whispered. He was no longer paying any attention to his surroundings. He didn't reply or look at me. I grabbed his arm and shook him, but Tom still didn't respond.

He walked toward the piano, and I followed a few steps behind.

We reached the piano, and I rushed to see the face of the pianist, hoping he could lead us to the emerald somehow. The pianist was wearing a long black coat and a black hat.

His face wasn't visible.

"Hello," I said as I approached him.

"Shhh," the pianist replied.

His head was bent over the piano keys. I looked at the fingers on the keyboard. Ten long slim pale fingers were pushing down the keys in a perfectly imperfect manner, in a way that only a true pianist could manage.

The music kept playing, and every time I tried to speak to the pianist, I got the same response: "Shh..."

"Tom? Tom?" I re-attempted to break the spell that Tom seemed to be under.

Tom just stared at the fingers playing the piano.

I looked up at the dark gray sky. The pianist didn't want to speak to us.

Tom and I had to continue our search for the emerald. The pianist didn't have the emerald, nor did he want to help. That much was obvious.

I grabbed Tom's arm and dragged him along.

The pianist played faster, and the leaves fell from the trees faster in turn.

In the end, there were so many leaves on the ground, they reached up to my knees. It was more challenging walking and dragging Tom at the same time.

"Tom! Tom! Wake up. Please, wake up!" Tom didn't respond. I slapped him lightly on the cheek, but he still failed to respond. Instead, he turned around and walked toward the piano again. I couldn't hold onto his arm anymore as I fell backward, landing on the leaves.

My eyes saw just the sky with the falling leaves.

The yellow, orange, and red leaves cascaded from the trees.

Deep... gray... sky. It was getting dark. We were running out of time! Even if we found the emerald, it would take time to get back.

I thought of my parents and Kate.

Would I ever see them again?

I also thought about Poppy and Charlotte. I hoped that they hadn't noticed that we were gone from the house. I didn't want them to worry.

Was I also hypnotized by the music? It was magical to listen to it while observing the falling autumn leaves. It would be so easy to give up...

"Tom," I shouted once I'd regained control of my mind, fighting hypnosis.

"Shhh," the pianist replied once again. The soft notes. The beautiful melodies.

I looked at the piano and saw the pianist still playing, and Tom standing next to him.

"Don't let the music stop you. Don't fall into the trap. You need to find the emerald. Everyone is waiting for you on the other side," I whispered to myself, stood up, and ran toward Tom and the pianist.

I shouted loudly, "STOP PLAYING THE MUSIC!"

The pianist stopped playing, and the music ceased.

The leaves stopped falling from the trees.

"What? What is happening?" Tom asked.

"We need to keep going, Tom. You were bewitched by the music. It's time for us to leave," I replied.

The pianist finally looked up, and I could see that he was a young boy with dark eyes, pale skin, a long and freckled nose, and a small mouth.

"Why did you want the music to stop?" the pianist asked with a calm but cold voice.

"I needed the music to stop playing so that we could find the emerald and return home to our friends and family. It's getting dark. We only have until midnight," I explained.

"My name is Music Head. I know two things very well: how to play music, and time. I can help you if you explain more about the reason you have to find the emerald before midnight," Music Head said in a monotonous voice.

"But we don't have time to explain," I replied, annoyed.

Music Head started playing the piano again and ignored us. Tom's eyes became fixed at the piano a second time, bewitched by the music once more.

"Fine, Music Head. I will tell you the reason," I said.

Music Head stopped playing and waited silently for my explanation, but didn't make any eye contact.

"Where should I start?" I asked.

"From the very beginning," he said quietly, his voice was soft and sounding like music.

"I visited my second cousins for the first time this Halloween. We found a recipe book and started cooking and baking with pumpkins from the farm. Everything was fine until a bunch of scarecrows chased us at night. We ended up in the library when we ran away from the scarecrows, and a book fell over our heads. The next thing we knew was that we were outside a big, gray castle. We were taken into it by a lady named Betty. She's a ghost, by the way," I said and rolled my eyes as I realized it must have sounded bizarre.

I continued, "Once we were in the castle, Betty introduced us to Duke Lukas, Danielle, and Isabel. They also have an eccentric friend called Dr. Herbert. The following morning, Isabel took us to the basement. She asked us to dig the ground until we found a precious emerald. She explained that we only had until midnight to find it.

"Otherwise, we'd be stuck in the castle forever. So, that's where we're at."

I took a deep breath; I'd summarized everything for Music Head as quickly as possible.

"We have to leave," I said and hoped that Music Head would understand.

"Oh," was the only thing Music Head said. He looked lonely. He was perhaps just sitting and playing piano alone all day long. He didn't seem to know what to say.

"Come with us if you want?" I said without hesitating. Music Head looked at me for the first time, surprised. Tom nodded in approval.

"Are you always alone?" I asked.

"Yes," he replied, looking down.

"Let's go," I told Music Head and held him lightly by his arm.

I realized how tall and slim the boy was when he stood up.

All three of us walked on the path, and no bewitching music held us back anymore. Besides, the lonely pianist wasn't lonely now.

"I hope it's not too late," I said as I glanced up at the navy sky.

"No, it's definitely not too late," Music Head said.

"How do you know?" Tom asked.

Music Head's narrow face appeared expressionless when he didn't speak. His face lacked the slightest trace of emotion. "I know the time in my head. It is 8:54:38... it is now 8:54:40."

He spoke so precisely, the same way a clock ticked without any faltering.

Tom and I stared, but he ignored us again.

"I have always known the time precisely. Don't you know the time well?" he asked.

Tom and I looked at each other, unable to believe what Music Head asked.

"No, we don't," I said.

"OK, ask me when you want to know the time," Music Head said.

"Thanks," I replied with a short and false smile. *I have a watch. But fine...*

We didn't say anything else and continued on the path. Music Head's long slim legs enabled him to move fast, and we had to speed up to keep the same pace.

The dark sky was covered with thick clouds. It didn't take long before the heavy rain started, making it difficult to continue.

"Let me use my umbrella," Music Head said. He pressed a button on the side of his hat, and a big black umbrella came out from the top, large enough to cover all three of us.

"Wow! Where did you get your hat?" Tom asked with great excitement.

"It's simple. I made it myself," Music Head replied.

There was a mountain ahead of us. Luckily, the rain stopped. The air became misty. We could barely see each other, but the ground was still visible. The walk up the mountain made my tired body suffer, and I was breathless, but we had to keep searching.

"Someone lives here on the mountain," Music Head said, and I didn't know if that was good or bad.

"Who?" Tom asked.

"The Mountain Beast. He has to give us permission to cross."

"Do you know of anyone who has managed to cross before?" Tom asked.

"No," Music Head replied bluntly.

"What happened to the ones who tried?" I asked with butterflies in my stomach.

"Oh, they burned to death," Music Head replied without any emotion as if talking about a movie he'd recently watched. The mist was too thick for me to see his expression.

"Why are we climbing the mountain then?" Tom asked. His face wasn't visible either, but his voice was more than anxious.

"There's no way for us to stop now. We need to keep going. The challenges on this journey, we can only overcome if we believe we can, if we do the right things, and trust our instincts," I said as I looked for Tom's face through the thick mist, but couldn't make it out.

"Do you have any other ideas?" I asked Tom and couldn't say another word because I was too breathless. It was difficult having to walk up the mountain and talk at the same time.

Tom didn't answer, but he was climbing faster than before.

My shoes were completely damaged. Hopefully, they would last until I got back to the pumpkin farm, at least. What should I tell my parents once I returned? I could say that my shoes got damaged while helping out. That was a white lie, of course.

Was thinking about being home a sign that we'd find the emerald and make it back?

Finding the emerald was just a part of the solution. Getting back to the castle, surviving the castle, and figuring a way back to the house on the pumpkin farm were other problems that needed to be solved. We had APPEARED in front of the castle. This meant that we had to DISAPPEAR back to the house again.

"We have to face the Mountain Beast," I said, walking ahead of Tom and Music Head.

"I know. We do have to," Tom replied. We continued climbing the steep mountain. From Tom and Music Head's heavy breaths, I knew that they were exhausted too.

"Who named you Music Head?" Tom asked between heavy breaths.

"People just started calling me that," Music Head replied.

The sky had turned pitch black.

"What time is it, Music Head?" I asked.

"It is 9:42:31."

The darkness had also made it more difficult climbing due to the lack of visibility.

I dearly wanted to sit down and rest, but knew I didn't have time for that. Even if we moved slower, we'd still get closer to our goal as long as we walked.

I looked down at my shoes but what caught my attention were small orange shifting objects on the ground.

What is this? I thought. I looked closely and noticed it was FIRE!

"Fire!" I shouted.

"We can cross. The flames are small," Tom said and carefully jumped on the fire-free patch on my path up the mountain. The mist disappeared instantly.

Tom and Music Head followed my steps.

Eventually, I reached the top, and a smile appeared on my lips. But it was short-lived. The heat stung my skin, and my cheeks turned red.

Small flames encircled me and spread up high toward the sky.

The fire smoke made me cough. There was no way to break free! I looked around to see if I could find a more suitable patch to jump over with fewer flames.

The picture of the old lady came to mind, and I remembered her advice: to follow my instinct. "I need to get past the flames!" I shouted loudly, feet firmly on the ground, fists closed tightly, my chest wide, head held high.

"I still have a lot of love to give to my family, my friends, and anyone else who may need my help. I have lots of love to spread into the world!" I said aloud and knew deep inside that Mountain Beast heard me. I could hear my heartbeat pounding like a drummer playing.

Sweat ran down my forehead, caused by the heat and the adrenaline rush in my veins.

"I need to find the emerald! Let me cross the fire!" Those were my final remarks.

The bright orange flames hurt my eyes, but I had to keep looking for an escape.

My eyes cast a look to the sky.

It was clear, and there was no way it would rain to dampen the flames.

The flame ahead of me changed color to orange, yellow… blue, and a path opened up! A shadow disappeared into the dark.

"Thank you!" I said as I looked at the spot where I'd seen the shadow disappear into the dark. Despite the darkness, I 'saw' Mountain Beast stop and turn around. Well, I couldn't see his gaze, but there was no doubt I could feel it.

What was left was the dark, empty space where the shadow had disappeared and my imagination of who the Mountain Beast was. I knew for sure that whoever he was, the most important thing was that he had a good heart.

Tom and Music Head rushed toward me.

"Lily! Are you OK?" Tom asked with worry. I'd known Tom for just a short period, but already knew he worried a lot. Maybe too much at times, but it also showed a caring side.

In that instance, he was right to worry. They must have witnessed me being encircled by the fire flames, with no way of escape.

"Don't worry about me. I'm fine. We have to hurry; we don't have much time left."

"Do you want to know what time it is?" Music Head asked.

"No, Knowing the time does not change anything as we have to just continue on our path to the emerald."

"OK," Music Head replied calmly. "But if you want to know the time, please ask."

We started to descend. It didn't take long before a green forest became visible at the foot of the hill on the other side.

"Look! A forest! Hopefully, we're getting close to the emerald. There's only one way to find out, and that is to get there," I said.

No one replied. Instead, we made our way swiftly down the mountain toward the forest.

It was much easier and quicker getting down the mountain compared to climbing up.

We continued walking down until we reached a small, old, wooden bridge at the very foot. It connected the mountain to the forest.

There was no way to get to the forest other than crossing the bridge, but it shook uncontrollably as soon as Tom placed his foot on it.

Is the wind shaking the bridge? Or is it the unsteadiness of the bridge? I thought.

The bridge shook and swayed violently. Tom held the ropes tightly on both sides to prevent falling. The shaking became so bad that Tom was unable to cross.

The bridge shook every time he set his foot on the bridge.

Tom tried crossing over and over, even running as fast as he could to reach the other side.

To no avail. The bridge shook from side to side and turned upside down, catapulting Tom off. He rolled until he managed to grab a stable rock and stopped.

He stood, walking toward us.

"We can't cross easily, but there has to be a way," I said.

"How else are we going to do it?" Tom asked.

"There must be a way. We just have to figure it out," I replied and looked at the still wooden bridge. The wind wasn't blowing, or at least not to a degree to move anything heavier than a feather. My mind went through all possibilities.

"The bridge is shaking... because we're rushing clumsily. Look how still it is now. It shakes uncontrollably only when we run! The only way is to take slow, gentle steps," I said.

"I'll try," Tom said and didn't hesitate.

He set his right foot slowly on the first wooden plank, and the bridge shook only slightly.

Tom stopped walking, and the bridge was completely still.

He continued walking slowly and paused whenever the bridge shook. He eventually reached the other side, but it had taken too much time. The clock was ticking.

"What time is it?" I asked.

I couldn't resist, despite having decided not to ask again before finding the emerald.

"It is 23:10:58," Music Head replied immediately.

I couldn't help but say, "Time is almost up!"

Music Head looked at me with no trace of emotion. "You can go before me. I have lived in this place a very long time. You two need to get back home."

I didn't want to waste time, but at the same time, couldn't let Music Head be left behind.

"We both have to get across. Let's get on the bridge together, co-ordinating steps."

"What are you waiting for? Just take gentle steps, and you'll be OK," Tom shouted from the other side of the bridge.

"Coming!" I replied and turned to Music Head again.

"Fine," Music Head said.

I stepped on the bridge, stood still, and instructed, "Get on the bridge now."

Music Head stepped on too, and the bridge shook. "We need to take steps simultaneously. Every time I say 'Step'. Ready! One, two, three, *step,*" I said. We both took a step forward.

"One, two, three, *step,*" I repeated and continued counting and coordinating our steps until we completed crossing the bridge.

It took us much longer than it had taken Tom, but the most important thing was that we had both crossed without leaving Music Head behind.

"We made it!" I said, and we all ran into the dark, dark forest without sparing a second.

The path was unclear, but we continued ahead without knowing where to go.

A brown owl sat on top of a tree, looking at us with big, round, piercing, yellow eyes.

The beautiful owl silently flew over to a nearby tree.

It turned its head through 180 degrees.

Then its head stopped moving and it dived down and captured something from the ground before flying up and landing on a branch again. A tail was hanging from the owl's beak.

It was a... mouse.

It was hard to see in the dark, but all three of us continued walking regardless.

"Where are we supposed to go now?" Tom asked.

"I don't know. There's no clear path," I said and stepped on a big rock next to a tree.

We had to decide which direction to take next.

The owl began hooting behind us, the sound echoing in the forest, making it sound as if there was a whole group of owls hooting at the same time.

Their sound was calming, as if the owl was trying to tell us that everything would be all right. The owl flew from one tree to the next.

We ignored it and continued, but the owl kept coming back to us. The owl then flew in the opposite direction when I gazed at it.

"Let's follow… let's follow the owl," Music Head said and was on his way before Tom and I could say anything. The owl didn't fly back and forth but kept moving in one direction, the opposite direction from which we were initially heading.

"Maybe. Let's see what happens next," I said.

Tom and I were following behind Music Head. He walked much faster than us. Soon we lost track of him as well as the owl.

My left foot snagged on something, and I fell.

Gallantly, Tom took my hand and helped me back to my feet.

"Are you OK?" he asked.

"Yeah. Let's see if we can find Music Head before it's too late," I said.

Chapter 8

THE FOREST OWL

Music Head was gone from our sight, but the owl's hooting could still be heard.

"Where is he?" Tom said, sounding frustrated. "Music Head! Music Head!" Tom shouted. He was looking around for a sign, but there wasn't any.

"I know. Let's find Music Head by following the hoots!" I suggested.

"Good idea," Tom replied. We both listened carefully. It was impossible to locate sounds in the forest. I rubbed my eyes and looked up, spotting the brown owl atop a tree, but there was no sign of Music Head.

"Tom, I think Music Head got lost," I whispered, hoping to be wrong more than ever.

"What makes you say that?" Tom asked.

"Look!" I said, pointing to the owl on top of the tree.

The owl spread its wings and flew to another tree.

"Wait a minute! We have to follow the owl to find Music Head," Tom said.

The owl flew from one tree to another.

The pitch-black forest reminded me of the time. Was it getting too late? Our ultimate mission was to find the emerald and return home. Instead, we were stuck in a dark forest and had lost Music Head. However, we couldn't leave him behind. We needed to find him.

"Do you think it's too late?" I asked Tom fearfully.

"I don't want to think about it," he replied. It was obvious that he also feared the fact that we hadn't found the emerald yet. Maybe we were doomed after all!

What if we had to live in the castle forever and never return home?

The owl flew to a tree on the left. Then ahead, then ahead again, to the left, to the left and ahead, and to the right. It was no wonder we had trouble following Music Head!

We were on the route to a secret place.

The owl had taken us in so many directions that my head was spinning.

"Do you feel dizzy too?" I asked Tom.

"I do," he said. The brown owl flew far in between two trees. Tom and I ran to find where it had landed.

We eventually found the owl sitting on a gigantic willow.

What forest is this? I thought.

The owl didn't move and kept hooting as if calling for us to get closer.

We moved toward the willow tree, and I noticed lights shining from the trunk of it. We moved closer and closer until an enormous door appeared on it.

Tom and I looked at each other, both surprised.

"Should we knock the door?" Tom asked.

"This must be the place the owl wanted us to find," I said before knocking lightly. The door opened just after a few short seconds. Seemingly, someone was expecting us.

A bright beam of light shone on our faces.

Our eyes were blinded by it. I opened mine slowly and saw an old lady standing at the door, the same old lady we had met outside the castle! The same lady who had given me advice after we had started our search for the emerald!

"Come in," she said with a smile. She had a friendly face full of freckles, just as I remembered from the first time we met. "I'm Willow Witch."

We stepped inside. The gigantic willow tree was Willow Witch's house!

The willow house had small windows opening to the forest. A wooden dining table and four chairs occupied the center of the hollow tree trunk.

A kitchen was visible under a solid wooden staircase, all part of the willow trunk. The staircase spiral reached up to the tree's very top.

The house had a mysterious atmosphere. It was such a cozy home!

Once I managed to gather myself, I looked around the room and finally noticed Music Head standing in a corner!

"Hello!" Music Head said.

"Music Head! We finally found you! We've been searching for you."

I felt so relieved to see him.

"Found me? I wasn't lost. You were. You should have followed me," he replied.

"Of course, but you were much quicker than us, and we lost sight of you." Tom took a deep breath. He had become overly anxious again.

I looked at Tom, but he ignored me as he looked around with apparent uncertainty.

"Thank you for letting us in," I said.

"You're most welcome! Sit down at the table. Have some chocolate chip cookies," Willow Witch said.

Tom and I sat next to each other at the table.

I was determined to not take a bite from the cookies offered to us. Willow Witch was a stranger, after all. "No, thank you," I said despite wanting to taste them so badly. "We need to leave soon because we have to find the emerald before midnight," I explained.

Willow Witch's small dark eyes were shining. She looked at me with a smile but remained silent. Then, she slowly moved toward us with her walking stick.

She set herself down at the table.

"Do you think you'll find the emerald?" she asked.

"Maybe. We need to find it before midnight and give it to Isabel. She's in the castle. We'll be stuck in there forever if we don't find it before midnight," I said.

Willow Witch's smile didn't fade from her ruby lips.

I couldn't understand how she could hear something so horrible and still remain calm.

"What did you do to get here?" she asked as she kept looking me in the eye.

"We dug the basement floor looking for the emerald, and then we somehow found an opening and entered…"

Willow Witch interrupted me. "No, no, no. That's not what I meant," she said. "What did you do to get so far?"

I was worried. My heart was beating like a trapped butterfly trying to spread its wings in a small glass cage. Suddenly, I realized what Willow Witch meant.

"We followed your advice. We followed our instinct, doing the right things."

The more I explained, the more I understood the tasks on our journey. The missing parts of the puzzle fell into place.

"We acted with kindness when we found the injured bird. Courage was all I needed when facing the monster in the pond. By facing my inner fear, I defeated my fear of the unknown.

"Only the truth was spoken when the Seal Monster asked us where we were heading despite the chances of getting hurt upon telling the truth."

I paused for a moment to think and continued.

"We persisted when we were surrounded by ice and the cave's rocky walls. Our surroundings seemed like a dead end, but we still found a way out of the cave because we had believed it was possible. Music Head wasn't left behind when we met him in the forest despite him being different from us, because of a strong feeling of empathy and friendship.

"We remembered others we loved despite being in immediate danger, fighting to reunite again. Great patience was the secret to crossing the bridge, and we finally reached our goal by being patient," I said, relieved that we had passed all the hidden tasks.

Willow Witch nodded. "Those were the only way you could have made it so far. You passed the lesson of kindness, the lesson of courage, the lesson of speaking the truth, the lesson of never accepting a temporary defeat as the final outcome, the lesson of friendship and empathy, the lesson of love, and the task of patience.

"All of these lessons are equally important." Willow Witch raised her bony index finger in the air to mark the importance of her words as the smile on her lips became wider.

"Thank you! But we still haven't found the emerald," I rushed to say.

"Don't worry about the emerald. You have already earned it."

Willow Witch opened her fist, and a magical, green beam of light shone in all directions. She held the precious emerald in her hand!

"Oh!" was the only word that came out of my mouth.

I was too mesmerized to say anything that made some sense. Now, I had a brief glimpse of how Tom must feel whenever he seemed stuck for something to say.

"Take it back to the castle... and don't worry about time."

Willow Witch placed the precious emerald into my hand. I absorbed the beautiful deep green radiation and felt the smooth surface.

We'd possibly be able to return home!

That was more valuable than all the emeralds in the universe.

"I can't thank you enough, Willow Witch! The value of the emerald isn't its beauty. The true value of the emerald is that... we can go home! Home to the ones that we love," I said joyfully.

"Where do I go? I don't have any family or friends," Music Head said.

Tom and I looked at each other.

"You're coming with us," Tom said.

"That's a wonderful idea!" Willow Witch replied.

"Do you know who all those people in the castle are?" she asked.

"Maybe some sort of... demons?" Tom said with his usual worried face. He hesitated to say the last word aloud as if the demons would magically appear if he mentioned them.

"You're right. After failing to find the emerald, all were converted to demons; night demons. They could not pass the numerous tasks along the path leading to the emerald."

Willow Witch continued speaking in a soft but serious voice. "Dr. Herbert was first. He's a scientist with ruthless intentions. Dr. Herbert experimented on animals in the forest surrounding the castle. The poor divos are the results of Dr. Herbert's experiments.

"He failed already at the first task by placing that poor animal in his pocket. His intention was to perform experiments on it later when he returned to his laboratory. That's why he's stuck in the castle. He failed the lesson of kindness. Everyone gets only one chance to find the emerald on their own. If they fail any task on the search for the emerald, they have to wait for the next person to find it for them," Willow Witch explained.

"How did he know about the emerald?" Tom asked.

"I told him about it one day when I saw him in the forest. What happened to him was only fair since he had the same chance to do the right thing as everyone else. The same instructions were given to him, but he was just unable to pass the tests."

Willow Witch took a sip of her drink before continuing, "By doing so, I could protect all the forest animals from his cruelty. I suspected he'd fail the tasks and get stuck in the castle as a night demon forever." She took a deep breath.

"As for Isabel, she discovered the castle accidentally and entered the castle. Dr. Herbert cleverly convinced her to search for the emerald in hopes of getting his hands on it and finally leaving the castle. The curse starts the moment you search for the emerald.

"Isabel... well, she couldn't pass the lesson of love. She told Mountain Beast that she had to find the emerald for her own sake. Isabel had planned to make a necklace of it. She described it as 'the most beautiful necklace in the world.' Isabel was willing to give away the opportunity and never see her friends and family ever again for the sake of the emerald. As a result, she ended up imprisoned in the castle alongside Dr. Herbert."

"Who was the third person trying to find the emerald?" I asked.

"Duke Lukas," Willow Witch replied in short.

"How did he get to the castle?" I asked eagerly.

Willow Witch got up and with her stick and walked over to the pot boiling away on the stove. She took up a wooden spoon from the drawer as she said, "Duke Lukas. Yes, he got to the castle by looking for his old friend, Dr. Herbert. Duke Lukas inherited the castle, but he was rarely there as he was afraid of the villagers. He was afraid the villagers would one day break in and burn him alive since there were rumors about him being a vampire."

Willow Witch paused and sat at the table again.

"Therefore, he was hiding in another estate, close to the castle. Dr. Herbert had promised Duke Lukas he'd give him an elixir to cure all kinds of diseases. The thing is children, Duke Lukas suffers from a terrible disease. A disease so bad it makes his skin blister, bubble and boil when exposed to sunlight. Imagine that!"

Willow Witch stared at me with her beady eyes, sending a shudder through me.

"These horrible blisters or boils leak pus, yellow goo and goodness knows what else. Urgh! And the smell! Believe me, it would put you off your food. And that's no lie."

Willow Witch shook her head and took a deep breath.

"Dear me, now where was I? Oh yes. So," she continued, "The villagers, who had never seen him out in daylight, only alone at night, starting spreading rumors, making out that Duke Lukas was out at night preying on victims, biting their necks and drinking their blood.

"This is a problem. When people see someone who's different like he is, they always need to make up some kind of a story. It's what people do. Unfortunately."

Willow Witch once again stood from her chair.

"Anyone who spotted him at night, would scream and run in the opposite direction to avoid the blood-sucking Duke," Willow Witch added. "Now, *you* don't honestly think Duke Lukas is a vampire, do you?" she asked.

"Err, no, I don't think he's a vampire, but I can understand why the villagers *thought* he was, if he was only spotted at night," I answered with a hint of doubt.

"He has no option but to stay indoors during daylight because of his condition. And, if you haven't already noticed, his skin is ghostly white due to his lack of sunshine."

Willow Witch paused once again and glanced at each of the children in turn.

"Sorry this is long-winded, but you need to know as much as possible."

"No, Willow Witch, what you are saying is fascinating," I interrupted.

"Duke Lukas wanted the elixir so he could get cured. He was tired of spending years in darkness. Daylight would cease being his greatest enemy if only he used the elixir.

"However, Dr. Herbert made a deal."

Willow Witch coughed before continuing.

"Excuse me. Duke Lukas would only get his hands on the elixir in exchange for the emerald. After their failed attempts, Dr. Herbert and Isabel were already stuck in the castle, hoping Duke Lukas would rescue them by successfully finding the emerald as he was desperate for the elixir," Willow Witch explained.

"Did Dr. Herbert's elixir really cure all kinds of diseases?" Tom asked.

Willow Witch laughed and said, "It did. It still does."

Tom appeared happier than I ever had seen him.

"Who has the elixir?" I asked.

Tom's mother could benefit from the elixir if we brought it to her!

"The elixir is still with Dr. Herbert," Willow Witch replied.

"Oh... that's tricky," Tom said. He was right to be worried. He looked down, trying to figure out a way to get hold of the potion.

"Will we get back to my cousins' house as soon as we return the emerald?" I asked.

"Finding the emerald allows you to leave the castle. Getting back to the house on the pumpkin farm depends on something else. Don't be too hasty. You will find out later."

Willow Witch smiled. "Everyone in the castle, except Betty, is a prisoner unless they break the curse by holding the emerald in their hand for seven hours."

"Why not Betty?" I asked, despite knowing the answer.

"Betty's a wandering ghost. She's neither good nor bad. Sometimes, she walks around in the forest, looking for people to bring back to the castle and search for the emerald. That's what happened when you first met her. She lured you to the castle."

Willow Witch got up, took her cup to the kitchen, and asked, "More drinks?" Tom and I looked at each other and answered *no* simultaneously.

"Tea for me, please," Music Head replied.

Willow Witch made a cup of tea for Music Head as she continued, "Betty brought her friend Danielle. What do you think happened?"

"She failed as the rest of them," Music Head replied.

"Indeed. Danielle failed... failed on the lesson of courage." Willow Witch turned around, laughed, and placed the teacup into Music Head's hands.

"What is the elixir made of?" Tom asked.

"I would have made it if I knew that. Everyone would! The only thing I'm sure of is that something so precious must be originating from nature. Our precious mother nature."

"You said we'll find out later," I said. "But I'm still worried about how we're going to return to the house on the pumpkin farm."

I was hoping that I'd get an answer despite not having asked a question.

Willow Witch smiled and said, "Everything is connected. You needed to get to the pumpkin farm, the house, and the castle to finally get here: holding the emerald in your hand!

I knew you were coming. Everything has been orchestrated for you to be here now in this moment, in this *very* moment," Willow Witch said, looking at me with her dark, small eyes.

"What happens next?" Tom asked.

"Time is not important as long as you are in this house. Time is always still here in the Willow House," she replied.

"Yes. Time has stopped," Music Head confirmed and placed his teacup on the table.

"What should we do with the emerald once we get back? Isabel wants to take it," I said.

"Remember, you have to hold the emerald for seven hours each. Try to hide from the night demons during this time as you risk losing the emerald... and you'll be stuck in the castle forever in that case," Willow Witch's voice became stern.

She continued, "Do your best to hide! The last one of you should bring the emerald to the Mirror Hall and place it in the center of the room. The sunlight shining through the emerald will purify the whole space, and the night demons will be unable to hold the emerald."

"Why are they called night demons, and why wouldn't they be able to hold the emerald in their hands anyway?" I asked.

"Because they are demons that turn into pitch-black crows, especially at night.

"Once you purify the castle with the emerald, they will become ghosts. The night demons turned to ghosts and would then leave the castle. Just like Betty, but they'll be harmless to the forest animals and anyone else."

"But can they turn into night demons again?" Tom asked in a worried voice.

"No, they'll never be transformed back to night demons once the reflection of the emerald's shining rays penetrates through them via the mirrors," Willow Witch said.

We all nodded in response.

"By doing so, you are also helping them," she added.

"What will they do if they get hold of the emerald?" Tom asked.

"At first, they'll use it to become humans again. Then, they each have a secret plan for it," Willow Witch answered.

"I have one last question," I said, knowing the answer would scare me.

But I asked anyway.

"You can ask anything you like," Willow Witch said.

"What would have happened to us if we'd failed to find the emerald?" I asked.

"What do you think?" Willow Witch said and laughed aloud.

"Besides being stuck in the castle eternally... we'd also have turned into night demons!" I replied, getting goosebumps.

"Once the last one of you has left the castle, you should all go back to the spot where you first appeared in front of it. Stand next to each other on the same spot," she emphasized.

It felt good hearing Willow Witch's last remarks about us returning home.

"Thank you for all your help, Willow Witch!" I said as I felt truly grateful.

"Thank you! You're very wise," Tom said awkwardly with a nervous smile.

"You would also be as wise if you were nine hundred and twenty-four years-old!"

"Nine hundred twenty-four years!?" Tom and I shouted simultaneously.

We looked at each other with astonishment.

"Thank you," Music Head said with his usual expressionless face, failing to show any reaction to Willow Witch's old age. She was amused by our response.

"Leave now. You still have a lot to do. Remember to look for the elixir."

"But how...?" I mumbled, but Willow Witch didn't let me finish my sentence.

"Come, let's go outside."

We were all standing outside the Willow House after a short while.

Willow Witch turned to face the three of us and blew hard. The next thing I knew, we were all flying high in the sky, floating like feathers in the wind toward the castle.

"Farewell and good luck!" Willow Witch shouted from afar, and her laughter echoed in the atmosphere. We traveled through the cold air with great speed. My eyes were shut tightly as I was afraid of suddenly falling into one of the terrifying places crossed on our path.

Chapter 9

THE MISSION

We were back in the basement, in the same hole we had dug earlier.

The difference was that we were more exhausted, Music Head was with us, and we had found what we wanted so desperately: the deep green, precious emerald!

"Let's get out of here as soon as possible. I'm claustrophobic," Tom said.

"I forgot how deep we had dug. There's no air," I said and took a deep breath.

Music Head was sitting in a corner. He appeared distressed but quiet.

"What's wrong?" I asked.

Music Head replied, "I'm not used to change."

"You're going to be all right, Music Head. This is not the best place to be. I also feel anxious here. We're in a hole in the ground of a dark basement of a very, very old castle in the middle of a forest. But we'll take you back to the pumpkin farm with us. You'll see how beautiful it is there! It's amazing, and welcoming," Tom said.

Hearing Tom's kind words made Music Head look more relaxed.

"Is it true?" he asked.

"Yes, you'll see for yourself once we get back," I answered.

"All right, we need to have a plan. We shouldn't get out of the basement without knowing how we'll complete our mission. Isabel and the other night demons will take the emerald away from us in no time if we aren't cautious," Tom said.

"Of course, we should have a plan," I agreed, trying to figure out how we should go about things. We were all quiet for a while, trying to think out the perfect solution.

"Isabel's expecting us. She might enter the basement any second now, being the one who ordered us to search for the emerald. Suppose we apply the knowledge we gained in the house on the pumpkin farm. In that case, we may be able to find the elixir, complete holding the emerald for seven hours each, leave the castle, and return home," Tom said.

"What a brilliant idea! We learned how to make pumpkin recipes that can make us fly, become invisible and bounce," I said.

"Is that true?" Music Head asked. I nodded.

"Wait a minute, we won't be able to get those powers if we don't have pumpkins from the farm. The magic's from the pumpkins themselves, the magical ones from the farm," Tom said and scratched his head.

Tom's right. We need pumpkins from the farm, I thought.

How were we going to complete holding the emerald for seven hours each, find the elixir and at the same time, hide from Duke Lukas, Dr. Herbert, Isabel, Danielle... and Betty?

"You still have the emerald on you, right?" Tom asked as he suddenly thought about the misfortune of us accidentally losing the precious gem.

"Don't worry. I have it," I said, my hand deep in my pocket, looking for the emerald.

Nervousness bloomed in me. *No emerald? What? Oh. Oh no!*

Tom and Music Head both stared at me, also worried, seeing me rummaging.

It took much longer to find it than necessary.

How could I lose the emerald we fought so hard for? I thought, almost sobbing.

Yes! I felt the emerald's smooth surface, but there was also something else in my pocket: a small, solid, deformed piece. I took my hand from my pocket, held my palm facing the ceiling, and there was the smooth, deep green, precious emerald...

AND a small piece of dried PUMPKIN!

Tom looked at me and said, "It's great, but will such a small piece be enough to give us special power?" Tom asked.

"Maybe it doesn't matter how little we eat as long as we consume some," I said.

"We'll only know if we try," Tom said. "We should make the recipe just in case the plain pumpkin doesn't work for certain powers. The first step should be to go to the kitchen and try to make the same recipe that made us invisible," Tom said.

"Who'll be the first to hold the emerald?" I asked.

I looked at Tom, and he looked at me, and we both looked at Music Head. He'd seemed in some degree of distress from the moment he'd appeared in the castle.

"Music Head should be the first because he never asked for any of this," I said.

"I agree. You'll feel better outside the castle in seven hours. Wait for the next person in the forest, and we'll bring you back to the house with us. You'll like it there. Charlotte and Poppy are both nice. Maybe you'll also be able to play the piano again," Tom said.

Music Head got up and said, "OK, that sounds good. Sorry I have to be the first, but I really don't like it here."

"Don't apologize, Music Head. We're in this together, and we'll need more time trying to find the elixir. I don't want to put you in danger for something I'm looking for," Tom said.

I stretched my hand toward Music Head. "Take it," I said, looked at him, and nodded.

Music Head then took the emerald in his hand and put it in his pocket.

"Let's leave before Isabel arrives. At least we have a plan," Tom said.

"Yes," I replied and knew our time was precious.

"What time is it?" I asked.

"It is 23:51:21," Music Head replied.

"Isabel will be here any minute. We've less than ten minutes to leave," I said.

"We should climb up out of the hole," Tom said and didn't waste any time. He managed to get out of it rather quickly.

"That was quick," Music Head said.

"Climbing's one of my favorite activities. Come on! You can do it too," Tom said. Both Music Head and I climbed, but we were much slower than Tom. Tom helped us both out once we'd reached high enough.

We all looked at the few steps leading up to the basement door.

"Let's go," I said and walked toward the door with Tom and Music Head following behind. I placed my hand on the doorknob and attempted to open the door. But it was impossible. "It's locked," I whispered.

Suddenly, I saw Music Head's hand moving toward the keyhole. He held a small black pin, placed the pin inside the keyhole, and turned it. The door opened effortlessly!

I knew I shouldn't make any sound and pushed the door open as slowly as possible. Light from the corridor shone on our faces as soon as the door opened.

Where's the light coming from? I thought and looked at the light source. I saw a lamp… and a hand… holding it! I looked up: Isabel was looking at me with a big smile!

"Hello, and welcome back!" she said.

Seeing Isabel's face made me jump. Her pale skin, dark eyes, and red lips were the only things in my visual field.

The smile on her face added an extra layer of creepiness.

"RUN!" Tom shouted from behind. He must have seen that I'd frozen.

Music Head was behind, and he started running, and so did Tom.

Finally, I was able to run as fast as I'd ever done in my life, without knowing in which direction to head.

Music Head was in front of me, already running far ahead. With his long legs, he could run faster. I decided to follow him, hearing Tom shouting behind me. "Let me go!"

Isabel was holding his wrist with her other hand.

"Give me the emerald! It belongs to me! I deserve it more than anyone else!" she shouted. Tom turned his wrist and freed himself from her grasp.

He shouted, "Run, Lily!" and I continued running.

We followed Music Head and ran through the big dining room. I was hoping we'd find a hiding place.

Music Head had opened one of the doors leading out of the dining room.

We got to a hallway, and I could still hear Isabel chasing us.

She was full of rage. "Wait 'til I get my hands on you! You'll see! You'll be punished if you don't hand over the emerald!"

Tom got ahead of me, my breathlessness getting worse.

Isabel's voice became louder as she came closer.

I could no longer keep up with Tom and Music Head, and fell behind.

The only way to escape was to quickly hide somewhere safe. There was a door further down the corridor. *Do I stand a chance? But what if Isabel follows me?*

I'll be trapped, I thought. A half-open window appeared ahead.

I should jump out of the window, I thought.

I first jumped on top of a short desk and tried to jump through the window next. I shut my eyes and pushed myself up with both legs, but something hit my face, and I fell backward. I couldn't think due to the excruciating pain.

Of course, I couldn't jump out of the window!

None of us were able to because we were cursed, imprisoned in the castle until we held the emerald for seven hours!

How could I have forgotten? Isabel laughed as she approached.

"Well, well, well. Now you really understand what I meant by saying that you'll be imprisoned. You haven't turned into night demons, and you were back before midnight. Hmmm... how come you're running away?!

"All of these things mean that you've got the emerald... congratulations!"

Isabel bent down and looked me in the eye as she held my wrists with her hands.

Her nails dug into my flesh.

The sharp pain made it hard to keep my eyes open or think clearly.

"That hurts!" I said and hoped that she'd release her grip.

"If you think I am going to have mercy, I have to inform you that you are wrong!"

She dragged me off the floor as she held my wrist firmly.

"Let go of me!" I said, fighting to break free.

"Stop it!" Isabel shouted.

She dragged me into a room, the same one in which we had found Duke Lukas and Dr. Herbert when we'd tried escaping the castle at night.

A divo was serving Duke Lukas, Dr. Herbert, and Danielle drinks. Isabel kicked the poor divo in the stomach as it was trying to cross the room with a tray full of drinks.

"Get out of my way, you little midget," Isabel shouted.

The poor divo fell over and dropped everything.

"Isabel, calm down," Duke Lukas said as he got up and looked at Isabel with a frown. He then spoke with a smile on his lips. "Bring more drinks immediately!"

The poor divo still couldn't get up but tried standing up when he slipped on the wet floor and fell again.

"You are useless!" Duke Lukas said with pure anger.

"Please don't say that," I said, despite my fear.

"What? What did you just say?" Duke Lukas said as he turned to me.

"Don't call him useless... please," I replied somewhat gingerly.

Duke Lukas looked at the rest of the night demons in the room and laughed aloud.

"Who are you to tell me what to do and what not to do?" he shouted. The sound echoed in my ears. "Do you have the emerald?" he asked, using a calmer voice this time.

I remained quiet.

"Have you searched her for the emerald?" Dr. Herbert asked.

"No. I just managed to capture her as she was running away with her friends," Isabel said.

"Search her now!" Duke Lukas ordered and clapped his hands.

Two chubby divos came in and searched my pockets, clothes, and even my dirty, damaged shoes.

They looked at Duke Lukas, held their hands in the air, and shook their heads.

Duke Lukas looked me deep in the eye for several seconds before saying, "Oh well, she hasn't turned into a night demon."

"I know. The child is not one of us... yet," Isabel said.

"That means they definitely found the emerald," Dr. Herbert said.

"They're three now. There's another tall boy with them," Isabel said.

"Search the castle!" Duke Lukas ordered again and clapped his hands twice.

Several divos started searching everywhere. They rushed in and out.

Duke Lukas turned to me with a smile. "Dr. Herbert, you have a new specimen to bring to your laboratory. Don't worry about your friends, Lily. We'll find them and fetch the emerald. Take her to the laboratory!"

All the night demons in the room laughed.

They all turned into big, black crows and flew around me in circles.

Their black feathers touched my skin. I protected my face with both my hands.

Suddenly, I couldn't feel their feathers anymore. I looked up and saw the night demons standing around me in their human form.

Duke Lukas clapped rhythmically and chanted, "It's going to be a special night! It's going to be a great night! Tonight is a special night! Tonight is emerald night! Tonight is the night we've been waiting for! It took over 500 years, but tonight is our special night!"

His singing echoed not only in the room but also, in the vast castle.

I could still hear Duke Lukas singing as two short but strong divos dragged me out. I couldn't move. *Is it over?* I thought.

***

Tom and Music Head didn't have enough time to make the pumpkin recipe, and seven hours was too long to wait.

The divos followed Duke Lukas's order and searched the entire castle.

They'd capture Tom and Music Head. All three of us could become Dr. Herbert's laboratory specimens. Just like the poor divos had once been.

What creature will Dr. Herbert turn us into? I got goosebumps from the mere thought.

There was no way that Tom and Music Head could leave the castle. They hadn't held the emerald in their hands for seven hours each yet. Therefore, they'd bounce back every time they tried to leave, just the way I had.

I felt numb and hopeless. *What is going to happen next?*

The divos were able to drag me away effortlessly. They took me to the ground floor, into a cold room. From the gray walls, glass bottles, and various pieces of science equipment, I could tell that we were in Dr. Herbert's laboratory.

I came to think of Willow Witch and her advice: *Trust your instinct and do the right thing,* she had said.

Could Willow Witch's advice be helpful in the castle just the way it had been on the route to the Willow Forest? I suddenly felt hopeful.

"I need to scratch my neck," I said, and one of the divos let go of my right arm and helped the other divo by dragging me by my left arm instead.

I took off one of my shoes and threw it outside the laboratory. The shoe must have hit an object as it made a loud sound.

The divos stopped for a moment, turning to look for the sound source.

After standing still and listening for a short while, they continued dragging me to the far end of the laboratory. They left me on the floor before they walked out.

One of the divos turned and waved at me before closing the door.

I waved back before I was locked inside.

Is the room full of bottles in the house on the pumpkin farm also a lab?

The noisy divos ran around the castle looking for Tom and Music Head.

Hopefully, they wouldn't catch them, and they were both fine.

What if I can find a tool that can be used to escape? I thought and started looking around in the dark.

There were laboratory bottles everywhere. The objects reminded me of my chemistry class—plenty of long glass tubes, glass pipettes, and solutions steaming on small fires.

I moved closer to one of the bottles and wanted to sniff it.

Suddenly, I remembered that my chemistry teacher warned us never to smell any unknown solution directly.

I ran my hand in the air over the glass bottle with my face away from it.

They smelled bad! So bad that I decided to stop exploring any further.

My legs were aching. I sat down on the floor far away from Dr. Herbert's solutions.

It was dead quiet in the laboratory for a while until the sound of footsteps, keys, the door unlocking, and door opening filled the space rapidly.

My gut feeling told me I should be on my toes.

Dr. Herbert was at the door! He strolled in.

This time, he was wearing a white lab coat, prepared for his experiment. He had a certain excitement on his face that I'd never seen before.

"Do you like my laboratory?" he asked with a smile, an *evil* smile.

Dr. Herbert entered, slowly closing the door.

The sound of his footsteps echoed in my ears. I couldn't tell which was louder: his footsteps or my heartbeats.

My vision got blurry, and I felt dizzy.

One... two... three, and Dr. Herbert was right in front of me, and he put on a pair of gloves.

I took a deep breath and gathered myself. Calmness was crucial to my survival.

"You have a nice laboratory," I lied.

"Do you really think so?" Dr. Herbert asked as he could surely tell that I was dishonest.

"Of course," I said, swallowing hard.

Dr. Herbert raised his eyebrows and screened the room. He walked over to one of the desks and got busy with something I couldn't see.

"Dr. Herbert, why do you *have* a laboratory?" I asked.

"This is my home, and I rarely leave. I even sleep on the couch over there." He pointed to a black couch, with his back still toward me.

Well, that hadn't even scratched the surface of my question.

He continued, "Duke Lukas, Isabel, and Danielle are not allowed in my laboratory."

"Why?" I asked.

Dr. Herbert got irritated by my questioning, looked over his shoulder, and replied with a frown, "Because I have precious things in here, of course. Why else do you think?"

Dr. Herbert looked inside a big black pot as he said, "You have been good! You deserve a treat." He seemed to be speaking directly to the pot.

Is he losing it? I thought.

The pot responded to Dr. Herbert by shaking viciously. It almost hit the wall. Some strange, somewhat screaming noise came from the black pot.

My tired eyes tried to find a way to do their magic, to see what appeared in the visual field from afar. But Dr. Herbert was blocking my view. He seemed scared and tried to quickly find the pot's lid. Unfortunately for him, he had placed it slightly further away.

He could not let go of the pot as it kept shaking uncontrollably, and he held it with both arms to prevent it breaking.

"You are the most precious! The most precious thing ever!" he said. Whatever was inside that black pot mesmerized him as much as it scared him.

He made another attempt to take the lid by reaching out as far as possible, but he was unable to grab it.

The mysterious object in the pot was getting out. I stood on my toes to see more, but something suddenly covered my mouth from behind.

My body twisted toward the entrance door, carried out so fast that I couldn't comprehend what was going on and had trouble orienting myself. Dr. Herbert was speaking in the laboratory, "Be still, precious. I'm going to give you a treat! Don't leave the pot. Stay there."

I looked down to see what was carrying me out of the laboratory, but all I could see was the floor as I floated in the air.

The thing holding my mouth had the shape of a hand.

I ran my hand in the air below me. Slowly I moved it away. There was an ear! A nose!

Tom and Music Head had become invisible by using the magical pumpkin recipe! They had found and saved me from the laboratory.

Had I given them the dry pumpkin piece? I thought but couldn't recall.

We entered a dark room further down the corridor.

Dr. Herbert shouted from the laboratory, "She escaped from the laboratory, that wretched, awful child! Bring her back!"

Once the door was closed, the light from the corridor was blocked by it.

Nothing was visible inside the room.

Tom spoke for the first time since they'd rescued me. "Are you OK, Lily?"

"I'm fine, but can't believe that you found me so fast," I said as I took a deep breath. A throbbing headache spread.

"You left a trace behind, remember? We found your shoe close to the laboratory. Once outside the laboratory, we could hear Dr. Herbert's voice. Music Head unlocked the door with his pin. Luckily, Dr. Herbert was busy. I'm not sure what we would've done if he wasn't," Tom said.

"You made it. That's what counts. Thank you," I said and looked in the direction from which I heard Tom's voice. "Music Head, are you all right?" I asked.

"Yes," he answered. I also tried to locate the direction of Music Head's voice.

"I don't know whose nose and ear I touched, sorry," I said. "It wasn't deliberate."

"Mine," Music Head replied.

"They'll probably search this room too. You better have some of this," Tom said and placed a tiny bit of food on the tip of my left index finger.

The door opened, a head appeared at the door, two big eyes looking me straight in the eye! It was Danielle, also looking for us.

I placed the food in my mouth and swallowed as quickly as possible, but Danielle kept looking at me.

Was the pumpkin quantity too small?

Danielle's gaze slid past mine and continued looking around in the dark as she took several steps inside the room. I didn't move or make any sound. I had to smoothly and quietly roll away from her footsteps.

She almost stepped on my hand, about to whack my face with her other foot.

I luckily rolled away again. We all needed to remain undetected for just a few more seconds, and Danielle would be done searching the room.

Danielle turned around to walk out. But she hesitated, looked down at her right foot, then ran her foot back and forth as if something was stuck on the sole of her shoe.

She then shrugged her shoulders and left the room.

"That was close," I whispered.

"My finger is hurting! She stepped on it and rubbed my finger with her shoe. Luckily, she gave up and left when I pulled my finger away," Tom whispered back.

I couldn't help but laugh uncontrollably. Tom laughed too.

Only Music Head remained silent.

"I'm exhausted," I said.

"So am I," Music Head replied.

"We still have time to find the elixir. We should sleep now. No one can see us because we're invisible," I said.

"I agree, but where do we sleep?" Tom asked.

I looked around. There was a double bed in the center of the room.

"Let's sleep underneath the bed. We're invisible, but the only way they can find us is if they walk into us or hear us," I said.

"OK," Tom replied. It soon became obvious that he was yawning. The three of us rolled under the bed, but all collided.

"We should roll one at a time," Tom said.

"I can go first," I said and rolled all the way to the other side, under the bed.

"I'm going next," Music Head said and rolled next to me.

"Make sure you bend your knees slightly," I reminded Music Head as his feet were sticking out.

"I will," Music Head replied.

We were all silent. Tom and Music Head had both already fallen asleep.

I could still hear the sound of divos searching everywhere for the three of us, everywhere besides underneath the bed in the dark bedroom.

The voices of Danielle, Isabel, and Duke Lukas also occasionally broke the silence in the room as they walked past the door.

My eyelids felt heavier and heavier until my eyes were completely shut.

My breaths became deeper and slower. My muscles started relaxing, and my thoughts slowing until there was no thought in my mind.

***

A loud banging noise woke me, sending my heart racing like a wild horse. My eyes were wide open as a reflex, and my muscles tensed.

I looked in the direction of the door and saw a pair of men's black shoes walking toward the bed. Duke Lukas!

We were hiding in his bedroom. He took off his shoes and walked around the room.

I hoped Music Head kept his legs bent so that Duke Lukas would not trip on them in the morning. He finally climbed into bed.

After some time, Music Head started snoring next to me.

I shook him gently, and he was silent again.

What if Music Head or Tom start snoring during the night? I thought.

Luckily, it didn't take long before Duke Lukas started snoring louder than anyone I'd ever heard snore before.

Chapter 10

SURVIVING

The following day, the first thing I did was check and see if we were still invisible.

I turned toward Music Head and couldn't see him: hopefully, we were still invisible and they hadn't left me here alone. They'd never do that to me, so I was reassured. How were we going to complete twenty more hours? Additionally, we had to find the elixir.

We had survived so far but with great hardship, but I wasn't sure we could keep on being lucky and clever for so many more hours. But we had to keep trying and believing.

What if we run out of luck? I thought and after a couple of hours, rolled out from underneath the bed and looked to see if Duke Lukas was still sleeping.

But he was gone.

"Wake up," I whispered as I stooped and looked under the bed. "Wake up. We're in Duke Lukas's bedroom. We should have something to eat. I'm starving, and can't remember when I last ate," I said.

"What time is it?" Tom asked.

"8:58:23," Music Head replied.

From the sound of their voices, I knew both had come out from underneath the bed.

"How are we going to communicate once we leave?" Tom said.

"What about holding each other's arms? We don't have to run or walk fast. We walk slowly and hold each other's arms so as not to lose each other," Tom suggested.

"That sounds good!" I replied. "I'll lead, Tom can go in the middle and Music Head at the rear." We held each other's arms, and I led the way as we walked toward the door.

"I looked around Duke Lukas's bedroom before leaving. A red, old Persian carpet was covering the floor. The rest of the furniture was as expected: old with a classic design.

Being perhaps the bravest of the three of us, I slowly opened the door and peeked out. Two divos walked outside the bedroom, laughing and making strange noises.

It felt good leaving Duke Lukas's room. One by one, we emerged from the bedroom. We walked up the stairs, through the Mirror Hall. Finally, we got to the very dining room we had entered when we had first come to the castle.

Duke Lukas, Dr. Herbert, Danielle, Isabel and Betty were all sitting around the table.

Everyone but Betty sat eating breakfast. The divos were going in and out from the kitchen, bringing more food. I was really hungry, and was sure both Tom and Music Head were too. What a delicious breakfast the divos had prepared!

I had an idea: we could go to the kitchen and help ourselves to food because the night demons wouldn't notice anything!

I pulled Tom's arm in the direction of the kitchen, but he didn't follow.

"We have to find the children. They have the emerald. We didn't wait centuries for some children to arrive at the castle, find the emerald and keep it for themselves," Isabel said.

I tried to pull Tom along once again, but it was impossible. He didn't move.

Why is he not following me? I thought, turned around and looked in Tom's direction.

A grape was floating in the air and disappeared suddenly.

Oh no! Tom is eating grapes! I thought, panicking as I didn't know how to stop him.

"What happened to the grape?" Danielle said.

"What grape? Can't you focus on what I'm saying for a moment?" Isabel asked, annoyed.

"There was a grape floating in the air... it then disappeared," Danielle said with a confused face that matched the tone of her voice.

"Oh dear, you must have imagined it! Did you not sleep well last night?" Isabel said with a mocking laughter as she took a bite of the bread in her hand.

How can they breathe in those corset dresses? Let alone eat food? They look so tight, I thought.

I had no choice but to pull Tom's arm as hard as I could this time as he was risking getting detected! Finally, he followed me slowly.

"Release the dogs. They'll be more helpful than the useless divos," Dr. Herbert said.

"In that case, the dogs shouldn't be fed today. They'll do a far better job if they are hungry," Isabel suggested.

The hair on the back of my neck rose.

"What a great idea, Isabel!" Duke Lukas replied, laughing.

We moved closer to the kitchen, and I turned my head as I sensed being observed.

Betty kept looking at me!

I looked at her and hoped she'd look away.

Could she see us? I moved and her eyes followed. I decided that it was best if I just continued walking toward the kitchen regardless.

We had to move aside multiple times as the divos kept coming in and out of the kitchen.

In the kitchen, the divos had placed a large selection of food on trays.

Everything appeared so chaotic. A handful of divos were each busy with a specific task. Some washed dishes, some cooked food over the fire, others placing it onto trays.

The chaos of the kitchen allowed us to eat without any of the divos noticing.

I took a slice of baguette from one of the trays and ate it as quickly as possible.

I hadn't eaten for a long time, but it felt like years. My hunger took control over me: I reached for olives and cheese and stuffed everything in my mouth.

Tom and Music Head were also enjoying themselves as bread, butter, grapes and pastries floated in the air before disappearing.

The divos continued with their chores. One of the divos was about to take out freshly baked bread from the oven. It smelled delicious.

Hmmm... fresh bread. I should have some! I want some! I thought.

Suddenly, the divo dropped the baking tray on the floor. He had burned his hand! He ran around in circles from the agony. It was absolutely horrible! The divo didn't seem to know what to do, so I picked up a cloth, soaked it in cold water and wrapped his hand with it.

The poor divo covered his eyes with his other hand.

The divo slowly looked around to see who had helped him. A broad smile appeared on his face and all his imperfect teeth became visible. He had irregular gaps between his teeth and his eyes shone from joy and relief.

He can't possibly see me, I thought.

The divo with the burned hand looked at me as he jumped up and down.

Maybe its behavior is a normal divo reaction? I thought optimistically as I tried to justify the circumstances. *The divos suddenly get excited and start clapping. I've seen it before.*

All the other divos stopped working, turned to me and clapped as well. They all looked at me. Straight at me... at... *me!* How could that be?

I looked around to see if I could see Tom and Music Head, but couldn't.

All the divos were looking at me, smiling. I didn't know what to do.

Suddenly it hit me. *Of course, I'm not invisible anymore*! I touched water when I tried to help the divo. How could I have forgotten? I frowned and scratched my head.

"Lily! Lily! You are no longer invisible," Tom whispered.

"What is going on?" Isabel's voice could be heard outside the entrance.

She was coming to the kitchen. The divo that I'd helped grabbed my hand and quickly took me through a tiny round door next to the oven and closed it behind us.

The divo placed its index finger in front of its nose, telling me to remain silent.

I nodded and hit my head lightly at the low ceiling. I had to bend down further.

The divo held the door closed with his hand and looked at me.

Can divos not speak? I thought.

It didn't seem as if they did. We were both quiet in the small space.

The space was enclosed in the wall or maybe between them. The interiors of the walls were bulky and uneven as if the divos had built the area themselves.

I had another look: there were tiny beds next to the wall, but I couldn't see much beyond the limited space in the dark. Small objects were scattered around the room in a mess, everything from wooden combs to small cups.

This must be where the divos stay when they aren't busy with their chores, I thought. Like some sort of a... divo-space.

"This is a divo-space," I whispered as I kept looking around.

"You need to clean up the kitchen. Stop wasting time being silly, clapping your hands for nothing." I heard Isabel's voice and her steps slowly moving away from the kitchen.

The divo standing next to me looked nervous and used his tiny hand to wipe the sweat from his forehead. Was he sweating because he was anxious or because of the temperature in the divo-space? It couldn't be the latter. The divo-space was much colder than the kitchen.

The divo was afraid since he had been helping me hide away from Isabel.

Someone knocked on the door and the divo was hesitant to open it at first.

"Lily, it's Tom. It's OK to come out now," a soft-spoken voice whispered.

The horrified divo opened the door cautiously. The divo slowly slid aside, away from the tiny door by what I imagined as Tom's hand.

"Music Head and I are coming in," Tom informed me, as he knew they were both still invisible.

"Careful with your head. Bend down before you enter," I warned.

We were both whispering. He must have followed my advice because I didn't hear the sound of any heads hitting the divo-space's low ceiling.

I moved further inside to give room to Tom and Music Head. The divo-space was much larger than I thought, and only the ceiling was low.

"They're going to release the dogs to search for us," Tom said.

"I heard that too. We need to stay away from the dogs. They'll notice us even if we're invisible because dogs have an incredible sense of smell," I said with a worried voice as I pictured the dogs in my mind. "We should hide but I don't think it should be in the divo-space because the divos could get into trouble because of us."

"You aren't invisible anymore and can't leave yet because there's a chance they'll detect you," Tom said.

"I agree," Music Head said.

The divo made a quiet unusual noise.

I was standing there, trying to figure out its purpose. Was that the divo's usual sound?

I kept observing the divo and tried to get familiar with the sound as we were going to be alongside them for some time. I didn't want to be ignorant.

A piece of paper flew up in the air, rolled into a cone, and landed by the divo's mouth.

"Here you go," Music Head said.

It became apparent that he was the one handling the cone.

"Thank you! What a great invention! We now have a voice! We can finally be heard by non-divos! And thank you, Lily for helping me with my burned hand," the divo continued with a gruff voice.

None of us said anything, amused as we were by the divo speaking.

The divo took the paper cone and placed it in front of his mouth and said, "You must stay away from Dr Herbert's dogs."

"The divo can speak!" Tom finally said, stating the now obvious fact.

"I could hear them perfectly, but noticed you couldn't due to the low volume of their speech," Music Head explained.

"Oh," I said with great astonishment. Also, I felt silly at the same time. The divo took the paper cone and placed it in front of his mouth again and said, "Can your invisible friends be visible again?" The divo was now looking at me, waiting for an answer.

"Hmm... yes, they can. They'll become visible once they touch water. That's how I became visible, when I soaked the cloth in water to treat your burnt hand," I said.

The divo ran out of the room before I could say anything else and came back after a few seconds, holding a glass of water.

"Nooo!" I shouted but the divo had already splashed water all over the visible empty space where Tom and Music Head were.

Tom and Music Head instantly became visible again!

The divo raised his hands in the air and ran in circles and was smiling, as if he had just reached the finish line at an Olympic competition and won a gold medal.

The divo also started clapping and jumping up and down joyfully. Tom and I looked at each other with disappointed faces and couldn't believe the essential magic was gone.

The divo took up the paper cone and said, "Great day! I'm being heard and you're being seen! What a privilege for us all!"

I was surprised by the divo's statement.

His explanation made his action seem perfectly rational. I'd never considered being seen and heard a privilege, but the divo was right, we were all privileged to be heard and seen.

The question was, how could we use these types of privilege better than being mute and invisible? And was the ability to have a voice or to be seen by others more powerful than the magic of having secretive communication or being invisible?

"Have you ever spoken up against the night demons?" I asked.

"No, we haven't, and they don't know we can speak," the divo explained.

"Have you ever tried?" I asked.

"No," the divo said.

"Why?" I asked.

"Too scared... we were *all* too scared," he said through the cone.

"Have you ever tried fighting them?"

The divo shook their head and replied, "No."

"In that case, we have a common goal: to defeat the night demons!" I declared proudly.

The little divo started shaking from head to toe.

"What's wrong?" I asked.

"I am frightened," the divo replied, still clasping his cone that as beginning to crumple in his shaking hands.

"How many years have divos lived in the castle?" I asked.

"Centuries. We've lost track of time. We came into existence as a result of one of Dr. Herbert's experiments," the divo replied.

"Well, would you like to be free?" I asked the divo.

The divo nodded as he briefly replied, "Yes."

"You should conquer your fear and demand freedom. We can all do something and if we're united, we'll achieve much more together than we ever will alone," I continued.

The divo looked at me without speaking for a while before saying, "I need to consult all the divos before making any decision. We've never challenged the night demons. Give me a moment, please."

The divo quickly left the divo-space and closed the door.

I looked at Tom and Music Head and waited patiently for the divo to come back.

Tom walked over to the door and looked through the keyhole. "The divo is talking to the others. We better hear what they have to say before we decide our next move."

"Yes, that's a sensible decision," Music Head said.

Finally, the divo entered the divo-space again, picked up the paper cone and said, "We were unable to reach an agreement about rebelling against the night demons."

"I understand, but we need to come up with a plan because the night demons are soon going to release the dogs. It's probably best if we leave the divo-space as we don't want you, or any other divo, to get into trouble for hiding us," Tom said.

He had barely finished his sentence when the sound of dogs barking made us all jump.

"We are visible, and can't leave the space yet," I said, trying to find a solution swiftly.

The divo stood with his back against the door. "Perhaps I'm able to help. There is a place for you to hide."

"Where?" I said, wondering. This space was going to be easy for the dogs to detect. I was about to shake my head in disagreement when the divo pointed behind me.

My eyes followed the direction of the divo's pointing finger: it showed the very dark part of the divo-space and I understood that the space extended much further!

No wonder it could house all the divos. There were too many of them in the castle and they all certainly needed a place to sleep, relax and have their personal belongings.

"Our space extends through the castle; we have built it inside the walls."

"Wow! That's brilliant!" I said and looked at Tom and Music Head.

"There are also various openings and connections in our space," The divo added.

"How can we navigate our way through the divo-space?" Tom asked as soon as he was less confused about the event.

"It's difficult. You can't really find your way if you haven't been inside the divo-space multiple times. The connections and openings can be very hard to find. We have lived here for centuries, built the space and know the place by heart," the divo said before adding, "Where would you like to go?" The divo looked proud to be able to help us.

I suddenly felt happier than I had in a long while as we had the opportunity to move around the castle seemingly safely.

Should we tell the divo that we were looking for the elixir? No, perhaps not, I thought.

Maybe not the entire divo clan will agree to help us. Trusting them was a great liability.

"I'm sure we'll find our way. Thank you for letting us use the divo-space," Tom said.

What a relief that Tom thinks the same as me, I thought.

"Let's find a way to defeat the night demons! You deserve more than being stuck in a castle, being mistreated and serving them all day long. Life's so much more than that.

"You should enjoy doing things that you love. Like reading, traveling, listening to music. Things YOU like," I said.

The divo looked at me with a somewhat confused face.

Suddenly it hit me: the divo didn't know what it meant to live in complete freedom. Perhaps they could not even name anything they enjoyed.

They had been serving the night demons for centuries, since their very existence!

"You'll see what I mean once you have freedom," I said.

The bell in the kitchen rang. The divo jumped up and ran out in a fraction of a second.

"Poor divos. The night demons are calling them," Tom said.

"Yes," Music Head replied.

"We should start exploring the divo-space," Tom said.

"Probably all we need to do is hide from the dogs as we look for the elixir," Music Head said. He had spoken the longest sentence since I'd met him.

"That's right! Finding the elixir should be our priority," I said and glimpsed at the dark extension of the divo-space.

The void looked frightening, but we didn't have any other option.

"It's best to get as far away from the door as possible because the dogs can smell our scent. Also, the divo-space door is quite visible in the kitchen, and the night demons may know about it. However, they may *not* know the divo-space extends through the entire castle," Tom said as he rocked his right foot back and forth in a nervous manner.

"These are all assumptions," Music Head replied wisely to Tom's comments.

"Maybe. But our time's running out," Tom said, slightly annoyed at Music Head.

Losing time, time, time. Everything is about time, I thought.

I didn't really want to walk further into the unknown divo-space, but our options were limited and I had to triumph over my fear.

"Who's going first?" I asked.

"I don't mind being first," Tom said anxiously and no doubt bravely, with both contradictory emotions coming out simultaneously.

"I can be the next," Music Head uttered automatically. I was happy that Tom and Music Head had volunteered to walk ahead. Tom started walking into the divo-space extension, Music Head and I followed him cautiously.

"It's too dark. I can't see the way very well," Tom said, trying to mask his anxiety. But I could hear in his voice that he was dead frightened.

A small lamp next to a tiny drawer caught my eye.

"Let's see if this lamp works," I said and turned the round metal switch on the side. A small fire appeared in the lamp and the vast darkness was defeated by the small bright light.

The divo-space became clearly visible. I handed the lamp to Tom, and we continued our journey further inside the unknown parts of the divo-space.

Tom, Music Head and I all bent forward to avoid hitting our heads on the low ceiling.

The ceiling gradually became higher as we continued further into the darkness, so our heads were not painfully bending forward.

The path ahead of Tom was visible even to my eyes as the space got wider.

The walls and floor were just like the ceiling, uneven and bumpy.

"The divos must have created this space with their bare hands," I said.

"It looks like it," Music Head agreed.

An unknown sound echoed in the divo-space.

We all stopped walking and listened to identify the sound.

It was Betty's voice! Where was she? She was singing a song, but the lyrics were unclear. Her voice became louder and louder.

None of us dared to say a word due to the chances of being caught.

Tom walked faster. Music Head and I did the same, following behind.

But the sound of Betty's voice continued to become louder despite us trying to move away. It didn't make sense.

I grabbed and squeezed Music Head's arm. He looked at my scared face and I signaled that we should walk back. Music Head shook Tom's arm in turn to catch his attention.

Tom looked at me as I indicated with my hand that we should change direction.

The sudden, unfortunate event of hearing Betty's voice had made us panic as we suddenly remembered that she was able to walk through anything, including walls.

Suddenly, I hit my head against the bumpy low ceiling while rushing back. The sound of Betty's voice continued no matter in which direction we walked.

Where should we turn? Where should we hide? Should we run back again? I thought.

I didn't know but there was no time to communicate with Tom and Music Head.

Surprisingly, Betty stopped singing and it felt immediately safer.

Now, the divo-space was as silent as the grave.

No one spoke. No one moved.

I took a deep breath in the belief that we had managed to get away from Betty. I was short of breath, but slowly and surely, took a few steps.

We had to return to the house as well as finding the elixir before leaving the castle, regardless of all the obstacles in our way.

Tom was behind us, holding the lamp now we had changed direction. I didn't have time to grab it from him, so we continued in dim light that broke the absolute darkness.

Once again, we were perhaps lucky despite being in a miserable situation.

Maybe life was a seesaw with luck on one end and misfortune on the other. This time, my seesaw had tilted slightly toward the lucky end in the midst of a dominating misfortune.

I turned around to see if we should again walk further inside the divo-space.

As I was about to speak with my lips slightly parted, a head came up from the uneven, muddy ground. It was Betty! Once again, her eyes were fixed toward mine.

Betty's pale face and smudged eye make-up were floating up higher and higher until her face was at the same level as my own.

"Where are you going?" she asked in a soft voice. My heart was pounding in my chest, my teeth were clenched, and I couldn't say a single word.

Fresh air! I needed fresh air. How could we initially have forgotten that Betty was a ghost and could easily find us? "Where... to?" Betty asked again, slower than usual.

She saw I was completely frozen.

Chapter 11

RUNNING AWAY

It felt as if I was the only one in the universe. Music Head and Tom were silent as if they didn't exist at all.

They must have seen Betty's head sticking up from the ground too.

"Answer my question," Betty demanded in a monotonous voice.

"We're... We're just walking," I said and felt stupid to have come up with such a simple explanation. *How could I not come up with something clever to say?* I thought.

It was hard to know what to say because it was the first time I'd been in a divo-space in a far-away castle and had a ghost asking me what I was doing, all while trying to hide from a bunch of night demons. Oh, and the dogs. The circumstances we were in were just... unique.

"Walking? I can understand that, but what are you doing here? I saw the three of you walking around in the dining room, but the rest couldn't see you," Betty said.

"For that, we're forever grateful to you," I replied, still avoiding her question.

"I still can, easily, give you away. Why should I be nice to you?" Betty asked, looking scarier than before.

Her eyes quickly turned red as if the blood vessels in her eyes had just ruptured, her face gradually becoming paler, so pale that I could see the change even in the dark.

"Because... you... erm, want to help?" I mumbled helplessly.

Betty kept her bloodshot eyes fixed on me as she sang again.

Her bloodshot eyes turned deep red, growing darker and darker until finally disappearing. Only two black holes were visible in her eye sockets. My jaw dropped, but my scream couldn't be expressed as I wished to disappear from the face of the earth...

Or wherever we were.

I really didn't want to be here.

I took several steps backward, noticing Music Head and Tom had already backed far away.

Betty continued singing, floating down until she was, fortunately, gone.

"Oh... never could I have imagined something this horrifying," Tom said.

Music Head was holding his ears.

"What is wrong?" Tom asked.

I couldn't speak and sat down to recover from what I'd just witnessed, looking worriedly at Music Head.

"I have sound sensitivity, especially to high-pitched singing sounds," Music Head replied and slowly uncovered his ears.

"Hope you get better now that it's stopped," I replied before saying, "Betty can see us even if we're invisible or hiding in here. She's a ghost so she can easily appear inside the divo-space." I felt overwhelmed by Betty's sudden appearance and disappearance.

"I wonder if she's going to tell the night demons about us being here? She didn't reply when you asked her if she was going to help us," Tom said and took a deep breath.

"We need to continue regardless," Music Head commented in a calm and gathered voice.

Tom and I turned to him. Music Head was looking at his nails, apparently wholly unshaken by the event.

He looked at us and asked, "Do we have any other choice?"

Both of us knew Music Head was right. He was sensible, intelligent, and calm, even under great duress.

"Let's go," Music Head said when he saw that we didn't have anything else to say. He continued, "We'll find a solution."

He took the lamp from Tom and walked further into the divo-space.

Tom and I rushed after him.

Music Head moved ahead with confidence as if he'd been in the divo-space multiple times in the past. All three of us were silent.

Betty could re-appear any minute. We all knew that. Music Head turned to the right. We reached another corner but continued until we got to a downward sliding muddy tube, a broken, rusty gigantic pipe.

Music head looked back at us.

Tom and I looked at each other before we finally nodded in agreement.

One by one, we slid down the enormous pipe.

My body glided through the pipe so fast that it was hard to slow and impossible to stop.

Where will we end up? I thought.

The tube went in spirals. Why didn't the divos mention the pipe to us? We finally reached the other end, rolled out of the pipe, and hit the wall, one after another. Thankfully, I was last to exit the pipe, and my fall was cushioned by both Tom's and Music Head's bodies.

We now had a choice. We could either head left or right. But a small dark brown door caught our attention just in front of us.

"It resembles the door that led to the divo-space in the kitchen," I said.

"Should we open it?" Tom asked.

"We should," Music Head replied.

"I will," I said determinedly and rushed to open the door because I was looking forward to getting out of the dark divo-space.

I grabbed the door handle and had to stop myself from rushing any further. I then turned the handle slowly and quietly.

Three figures stood outside the divo-space: Duke Lukas, Isabel, and Dr. Herbert.

It was the same corridor that led to the laboratory. Luckily, they didn't notice me peeking.

Dr. Herbert said, "As you know, I don't like having anyone in my laboratory unless I'm doing experiments on them. Please wait here."

Duke Lukas and Isabel nodded as they watched Dr. Herbert head toward the laboratory.

"He is so protective of his laboratory," Isabel said.

"In all these centuries we have lived in the castle together, Dr. Herbert has never allowed me in there," Duke Lukas replied.

Duke Lukas's eyes started slowly wandering in my direction. I closed the door cautiously before he saw me.

"We have to remain here and find another exit. Duke Lukas and Isabel are both standing outside. Dr. Herbert walked to his laboratory just now," I whispered as soon as I'd moved away from the tiny door.

"Did you see any dogs in the laboratory, Lily?" Tom asked.

"I didn't, but I saw a big black pot that seemed to have a living being inside. I don't know what it was. You carried me away before I could see anything," I replied.

"Well, would you rather have stayed?" Music Head said.

It sounded like a joke. Having spent some time with Music Head, I knew he had asked a question and expected an answer.

"Never! It's a very smelly and scary place with a lot of weird stuff in it," I answered.

Tom looked more worried than usual.

"What is it?" I asked, looking at Tom.

"I'm worried that we may never find the elixir. We aren't invisible anymore, and we have limited time. Music Head leaves in less than five hours. It will be just the two of us left. The last one of us will be left behind alone in the castle for another seven hours. Things will get harder over time because we have to leave one by one. The night demons will also get more determined in finding us and take the emerald," Tom said.

"Don't worry, Tom. We'll find the elixir. We all have to think about our next step, but let's start by moving away from the door. Otherwise, the dogs will find us." I took the lamp in my hand and continued walking as I said, "My gut feeling tells me that we should walk toward the laboratory." We walked in the same direction as Dr. Herbert had walked in the corridor.

Both Tom and Music Head walked along without objecting to my suggestion.

"The best place to hide is perhaps the laboratory divo-space. If we find the way leading there, of course. Since they are Dr. Herbert's dogs, they'll most likely be released from the laboratory or somewhere close to the laboratory," I said.

"That sounds like an excellent plan," Tom said while walking swiftly to reach the laboratory divo-space as soon as possible. Deep inside, I was just hoping that I was right about my assumptions. I didn't want to disappoint Tom, or Music Head, who had put his fate in our hands by trusting and following us.

"There's also another scenario, the dogs entering the divo-space," Music Head said.

I stopped and looked at Music Head. He was right. Yet we didn't have any choice but to carry out our plan.

An imaginary picture of two horrifying dogs came to my mind. They were enormous with sharp teeth... I had to control my mind to not think about them, at least not now.

The path ahead of us became a bit bumpier, and I moved forward but noticed a wall blocking the way.

That's it! I thought and said, "We can't continue toward the laboratory as a wall blocks our path." Tom and Music Head were behind me, and couldn't see the way ahead as well as I did.

Music Head walked past and started tapping the wall.

"What are you doing?" I asked.

"I'm trying to identify what is behind the wall," Music Head replied.

His action didn't make much sense to me at that time.

I turned around and walked back to see if any other route led to the laboratory.

Tom walked next to me and said, "Let's go back and find a way out of the divo-space. What if this is a dead-end, and we're stuck here forever if we don't act?"

"Maybe we should see how we can get back out again," I said and held the lamp in the air to look for an exit out of the divo-space.

Music Head kept tapping on the wall continuously, and the tapping noise was the only sound in the dark divo-space. Suddenly, my peripheral vision detected a moving object, and I focused my gaze, trying to see what it was.

"That must have been one of the divos... Hello?" I said, somewhat hoping to see a divo.

No reply.

A shining object from afar got closer and closer to us.

It seemed to be coming out of the pipe, and it was... continuous... elongated, dark, and had rough shiny skin! My mind couldn't comprehend the information received from my vision, as if there was a sudden shock leading to disconnection between my senses and brain.

"Snake! run... run... now!" I shouted and ran the opposite way toward Music Head.

Music Head had formed a small wall opening, and it seemed as if he'd found a way out.

He turned around, looked at me, and saw the black, enormous snake coming toward us.

He jumped up and kicked the wall firmly in a way that made even the ground shake.

The solid wall came down, and we all ran through the—now big enough—opening, and we ran for our lives.

After gathering all my courage, I looked behind to see how far we were from the snake.

Betty was standing behind the monstrous snake with her arms crossed.

She said, "Dr. Herbert decided to release his favorite pets when I told him that you had entered the divo-space in the kitchen." *Did she say pets? Is there more than one? Oh no!* I thought. I didn't know where we were anymore as I couldn't think straight.

We were all out in the corridor! Out of the divo-space! Out of our shelter!

Music Head had wrongly and rightly formed an opening in the wall for us to escape the snake, but it had led us to the corridor where the night demons were!

The monstrous snake was right behind us. I could hear it hissing.

Music Head ran ahead and something fell out of his pocket. It was the emerald!

"Oh, as I thought. I see you have my precious emerald. Give it to me! It belongs to me!" Isabel's familiar voice came from nowhere.

She was standing next to a wall in the corridor.

Music Head took several quick steps back, fished up the emerald from the floor, and ran again. We kept running, but somehow, Duke Lukas appeared just in front of him.

"You're trapped now! There's no escape! You had better hand me the emerald!" he said.

A barking came from behind, and I looked over my left shoulder.

Dr. Herbert was standing on the other side holding two murderous dogs on leashes. They were far, far scarier than the hounds I'd imagined. We were truly trapped.

The two dogs were tall, white, and had mouths that resembled crocodiles' mouths.

"Look at my beautiful precious dogs! You have a choice. If you hand me the emerald, I won't ask them to come and say hello to you," Dr. Herbert said with a vicious laugh and an animated facial expression.

Danielle also appeared on our left and said desperately, "I have always been nice to you, children. Why don't you give the emerald to me?"

The night demons, Betty, the murderous dogs, and the enormous snake surrounded Tom, Music Head, and me.

They had formed a circle around us that we were unable to break.

Isabel, Betty, and the enormous snake were behind us, and Duke Lukas in front.

Dr. Herbert and his two murderous dogs were on our right side.

Danielle appeared on our left.

They all got closer and closer, the two dogs now too close for comfort.

"Hello, night demons!" a familiar gruff voice said unexpectedly.

Everyone was caught by surprise and looked in the direction of the voice to see who it was. It came from the top of the staircase. A short, blue figure held a paper cone in front of its mouth, standing there and looking down at us.

It was the divo with the burned hand that I'd helped in the kitchen! The divo's right hand was still wrapped in the cloth I'd given him.

"I know you are surprised to hear me speaking. Especially on such an important occasion," the short, blue divo said courageously. No one in the room moved. All eyes were on the divo. Even those of Dr. Herbert's experimental, monstrous pets.

The night demons and Betty were all in disbelief, with a facial expression that could easily be read: *The divo, the slave divo, the insignificant experimental animal is speaking! How dare the divo have a voice?*

I smiled and whispered, "He made it. He's using his voice to fight the night demons!"

"I know what you are thinking. What is this small insignificant creature who we treat so badly doing here? Why is this little blue divo destroying such a glorious moment when all we want is to finally get the emerald? You are all greedy, obnoxious, and selfish," the divo said with his somewhat cute, gruff voice.

He was standing up straight on his tiny chubby legs. He supported the paper cone with one hand and tried simultaneously to balance his other arm.

The divo's blue rough skin, his round belly and red hair, contrasted the light background even from afar. The night demons looked completely unimpressed.

"I'll deal with you later! We don't have time for this now!" Duke Lukas shouted at the divo and started walking toward us again.

The divo coughed before saying, "I'm not done with my speech yet. I declare that from now on, all divos in the castle are free! We'll no longer serve you." The divo raised his arms as if he had just declared himself king of an unknown kingdom.

"Be quiet! You silly little creature," Isabel said and started walking toward us, and so did the rest of the night demons and Betty.

"Wait! I have a surprise for you," the divo said, and all we could see were hundreds of divos rushing out from every corner. "One... two... three... go!" the divo shouted, and the hundreds rushed past the night demons to encircle us.

The night demons couldn't move.

The divos created a barrier around us, and no one could get close.

They were protecting us.

Duke Lukas walked toward us, shouting, "What nonsense is this? Give me the emerald now!" But he could not get close as the divos quickly stood on each other's shoulders, creating a wall around the three of us.

"Attack, boys!" Dr. Herbert ordered his murderous dogs and released them from their leashes. The dogs attacked the divos with their crocodile mouths and sharp teeth! I closed my eyes so as to not witness the scene. Once I'd opened my eyes, I saw that the divos remained unharmed and the dogs had broken their teeth.

"Useless dogs!" Dr. Herbert shouted angrily as the dogs quickly escaped the scene following their injuries. "Attack them now!" Dr. Herbert ordered.

But the dogs have run away... I thought.

I was wrong. Dr. Herbert wasn't ordering the dogs!

The monstrous snake had now approached the divos' protective ring.

There's no way to escape! I thought as soon as the snake got closer to the ring of divos and elevated its head, a pair of shining, small, red eyes looked at us.

The snake hissed and its tongue flicked in and out as it moved directly toward us. Slowly, the snake encircled the ring of divos, all the time keeping its eyes on us, and gradually made the ring smaller by squeezing the divos into the center of the circle.

The circle became smaller and smaller until the pressure was so great, a number were launched into the air, many landing on their heads before slowly standing again.

A small group of divos grabbed the monstrous snake's body and pulled, but the snake was too strong for them to even move it one single inch.

"Good job! Get to the children!" Dr. Herbert instructed.

The snake squeezed the ring even further, and more divos were removed from the wall created around us. The snake was getting dangerously close, so we had fewer to protect us.

There was almost no protective barrier left between the three of us and the snake.

The night demons suddenly transformed into four big, black crows.

They flew above our heads before attacking us with their beaks, but they also tried to snatch the emerald as they poked our pockets.

We bent down and protected our faces with our arms.

The snake just continued making the ring smaller while the crows were attacking.

"We have to do something," Music Head said.

"I agree. This is not looking good for us," I said, trying very hard to protect my face.

Tom tried to say something, but didn't seem to find any words.

All we could hear was the snake's hissing and the sound of crows flapping their wings and cawing above.

The snake's thick body was at least one meter high, and he was at least twenty meters long. It was huge and getting closer.

Once again, I remembered Willow Witch and my recent experiences.

'Follow your instincts and do the right thing, Willow Witch said," I whispered to myself as the snake was just several inches away.

The poor divos tried to help, but couldn't do more than they'd already done. The crows became silent suddenly, and I couldn't feel their beaks poking me anymore.

"Give me the emerald, and I will make the snake stop," Dr. Herbert shouted as they all transformed back into their human forms.

"No, we're not going to give you something you haven't earned. We earned the emerald, and that's why we have it. You had the same chance as us to find it," I shouted back.

But I still didn't know what to do next.

I stood up straight and looked around.

There should be a way out of the situation without giving away the emerald.

I put my hands in my pockets as I looked at the faces of everyone around.

Isabel, Dr. Herbert, Duke Lukas, Danielle, Betty, and all the divos, in addition to the gigantic snake about to squeeze the three of us to death.

My heart wasn't pounding in my chest anymore. There was a way.

I was holding a small, dried piece of pumpkin that I'd amazingly found in my deep pocket! I grabbed the magical pumpkin piece from the pumpkin farm, and quickly placed it in my mouth. I had to try as there was no other option now.

The snake elevated its head and made strange movements as if sensing it could never get us if it didn't act quick enough. With one arm, I grabbed Tom, and with my other, grabbed Music Head. They, too, held onto me tight as if they knew what was about to happen.

I floated up in the air and lifted Tom and Music Head along with me.

We were flying above them all.

The snake was below my feet, its big mouth opening beneath us. It had two gigantic teeth resembling two sharp swords.

Hundreds of divos pulled the snake's tail simultaneously, and this time, dragged it down to the floor successfully.

The weak divos' strength overcame the one, strong, monstrous snake.

"The children are running away! We have to stop them! They have my emerald!" Isabel cried out, clearly angered.

"What do you mean by YOUR emerald!? It doesn't belong to you, Isabel! If there's anyone who should have the emerald, it's me, I'm afraid!" Duke Lukas said with an irritated voice, looking over at Isabel.

"Dear Duke Lukas, how can you forget that you are actually not deserving of the emerald more than I do? I'm the one who created the divos for you. I provided my own creations, the dogs and the snake,' Dr. Herbert replied determinedly.

"I have been the nicest of all to you children. Don't you remember? Why don't you give it to me?" Danielle said from below our feet, looking up at us.

"Danielle, stop already. You should all remember that I own the castle. Be grateful!" Duke Lukas said. They all started arguing with one another about who deserved the emerald the most. The night demons forgot to pay attention to the fact that the emerald was being carried away and that they didn't have it in their possession yet.

Upset about each other's claims, they got distracted from the fact that the snake was pulled by the divos and could no longer capture us.

Having found the golden moment, the divos dragged the snake further away with an even greater force than before. Now able to see what they could achieve together, they smashed the snake to the ground, and the sound of an explosion filled the space.

The gooey pieces of what remained of the monstrous snake covered the floor.

The divos jumped up and down with their hands in the air happily.

They had defeated something much more powerful and bigger than themselves!

"Nooooooo! My poor darling!" Dr. Herbert screamed as he ran to the spot where the snake's head had been.

We had reached the high ceiling, and I had to aim for the staircase.

But my hands were full.

"Use your hands... grab the staircase rail! You are... heavy, and I don't know how much longer I can hold you," I said as I tried hard to keep holding Music Head's arm.

It slipped from my grip, and I had to fight to hold onto his hand... and then his fingers... He was sliding from my grip.

"Don't let go!" Music Head warned. Tom was silent and focused on directing us to the second floor with all his power.

The divo with the injured hand grabbed me by my ankle and pulled me toward the staircase, trying to help Tom. Tom could then pull us to the first floor. Luckily, we landed safely before Music Head fell to the night demons below.

The night demons finally realized that we were escaping, stopped arguing, and all ran upstairs toward us.

"What should we do now?" Tom asked and turned to me.

"I don't know," I replied.

"Do you have any pumpkin pieces left?" Tom asked.

"No," I replied, disappointed. The divos were all downstairs, appearing exhausted from all their efforts in destroying the snake.

The night demons rushed toward us competitively to get to us and the emerald.

"We need to run away!" I said and looked around for an escape.

"Where should we go?" Music Head asked.

We could always run anywhere on the first floor, but there was a chance we'd be trapped if we walked into a room.

Suddenly, it hit me that we should follow our first plan: hide somewhere unexpected!

The perfect hiding place was still the laboratory! No one except Dr. Herbert could go there. It would be much easier to handle only Dr. Herbert than all four.

"I have a plan," I said with a smile. "Follow me!"

The corridor on the first floor ended in a big room with lots of windows.

I ran back toward the stairs with Tom and Music Head following behind.

Duke Lukas and Isabel walked toward us, smiling as they were just a few steps away.

"You can't get away now!" Duke Lukas said as he came closer.

He stretched out his hand toward me and said, "Give me the emerald."

"I don't have it," I said. This was true because the emerald was with Music Head.

"Don't waste my time! Tell your friend to hand me the emerald!" he shouted.

"Give it to me! Duke Lukas, don't you remember our agreement? Even if you get the emerald, you won't have the precious thing that only I can provide you with," Dr. Herbert said, short of breath as he struggled up the very last step. His chubby abdomen had prevented him rushing up the stairs as fast as the rest.

Precious thing? That must be... the elixir! I thought.

"We can talk about it later. I'm sure we can make another agreement," Duke Lukas replied, trying to reassure Dr. Herbert.

"No! I should have the emerald, then you can get the thing that you need so badly," Dr. Herbert argued vividly.

Duke Lukas rolled his eyes, turned to Dr. Herbert, and said, "Things are different now."

Duke Lukas and Dr. Herbert ignored us and kept arguing about who deserved to have the emerald again. This was working in our favor as they were now focused on their argument.

Isabel saw the opportunity to approach us and get the emerald for herself.

Her face was pale as usual. She smiled and approached us quietly to avoid attracting attention from the others.

My focus was on Isabel when I suddenly heard a burst of laughter behind me.

It was Danielle.

"Isabel, let's be honest. It just isn't yours!" she said.

Isabel just looked at her for a moment.

"Maybe we can take the emerald and not tell them," Isabel said and pointed to Dr. Herbert and Duke Lukas. "That way, we can discuss it later, just the two of us."

Isabel had noticed something Dr. Herbert and Duke Lukas hadn't.

She knew they should be fighting over the emerald once it was in their possession, not losing it by fighting each other prematurely.

Danielle took a deep breath and nodded.

Then, the two women approached slowly but surely, each from a different direction, with us standing in the center. The wall and the staircase railing made up the other two sides.

I looked at Isabel's face and then at Danielle's. They were both smiling and were now so close that I could smell their strong, musky perfume.

I grabbed Tom and Music Head again by their arms. I closed my eyes, jumping over the staircase railing.

Chapter 12

FLY, LILY! FLY!

We flew off from the first floor, the night demons completely silent behind us. They didn't say a word, but I knew they were looking at us in astonishment.

"Fly, Lily, fly," Music Head said as I was struggling to carry both Tom and Music Head. I had to focus on flying as I was moving slowly, and heading downwards much faster than I flew up because of the weight I was carrying.

"You are... heavy," I said and tried my best to reserve some energy for when it was really needed.

"Ouch!" Tom shouted.

"What?" I asked.

"They're throwing things at us," he replied.

The night demons were all observing me, and I tried to avoid looking at them so I wouldn't get nervous.

Isabel had taken off her shoes. She had thrown one at Tom, and was aiming her other at me. It hit my chest. I felt intense pain, but had to stay focused. Giving up wasn't an option, and we all had to get away from the castle.

The only option was to slowly land on the ground floor.

Another thing will be thrown at us soon! I thought.

True enough, Duke Lukas followed Isabel's example by picking something from his pocket. I couldn't see what it was from afar.

He aimed at me. I was trying to move away to avoid getting hit, but couldn't coordinate due to the heavy weights I was carrying.

The object flew toward us, bouncing up and down, passing through the air.

The 'object' was a living being!

Two wings spread out, and a small head became visible. The creature's teeth resembled two sharp needles completely red—red from blood!

The creature flew around us. It was a type of bat with thin wings! But much bigger than I imagined a bat. It flew toward me and bit my left arm, hard and deep.

The intense pain prevented me carrying Music Head anymore as my arm turned numb, and he fell down to the ground. I followed his fall with my eyes and witnessed Music Head landing on the hard, rocky floor. He didn't move.

The bat flew back to Duke Lukas. He grabbed it in his hand and said, "Good job! Do it again for us!" Once again, Duke Lukas released the bat.

The big, black bat was hurtling toward me with a greater speed this time, aiming for my other arm! *Tom?* I thought and looked at him hanging from my arm, just to find out that he had fainted. *Move! Move!* I commanded my body in my head. The big, black bat bit me hard a second time. My desperate attempts to move away from it failed.

Both Tom and I fell as I could no longer keep my balance, injured badly. Luckily, our distance to the floor was minimal.

The numbness in my body was spreading, but I could still move.

The night demons smiled grimly as they made their way toward us from the first floor.

Are the others fine? I thought and looked for them.

Music Head was gone.

Fortunately, Tom had regained consciousness. He attempted to get up off the floor as he held his head with one hand.

The sound of the night demons' footsteps became louder as they approached us. Betty stayed on the first floor, singing with a high-pitched voice.

Why does she sing at such odd times? Perhaps ghosts enjoy singing? I thought.

Music Head appeared from nowhere, helped me up, and said, "Quick, follow me." We followed him into another room.

"This is a bad idea!" I said. We'd get trapped!

"They're coming," Music Head said and walked toward the window.

He wants us to jump out? Has he forgotten we're unable to leave the castle?

Music Head pulled back the curtain slightly, and the divo with the injured hand was standing next to the wall, smiling at us.

He pushed the bottom part of the wall, and there was a small opening leading to the divo-space. The divo pointed at the open entrance and nodded as he wanted us to rush in.

I felt hesitant to enter the divo-space in fear of running into Betty or some other dangerous creature. But the sound of the night demons meant they were already on the ground floor.

"You are unable to run away, Lily. The bat bites are going to make you sick. *Veeeery* sick!" Duke Lukas said and laughed for a moment before continuing, "We'll find your dead body and take the emerald from your friend. We are going to destroy all of you!"

The divo covered the divo-space entrance door with the curtain before joining us, then closed the door by pulling the handle firmly from inside.

It walked away from the door, and we followed. It then passed behind a small wall away from the entrance and took up its paper cone.

Tom asked, "How are you, Lily?"

"I'm OK," I said and tried to look well, even if I wasn't.

"Duke Lukas said you'll get very sick from the bat bite. You have to let us know if you feel unwell," Tom said.

"I'm feeling OK," I said again to reassure Tom.

"Really?" Music Head asked.

"It was a bad bite! I saw that with my own eyes," Tom said, not convinced by my reluctant reply.

I took a deep breath and said, "The bites were very painful, but I'm not feeling too bad. Don't worry. I'll let you know if I feel sick."

The divo listened and looked a bit restless as he wanted to speak.

All three of us turned to him to listen to what he had to say.

"I can help you get around the castle. I know all the connections and openings in the divo-space," the divo said quietly, afraid the night demons could hear.

"How? They seem to know about the divo-space. That's how they were able to release the snake into it," Tom said.

The divo shook his head. "No, Betty told them that you were all in the divo-space in the kitchen. The night demons don't know the divo-space extends beyond the kitchen and has such a vast network of connections in the walls, ceilings, and floors."

"How do you know?" Music Head asked.

"They called us for help. As soon as I got back to the kitchen, I saw Dr. Herbert and Isabel. Isabel showed Dr. Herbert where the opening to the divo-space was, and she opened the door. He took out the snake from a pot and released it into the divo-space." He added, with sadness. "I'm sorry I couldn't stop them."

"Don't worry. You couldn't have stopped the night demons," I replied with a smile.

"Betty's the only one knowing about the divo-space connections because she's a ghost and can walk through anything." The divo took several steps back and forth.

He was looking at the ground, trying to focus on what to say next. The divo wasn't used to being heard after all. "We made a deal with Betty, and she's not going to tell the night demons about you being in here or about the connections."

"When?" Music Head asked calmly.

"We made the deal just a moment ago. Betty started singing to distract the night demons," the divo said with a worried face.

I finally understood why Betty had been singing!

"What does Betty get in return?" I asked, knowing she wanted something from us.

"She wants to... leave the castle with you!" the divo said and covered his eyes. My jaw dropped, and I didn't know what to say.

"Leave the castle with us?" Tom asked, shocked.

"This was the only way she'd agree to help. She can find you wherever you go and tell the night demons," the divo replied.

I suddenly remembered what Willow Witch had said: *Betty is a ghost. She's neither good nor bad.* Maybe the divo was right, and we had to have Betty on our side.

"At least we don't have to worry about her anymore," I said.

"Yeah," Music Head agreed.

Tom took a deep breath and shook his head as he said, "How?"

The divo took up the paper cone and spoke. "I'm here to help. You helped us to use our voice. I want to return the favor."

"It would be great if you could help us get around in the divo-space! Last time, we couldn't find our way," I said and remembered the opening in the corridor. "What happened to the damaged wall?"

"Don't worry about the wall. The divos quickly covered it with bricks," the divo replied.

"Perfect!" I said.

Everything seemed to spin around my head, but I ignored it. We still had to find the elixir before leaving the castle.

"What's your name?" I asked, looking at the divo.

"I don't have a name."

Music Head said, "I also didn't have one until one day, someone called me Music Head."

"What will you call me?" the divo smiled.

It was an unexpected question. What name could we give the divo who had stood up against the night demons despite its small size and after centuries-long oppression? I suddenly knew the perfect name.

"Brave! You should be called Brave because you bravely spoke up against what you thought was wrong," I said.

Brave jumped up and down with his hands in the air. He then clapped his hands intermittently and joyfully. He took up the paper cone and said, "I am brave! I am brave!"

The way he celebrated put a smile on our faces.

"What next?" Tom asked.

"Let's all think about what we should do and tell the rest," I said.

"OK," Tom replied.

My head was still spinning, and I had to sit down in a corner.

What disease do bats cause? I remembered the TV program I'd watched about bats.

Rabies! What are the first symptoms of rabies? I couldn't remember.

My headache was getting much worse.

"We need to find the elixir. I don't feel good," I said.

"You look sick. Where can we find the elixir? We only know we need it," Tom said worriedly.

"Where can it possibly be?" Music Head said. We were all still.

I also felt feverish.

The elixir had to be found. If not, I could... die here in the castle.

Tom and Music Head had no idea how unwell I felt.

They shouldn't find out either, as they'd panic.

Where can I find the elixir? I thought. *Follow your instincts*, Willow Witch had said.

Where would I place the elixir if I were Dr. Herbert? I looked down, and suddenly I knew. *I'd hide my most beloved discovery in the... laboratory! That was why he didn't let anyone else enter! He was keeping it hidden, out of sight.*

What had I seen in the laboratory? I tried to remember.

Have I seen the elixir?

Was it in one of the bottles? I'd seen a big black pot, but it couldn't possibly be the elixir because it was moving. I also remembered smelly mixtures, but the remedies were too awful smelling to be the magical elixir healing all kinds of diseases.

If anything, that would probably be an elixir causing all sorts of disease, I thought.

What had I observed Dr. Herbert doing? He talked to the big black pot and kept talking to it as if it was the most valuable thing in the laboratory. I knew where the elixir was.

The elixir was in the big black pot!

Chapter 13

BRAVE

"The elixir is in the laboratory! It's in the big black pot next to the wall. I can show you as soon as we're in the lab!" I said joyfully.

Tom, Music Head, and Brave looked at me as if I'd gone mad.

"What makes you think that?" Music Head asked.

"Yes, what makes you think that?" Brave repeated before continuing, "And also, what is an elixir? Is it for taking baths and smelling good?"

We all looked at Brave and didn't know what to say, all surprised that he didn't know what an elixir was. He then held the paper cone in front of his mouth.

"What is it? Is it a hair softener? For my rough hair?"

We all burst into laughter as Brave stood entirely still, still wondering what an elixir was.

"What?" he asked and lowered his straight arms next to his small, round body. The paper cone was now touching the floor since he had stopped paying any attention to it.

Brave was waiting eagerly for an explanation.

I forgot about how unwell I felt and tried stopping myself from laughing to explain.

"You're almost right. The elixir is good for your body, and it's believed to heal all kinds of diseases. I'm not sure if it can make your hair soft," I replied.

Brave smiled, brought the paper cone next to his mouth, and said, "Good! You can have the elixir because you are sick."

I knew I was sick, but didn't want to use the elixir. Tom's mother needed it too.

"The elixir is for those who are *really* sick. I don't need the elixir that much," I said.

Brave shook his head and scratched the red, rough hair on it with his tiny blue hand as he said, "You'll get very sick soon. Duke Lukas's bat is an extraordinary animal.

"The bat flies to different caves at night and gets back to the castle after attacking and sucking the blood from humans. I once looked out of the window and saw the bat sucking blood from one of the villagers. Bright blood ran down from the bat's mouth, and the villager was fighting hard to escape."

Tom, Music Head, and Brave all looked at me without saying anything further.

"What is it?" I asked.

"You are pale," Music Head replied.

"I think the bat has sucked a lot of blood from you," Tom said as they all continued looking at me.

I smiled and tried to say something, but didn't know what to say.

Horror grew inside me. I didn't want to die in the castle!

My friends and family were waiting for me.

Will my ghost be stuck in the castle with Betty forever? Will Tom and Music Head leave me behind? I will have to live with the night demons eternally, I thought.

The only way not to die was by having the elixir!

What will happen to Tom's mother without the elixir? I thought and felt as if we had already failed to help her. The elixir didn't need to be used!

"There's no point in deciding to use the elixir yet. We should just try and find it first. As I said, I'm not feeling too bad." They all nodded with a frightened look.

"Brave, can you please show us the way to the laboratory?" I asked.

"Yes! I am the master of the divo-space connections! I know how to take you anywhere you want to go," Brave said.

"How old are you, Brave?" I asked.

"Hmm, around three to four," Brave replied.

"Years?" Tom asked.

"Centuries," Brave said.

We looked at each other with astonishment and followed Brave.

"Did you know you were able to speak in all these centuries?" I asked.

"Not really. I didn't think I could talk to non-divos," Brave answered. "You helped me, and all the other divos, find our voice. I feel strong now I can speak," Brave added.

"It's important to have a voice," Music Head said.

"If I die in the castle, at least I die happy because I helped you to find your voice and use it against the evil night demons," I said. Everyone stopped walking and looked at me.

"Do you think you are going to die?" Tom asked.

I didn't reply for a moment as I'd run out of white lies to tell, and my appearance was probably also giving away how I truly felt.

"Maybe we'll all die here. There's no way we can be sure to escape as the night demons keep searching for us and can harm us. So far, we've fought with the night demons in their crow form, a bloodsucking bat, the murderous dogs, and the monstrous snake. Perhaps they have many more forms. We have the emerald, but still have a long way to go," I said.

"I can't believe we've only completed a few hours without even finding the elixir. It feels like ages!" Tom said.

"It does," Music Head replied.

Brave continued leading the way in the dark divo-space, and we were all silent.

"It's boiling in here," I said.

"It's not hot. It's very, very cold. Much colder than inside the castle," Tom said.

Of course, I had a fever, which was why I felt so hot. I was getting worse.

"Me too, but I always feel hot because of my tough skin. That's why divos enjoy being inside the divo-space. We really dislike the kitchen because of the hot oven," Brave said.

"Maybe you have a fever?" Tom suggested.

"No," I lied and thought I shouldn't have said anything.

"Yes, you do," Music Head said as a fact.

"I don't," I said again.

"We're all freezing, except Brave. How can you feel hot?" Tom said.

"OK, maybe I do have a fever, but it doesn't mean anything," I said, knowing I couldn't win the argument.

"Of course, it does. It changes everything! This means we have to hurry up and find the elixir before you get too sick," Tom said, annoyed.

"Brave, how long does it take to get to the laboratory?" Tom asked.

Brave hesitated to reply, but he finally said, "It may take some time."

"Some time? How can it be? We're at the same level as the laboratory, and we know the laboratory is just meters from the room we were in just now," Tom said worriedly.

"I walked the route to the laboratory only once by mistake two centuries ago. I finally understood why it took such a long time to get there.

"Divos try to avoid going near the laboratory because we're scared of Dr. Herbert. He's usually in there, and we don't like to get close to him," Brave said.

"Are we sure there's even a connection leading there?" I asked.

Brave took a deep breath and placed the paper cone in front of his mouth.

"Yes. I'm sure. The route leading to the laboratory is not as advanced as the other divo-space connections because we don't use it.

The other connections are well maintained. Here, the ground is bumpier, and the walls aren't as smooth as the other parts of the divespace."

"Yes. I've noticed," Music Head said. Music Head had observed all the most minor details in his surroundings. Tom and I hadn't.

"What if Dr. Herbert is in there?" I asked. Brave shook from head to toe. His rough red hair stood up, but still he kept walking.

"That would be *veeeery, veeeery,* unfortunate," Brave said, and it was apparent that he was nervous about encountering Dr. Herbert in the laboratory.

"Don't worry, Brave. We're not going to do anything that puts you in danger," I replied.

"Lily's right. We'll be careful," Tom said as we walked on the uneven ground.

My steps were slow as I tried to keep my balance. My dizziness became worse.

"Well, I said I'd bring you there, and I will!" Brave said.

I didn't know how much longer I'd be able to keep taking steps.

We walked for a long while and passed through bends and bumps.

My legs felt weaker.

Brave stopped walking, and so did we. He turned his head right and left for a few seconds as if looking for something. He then moved a big rock to one side before continuing.

"We're almost there. I remember seeing this rock before on my way to the laboratory," Brave said.

I was glad to hear that we were close.

Brave walked a few more meters, stopped next to the wall, and started knocking lightly on the wall. I couldn't stand up anymore and had to sit.

"Are you not feeling good?" Tom asked.

"No," I answered briefly. Brave didn't pay any attention to us and started examining the wall as if trying to identify the exit.

"I think we're in the laboratory divo-space," Brave said while still facing the wall. He dropped the paper cone to the ground and touched the wall with both hands. I felt confused, and had to try hard to remember where we were and what we were doing.

"Lily, you are drooling," Music Head said, looking at my face.

I didn't feel embarrassed as I was too sick to care.

"Say something, Lily," Tom said. Tom bent down and held my shoulders as he looked at my face. "Do not give up! We're almost there!"

My body couldn't function anymore. I couldn't speak.

I tried my best and said, "I won't."

Tom stood up again and turned toward Brave. "Lily is very sick. We need the elixir. Are we there now?"

"Yes, I think so, but I have to find the exit," Brave said.

He stood suddenly still and put his ear against the wall.

He took a few steps toward us and said, "We have found the laboratory, but Dr. Herbert is in there. He's speaking... I can hear his voice."

Music Head took several steps back and leaned against the wall as he said, "I will never give you to anyone. You're my greatest discovery... That's what Dr. Herbert is saying," he whispered softly with his eyes shut.

"How do you know?" Tom whispered to Music Head.

"It's because my hearing is very good," Music Head replied.

He could hear the divos speaking even when they didn't use the paper cone when we couldn't. Music Head was special, and I'd known that ever since we'd first met him.

I tried to figure out how we could enter the lab without Dr. Herbert seeing us.

"It's best if we wait until Dr. Herbert has left," Tom said.

"She's sick. Very sick," Music Head said, wanting Tom to realize that waiting much longer wasn't an option.

"Dr. Herbert is in the laboratory most of the time. He rarely leaves," Brave said.

"Oh, that makes things harder," Tom said. Everyone was silent for a while, and Tom started speaking again. "We can try to..." he stopped talking and stared at the wall behind Music Head. Everyone turned around to see what he was looking at. It was Betty!

Betty had found us once again, but luckily, she was on our side this time.

"Betty, you found us," Brave said.

"Yes," Betty replied.

"Maybe you can help?" Brave asked.

"We made a deal," she replied.

"Yes," Brave said bravely with his head held high.

He turned toward Betty and walked up to her.

Brave looked Betty in the eye, his neck completely extended backward because of his shortness. He continued, "Lily is very sick. We need to get to the laboratory... and find the elixir. Dr. Herbert is there, and we can't enter because he will see us."

"Do you want me to distract him?" Betty asked.

"Yes! It would be great if you could," Brave said.

Betty glanced at me, and I got goosebumps despite having a high fever.

She had a chilling aura and knowing that she was on our side didn't change that I was still scared of her. Betty didn't say another word and disappeared.

"Is she going to just walk in?" Tom asked.

"No. Dr. Herbert doesn't let anyone in," Brave said.

"But Betty is a ghost. She can go wherever she wants," Tom said.

"Even she stays away from the laboratory, I think she's going to help," Brave said and continued looking for the opening. He touched the wall until he suddenly turned around and smiled. He took up the paper cone and said, "I found the opening! I found it!"

Pure excitement filled Brave's face, and he was jumping up and down with his short legs as he was expressing his feelings.

Brave also raised his hands up in the air, just the way he always did when he felt happy.

"OK. Dr. Herbert is still there," Music Head said in response to Brave's celebration.

Braved stopped jumping up and down, his smile fading away.

Everyone looked at Music Head to see what he had to say because he could hear everything in the laboratory.

Music Head was silent.

I was still sitting next to the wall and couldn't move, but sitting still made me feel better.

"Betty's now at the entrance talking to Dr. Herbert," Music Head said.

"What are they saying?" Tom asked impatiently. Music Head closed his eyes again as he was concentrating.

"Betty's telling him that she has seen us and she can't find the other night demons," Music Head said, and he continued listening again.

We all held our breath to see if Betty could make Dr. Herbert leave.

"Dr. Herbert is telling Betty that she shouldn't tell the other night demons she's found us. He wants the emerald for himself," Music Head said and continued. "Betty said she won't tell, but she needs something in return."

Music Head became silent and took a deep breath in a way that worried us all.

What if Dr. Herbert's deal with Betty is better than ours? I thought.

"Something? Like what?" Tom asked.

"He promised to show her his laboratory," Music Head replied. "Betty's now going to show Dr. Herbert where you are," he explained further. Everyone smiled, knowing our deal with Betty was much better than Dr. Herbert's.

I felt something cold underneath my hand. It was water! I jumped up, frightened.

"It's just water, Lily," Music Head said calmly. But it didn't matter; I didn't want to get close to water.

Tom looked at me and said, "Oh no. She's much worse. We need to hurry."

Music Head said, "She has hydrophobia. She's scared of water. That's a symptom of rabies." He looked over at Brave and said, "I can't hear Dr. Herbert anymore. He must have left the laboratory."

Brave pushed the wall, and the light shone into the dark divo-space.

We had found our way to the laboratory!

Brave cautiously moved his head from the divo-space and looked around before taking a step forward and entering the laboratory.

Music Head said, "You go first, Tom. I will carry Lily."

Tom looked at me and at Music Head before saying, "No, I will carry her. You go ahead." I hadn't realized how sick I was, but it became apparent from their conversation that I was too ill to walk. "I'm OK," I said and stood up on my feet but fell.

Music Head turned around and walked out first.

Tom carried me into the lab. I was happy we'd finally made it with Brave's help.

Dr. Herbert's laboratory was just the way I remembered.

The only difference was that we had entered via the divo-space, and I was there voluntarily this time.

The laboratory smelled worse than before, as if Dr. Herbert was mixing and boiling dead animals in a pot along with rotten eggs.

"Oh! This is the worst smell ever!" Tom said. "Putrid!"

I was too weak to cover my nose with my hand, and I breathed in the smelly air.

Brave walked around slowly, but couldn't see much.

He was too small, and the objects were large.

On the other hand, Music Head was tall and could easily see all the bottles and pots on the laboratory shelves and tables. He didn't waste any time and looked around.

Everything appeared blurry. I felt exhausted, but knew I had to stay awake.

"We need the elixir now! Time is running out for Lily," Tom said.

He put me down in a corner.

"In the black pot," I said with great effort as I tried to make Music Head stop being distracted by the things in the lab. He had to find the item that mattered the most: the elixir.

The big black pot was close to the wall, easily visible.

Music Head walked over to the black pot.

Tom and Brave were standing one step behind him, and I couldn't see well with my increasingly blurred vision from the corner where Tom had placed me.

Music Head looked inside the black pot, but had to take a step back as the pot started shaking uncontrollably, the same way I'd seen it shake when I was in the laboratory before.

"Oh," Music Head said and backed away further as if seeing something incredible inside the pot. Everyone held their breath and had their eye on Music Head as if he was looking into a crystal ball, seeing our destiny in the castle.

"What can you see?" Tom asked, but strangely, Music Head, who always was in control, didn't find any words to say.

"What's in there?" Brave asked. We were all losing patience, worried that Dr. Herbert would come back any minute.

"A white snake," Music Head said. He seemed blown away by what he'd observed.

"A white snake? Is there a snake in the pot?" Tom cried out anxiously.

The pot shook vigorously now.

I was doubtful that we'd finally find the elixir. Was Music Head seeing the twin to the monstrous black snake the divos had killed earlier?

Music Head eventually said, "There's a small bottle in the center of the pot. A big, white snake is wrapped around it."

"Is there another snake beside the monstrous one that chased us earlier? How many snakes does he have?" Tom asked with a shaky voice that indicated that he was feeling faint.

"He likes snakes!" Brave announced like a TV presenter but hid completely behind Tom.

My legs were weak, my body was exhausted, and my eyes were almost shut.

Music Head did something unexpected.

He put his hand courageously inside the black pot and held it there.

"Music Head! Careful! You're going to get hurt!" Tom mumbled, and his jaw dropped. Brave jumped up on Tom's shoulder and hugged him tightly from behind as he trembled.

"It's OK," Music Head replied with a calm and controlled voice. The snake was wrapped around Music Head's long arm!

He kept his whole arm inside the big, black pot for a while before gently taking it out.

"Tom, take the elixir out now!" Music Head commanded. Tom took several slow steps toward the pot, closely watching the snake wrapped around Music Head's arm.

Will Tom make it? I thought.

Not only did I have blurred vision, but my eyelids also felt very heavy.

I was struggling to hold my eyes open.

Everything started spinning around me and turned black.

Chapter 14

THE ELIXIR

"Lily! Lily! Open your eyes!" I heard a voice say. It was Tom's voice. I had to fight very hard to keep them open and stay awake.

"Where am I?" I asked.

I was neither oriented in time nor place, but still knew who I was.

"In the laboratory! Open your eyes and look!" Tom said, holding an object in front of my eyes. My vision was still blurry, and I struggled to see what it was.

"What?" I asked. I couldn't make any sense of Tom's words or the thing he held in front of me. It appeared as a blur. I simply couldn't focus on anything.

"Come on! Open your eyes! You're almost there!" Tom said again.

"Lily, open your eyes!" That voice was also familiar. It was the voice of Brave.

With great difficulty, I opened my right eye and saw Brave's blue face and small eyes. His bright red hair was barely visible behind the paper cone he held in front of his mouth.

The sharp edge of it was tickling my face.

"Hmm," I said in response and did my best to open my eyes.

"Music Head removed the snake by having it wrapped around his arm. I could then take the elixir out of the pot. The snake was guarding the elixir and fighting back," Tom said.

He paused for a while before saying, "But... but... Music Head's been hurt."

I gathered all the energy that I had left, sat with my eyes wide open, and looked for him.

Where is Music Head? Where is the white snake? I thought.

To my surprise, I couldn't see Music Head.

"Where's Music Head?" I asked, but no one answered. "Where is he?" I asked again.

"He's over there," Tom said and pointed to the other side of the laboratory. Music Head was lying on the floor.

He didn't move, but a smile appeared on his lips.

Half of the snake lay on the floor close to Music Head, and the second half was on the other side of the laboratory.

"What happened?" I asked.

"I did my best to stop the snake from biting Music Head," Brave said. My eyes were shut again. I just couldn't keep them open.

"Have the elixir, Lily," Tom said.

I replied, "What about Music Head?"

No one said anything, and I heard Music Head replying from the other side of the room.

"You're sicker than me. Please, take the elixir." He sounded well, and one could never have guessed that he had a snake bite injury.

I took the bottle in my hand and looked at Tom.

"Tom, I'm sorry. The elixir was going to be for your sick mother," I said and looked at Tom's sad face. A smile appeared on his face despite all the pain.

"It's OK. Have it," Tom replied.

Despite my blurred vision, I could just about see the elixir bottle. It was much smaller than I'd imagined, even smaller than my index finger.

A spicy and floral scent filled the room and covered the rotten, dead animal laboratory smell. I took the small, deep blue elixir bottle in my hand and removed the wooden top.

I lifted up the bottle and took it to my mouth. Is this the elixir? I thought, but knew it was a magical solution from the smell.

A few drops touched my mouth, and I lowered the bottle again.

I had a strange taste in my mouth. The elixir was sweet, strong, and spicy.

I placed the wooden top onto the bottle and said, "Music Head, catch."

"No! No, Lily! Hand it to me, I'll take it to Music Head. We don't want the bottle to smash and lose the elixir," Tom said loudly. He took the bottle and handed it to Music Head. He, too, drank from the elixir until the very last drop.

Tom and Brave were sitting on the floor between Music Head and me, waiting to see if the elixir had any effect on us. We waited a few minutes, and nothing happened. My legs were still weak, my head was spinning, and I still couldn't open my eyes.

Music Head didn't make any sound either, and I knew he was feeling sick.

He too was becoming worse by the minute.

This is it for Music Head and me, destined to be ghosts in the castle forever, I thought.

"Tom, remember to take the emerald from Music Head," I whispered. Everything was still. Silence had filled the laboratory.

I took a breath and a second breath, and a third breath, but nothing happened.

These could be my last breaths.

Unexpectedly, a few water droplets fell onto my face.

I opened my eyes, and saw Brave holding a glass pipette above my face, dripping water over me.

"Don't do that, Brave!" I said as I felt irritated and sat up.

Brave had just ruined such a beautiful sentimental moment before my death!

We forgot the special moments in a matter of seconds.

"She is well again! She is well!" Brave dropped the glass pipette and started making his usual celebratory dance. "She's not having— what did you call it, Music Head? Waterphonia?" Brave asked.

"Hydrophobia," Music Head replied from the other end of the laboratory. I opened my eyes, and hesitantly, stood up and shook each leg before jumping up and down.

I wasn't exhausted anymore! My headache was gone too.

"It worked! It worked!" I said happily.

Music Head was already standing and adjusting his clothes.

However, he didn't show any excitement.

"Yes! You both look well again. I was so worried for you both," Tom said.

Brave continued the classic divo-celebration he spared for his many exciting or jolly moments. He raised his hands in the air and waved them around.

He ran toward the paper cone, held it in front of its mouth, and said, "Hurray! It worked! Hurray!"

I stopped smiling and looked at the deep blue, empty elixir bottle on the floor.

I walked over, and picked it up. Not a single drop was left. I gently held the bottle up against the light and hoped I was wrong, but I wasn't.

Tom, Music Head, and Brave were all standing before me, wondering what I was doing.

"Well. That's it. We came so far and used the elixir ourselves," I said, disappointment in my voice.

Footsteps from outside the lab broke the moment of silence.

A key turned inside the keyhole, unlocking the heavy door.

We all looked at each other and knew immediately that we had to run into the divo-space.

I was closest to it and ran in first, the rest following.

Music Head closed the door firmly once we were all back in safety.

Brave signaled the rest of us to follow him.

He moved his tiny legs fast and accidentally dropped his paper cone on the floor. He stopped and looked at it with a worried face.

Tom picked up the cone and continued running behind Brave.

We didn't know where Brave was taking us, but we just couldn't stop running.

A few stairs appeared in front of us.

We ran up the stairs and reached another corridor. The divo-space with all its connections was highly confusing. I was sure Dr. Herbert wouldn't find us for the exact same reason.

"Where is Brave taking us?" Tom whispered.

"I don't know, but I trust that he will bring us somewhere safe, far away from Dr. Herbert," I whispered back.

"We should just follow him. I trust Brave," I added.

"Me too," Tom replied.

Brave took us far from the laboratory. We didn't ask him where we were heading because we knew we were in good hands.

Everyone walked ahead of me in the narrow space.

Something bright appeared on the dark, stony wall.

I ignored looking at the spot, having a bad feeling about it, but it kept following me. Finally, I decided to turn toward the bright spot and face it as it didn't disappear.

It was Betty again!

"You are always trying to hide from me," she said.

"Betty... no... I haven't tried to hide. The elixir... we found it," I told Betty with an anxious voice before I could stop myself.

The rest continued walking, but I'd stopped to talk to Betty.

"Oh, you took the elixir? That's why Dr. Herbert's gone mad! He's looking under every small stone to find you because he knows you are responsible. Don't worry, he will stop if you give the elixir back," Betty said with an amused voice.

"We can't return the elixir," I said.

"Why not?" Betty asked.

"It's because... we had to use it. We had to use *all* of it," I said.

"You *used* the elixir!" Betty asked.

"As I said, we *had* to use the elixir. Both Music Head and I were very sick," I replied.

"What a shame," Betty said with an exaggerated sad voice. "Well, Dr. Herbert is going to do everything in his power to get you. You took away his most precious discovery."

My hair stood up from the moment Betty had appeared, and rightly so, because not only was she scary, but she was also the bearer of bad news.

"Do the night demons know about the divo-space and the connections in the castle?" I asked once I was calmer.

"No, not really. Anyway, it doesn't mean no one will find out," Betty said and started singing.

"You aren't going to tell them, right?" I asked, but Betty had already disappeared. I looked around and saw I was left alone as the others had walked away.

"Brave? Tom? Music Head?" I shouted. No one replied.

I walked in the same direction I thought they had gone.

How stupid of me to stop and talk to Betty. Betty the ghost. Maybe she did that on purpose, to distract me. Why didn't the others wait for me? I thought.

"Tom? Music Head? Brave?" I shouted again without hearing any response.

I realized that I was... lost. Lost and alone. Water droplets fell to the ground, the only sound in the divo-space.

There was no trace of the others. Once again, I had to follow Willow Witch's advice.

I stood still for a moment and tried to guess where Brave was taking us.

We had rushed out of the laboratory to run away, but we hadn't decided where to go.

We had just followed Brave.

Brave was running to... running to? The kitchen? No, it can't be since the kitchen divo-space is known to the night demons, and it would be one of the first places they'd search.

Where would I go if I were Brave? He took them far from the laboratory.

He took them to... another floor!

I thought and found my answer. *The laboratory is on the ground floor. Brave most likely moved up to the highest floor possible to hide them in the divo-space as far away as possible from the laboratory and the kitchen.*

Now I knew where I could find Tom, Brave and Music Head.

The night demons were going to search the castle inch by inch, floor by floor, corner by corner, but never wall by wall unless they found out about the divo-space.

Before moving toward them, I thought how we'd complete our remaining time here.

Music Head would leave in less than four hours.

We had already got into so much trouble in just a few hours, so another eighteen more were too long of a wait for us to not have a good plan.

"It must be getting dark by now," I whispered. Suddenly, I knew what I had to do! We got into trouble because we had been looking for the elixir.

We went from the basement to the dining room, kitchen, and even Duke Lukas's bedroom. We needed to stay in the same place for the remaining time in the castle and hold the emerald one by one for seven hours each.

We ensured the ones staying behind wouldn't get into trouble or get lost.

How can we stay in the same spot for such a long time? Music Head has to be still for four hours, the second person to leave has to be still for eleven hours, and the last person has to stay still for... eighteen hours! I thought.

That was a long time to be entirely still, especially as the night demons were trying their best to pin us down. Another droplet fell, and an idea appeared in my mind.

I had to find something that could put us to sleep.

Brave can wake us one by one when it's time to leave.

What can make us fall asleep? Lavender could help with sleep but not for more than an hour, let alone eighteen hours.

What if Dr. Herbert has a solution in his lab that could help us sleep for an extended time? I'm sure he has, but I'm not sure we'll be able to wake up... ever again, I thought.

I walked in the direction that I suspected the rest had gone.

The only way to the highest floor in the castle was to move upwards instead of down. From where I stood in the divo-space, the stairs headed off up and down, but I knew I had to avoid them. So, I walked and got to a wooden plank with ropes attached. It was a primitive elevator! The divos had creatively shaped the divo-space.

There was also a narrow tunnel leading away from the elevator.

There was no way that Brave would take this route as not all three would fit on the wooden plank. Music Head was also too tall for the elevator.

I entered the narrow tunnel and imagined it to be the route that Brave and the rest had taken. The dark, narrow tunnel was scarier than the other parts of the divo-space and perhaps a claustrophobic person's worst nightmare. But there was no time for hesitation. I'd never find the others if I stood still; I had to keep walking and looking for them.

Betty should never have distracted me, and I should never have stopped following behind Music Head! That I knew for sure.

My steps were slower than usual as I couldn't see anything in this darkness.

Luckily, I could use my sense of touch. My hands touched the tunnel's walls, and I moved cautiously to feel for any sort of obstruction.

The quiet tunnel wasn't dead anymore.

What is that noise? And where is it coming from? I thought.

Suddenly, I felt something soft and furry behind my left foot. I ran as fast as I could within the darkness, but the furry creature kept chasing me. I could feel its tail!

It was a mouse!

I hate mice!

It didn't take long before I hit a wall, fell backward, and landed on my back. The mouse ran toward my head and smelled me before disappearing into the dark.

I was still lying down when I heard a new, faint sound.

This time, it wasn't the sound of a mouse or any other furry animal. The sound was... words... that I could understand!

"Where can she be? How did we not notice she wasn't following us anymore?" That was Tom speaking.

"Don't know," Music Head replied.

"Don't worry. I will find her. I know the connections back to the laboratory," Brave said.

"What if Dr. Herbert's captured her?" Tom said in his regular anxious voice.

"No. Lily was just behind me," Music Head said.

I sat up quickly as I could hear the voices almost disappearing again.

"I'm here! I'm here!" I shouted. My voice echoed in the tunnel, and it didn't take long before I heard a reply.

"Lily! Lily! Where are you?" Brave replied, but his voice was still very faint.

"In the tunnel. It's so dark here. I can't see anything," I replied.

"Wait on the same spot, Lily. Don't move. We'll lose you if we all start moving around simultaneously. Just keep on talking to us so that we can find you," Tom said. I could hear his voice getting louder as he spoke, and could tell they were getting closer.

"You're moving in the right direction. Your voice is getting louder," I said and listened to see if I could get a reply. I was over the moon that we were about to be together again.

"Yes, we can also hear you clearly. It's very dark here. Keep on talking," Tom said.

I didn't know what to say, but suddenly, I knew: I could tell them about my plan.

"I have a plan for getting through all eighteen hours without any problem!" I said.

"And your plan is?" Music Head asked.

"I think we should find a safe spot and stay there until we've completed our seven hours holding the emerald each. We're searching for nothing else since we already found, and used, the elixir. We'll just get ourselves into trouble if we keep walking around the castle as the night demons will find us. We need to fall into a very long sleep and leave the castle one by one when time's up for each of us," I said and looked up.

Tom's face was barely visible on my right-hand side.

Chapter 15

FALLING ASLEEP

"Lily, here you are!" Tom said. I got up on my feet and smiled.

"Your plan sounds good but let's talk about it because maybe it's not that straightforward," Tom said.

"It's a great plan," Music Head replied. He must have been standing far back behind Tom as his voice was quieter and seemed to come a long distance.

"I can assist you with your plan," Brave said.

The sound originated somewhere between Tom and Music Head.

"I'm so glad you're all here. I was so worried I'd never see you again and have to stay in this castle forever," I said and noticed for the first time that I'd been trying to suppress my fear of being left alone.

"Did you pass through the tunnel earlier?" I asked.

"No, we didn't. There's a shortcut behind the elevator that leads to the other side of the tunnel. The tunnel's too narrow, and the divos don't usually use it," Brave said.

"We should get out of the tunnel because there's a good chance that it's blocked halfway. There's also a risk of falling stones," Brave said.

We all then walked back in the direction we had entered the tunnel.

"There are mice in here," I warned.

"Yes, this is probably one of the places with the most mice in the divo-space," Brave said. I got goosebumps from just the thought of the mouse that had followed me.

"I see," I said and hoped that we'd exit as soon as possible.

Luckily, we weren't far in, and it soon became brighter.

Tom, Brave, and Music Head were all visible under the brilliant light from the tunnel's opening. It was so good to see them again, instead of just hearing their voices.

"Tell us more about your plan," Brave said impatiently before anyone else had the chance to speak.

"As I mentioned earlier, we need to find a safe spot to hide away from the night demons until our very last day. I think it's great to be in the divo-space, but we should stop moving around and stay in one spot," I explained.

"That's impossible, Lily. The last person has to stay in the castle for about eighteen hours. That's too long to be staying in the same spot," Tom said and scratched his head.

"Tell us more," Music Head said optimistically.

"We need to find a safe place within the divo-space where no one disturbs us. We should sleep there until we can leave the castle," I added with great enthusiasm.

My plan was simple yet sounded perfect.

"How will we be able to sleep for so many hours?" Tom asked.

Tom was right; it was one thing to say that we'd sleep, but it was another thing to actually stay asleep for more than eight hours.

"We need to find out how to sleep for that long," I said.

"It may work if we get hypnotized to sleep on top of a lavender bed," Music Head suggested. We all looked at Music Head, and no one said anything as we were unsure if his idea would work.

"How do you know this?" Tom asked.

"I tried it before," Music Head replied.

"How does it work?" I asked.

"Hypnotism helps you to fall asleep, and the lavender bed keeps you asleep," Music Head explained.

"Hurray!" Brave said joyfully.

"Amazing! That was the part of the plan that I didn't know how to arrange," I said and turned to Tom to see what he thought about Music Head's suggestion. It was apparent from Tom's expression that he wasn't sharing the same optimism as us.

"What do you think, Tom?" I asked, noticing that Tom didn't say anything.

"I don't know. I don't think it will work," he replied, and I knew he was being honest.

"You can try it first on me. That way, we'll know whether or not it works. If it doesn't, we'll have to figure out something else," I said.

"All right. I guess it doesn't hurt to try," Tom said.

"Do you know where we can sleep without being disturbed for days?" I asked Brave.

"You can sleep in the divo-space on the last floor," Brave said.

"Is that where you were taking us?" I asked.

"Yes, that's the place other divos don't usually go, and I wanted to hide you there," Brave said. We were all silent for a while and thought about the plan.

"The location you suggested sounds good, Brave. But we also need to be close to the Mirror Hall. The last person needs to place the emerald in the hall's center. Willow Witch told us to stand on the same spot as we appeared when we first arrived outside the castle.

"We need to stand there together when we're ready to return to the house. This means that the first two have to wait in the forest until the third person comes out," I said.

"She said that, but she never said how we actually would be able to get back," Tom said.

"I don't know. Willow Witch only told us that and said we'd find out how later," I said.

Brave looked unhappy, and he was completely quiet, which was unusual.

It suddenly hit me: the three of us would leave, but what about Brave? Would we leave him behind? Did he want to stay in the castle?

"Do you want to come with us to the house on the pumpkin farm?" I asked.

A smile appeared on Brave's face. He jumped up and down from joy.

He dropped the paper cone on the floor and started celebrating the same way he celebrated every time he was joyful. He jumped up and down on his short blue chubby legs.

"Lily, you can't be serious? Do you really want to bring Brave to Charlotte and Poppy's house?" Tom whispered.

"We can't leave him behind. Besides, Charlotte and Poppy's home's so big that it can house hundreds of people," I whispered back, hoping Brave wouldn't hear us.

Brave didn't notice us whispering. He was too busy celebrating.

"People, Lily, people. They can house people. Not a creature called divo with blue skin and rough red hair, living inside walls!" Tom said, trying his best to keep his voice down.

"Everyone should be welcome to any place that's considered great. The house on the pumpkin farm is a great place. Therefore, any creature in any form is welcome as long as they are kind and do no harm," I whispered loud enough for Tom to hear.

Music Head looked at me and smiled for the first time.

"I agree with Lily. Any truly great place accepts anything and anyone who is different. I'm not going to leave Brave behind. I won't come if Brave doesn't come with us," Music Head said.

Tom looked at him and me before taking a deep breath. "Brave, we're more than happy for you to come to the house on the pumpkin farm with us."

Brave continued shaking his backside rhythmically from side to side in dance moves. Everyone, including Brave, started laughing.

"What about Betty? Is she kind?" Tom asked as soon as he'd stopped laughing. He awaited an answer, and his statement had been clever.

"She's not good, but neither is she bad. Besides, we really had to make a deal with her. She also helped us enter the laboratory," I argued.

"Sorry, I don't mean to sound awful. I just worry about Charlotte and Poppy. What if they get mad?" Tom said.

"Well, we have to see. I'm sure we can come up with something if Poppy and Charlotte get mad," I replied. Tom nodded in response.

"Thank you, Lily!" Brave said, jumped up, and gave me a hug.

I fell backward, not ready for Brave's tender clinch.

"All right," I said, laughing. "Back to the discussion about our hiding spot, can you take us to the divo-space in the Mirror Hall?" I asked.

Brave took several steps, picked up the paper cone, and said, "Certainly! The Mirror Hall divo-space is wide and undisturbed," Brave said.

"Good! We need to take the same way leaving the castle as when we first arrived. That way, we'll easily find the spot we first appeared,' I said.

"There are so many exits. It's hard to know exactly how you entered," Brave said.

"We might not find the spot if we take the wrong one," Tom said, rubbing his eyes.

"Betty can help us leave. She brought us in. Maybe she knows which way we took?" I said and could finally be really proud of Brave for his deal with Betty.

"Good idea! She won't say no because we made a deal. Besides, she's coming back to the house on the pumpkin farm with us. We have to talk to Betty next time we see her," Tom said.

"We have a plan!" I said and hoped it wouldn't fall apart.

"I'm starving," Music Head said.

"Me too. We need to eat before we sleep," Tom said.

"Do you think we can go back to the kitchen and have something to eat, Brave?" I asked. Brave scratched his head and thought for a moment.

"No. I'll bring you food if you want. We shouldn't go back to the kitchen as the night demons show up in the kitchen from time to time. No one will be suspicious as divos aren't allowed to eat anywhere other than inside the divo-space," Brave said.

"Fine. Where should we wait?" I asked.

"I'll take you to the Mirror Hall divo-space first. You can wait for me there...." Brave stopped speaking as an unexpected sound came from the other side.

"Hurry! Hide inside the tunnel. Don't come out until I say so," Brave said quickly and quietly.

Tom, Music Head, and I ran inside the dark narrow tunnel and stood still next to the wall. I was the closest to the tunnel opening, but couldn't see much in the dark.

I didn't want to look because there was a chance we'd be discovered by whatever we were hiding from.

"I can..." Tom said before I squeezed his arm and signaled him to be quiet. Tom's voice echoed in the tunnel, and I hoped we wouldn't be discovered.

Two shadows moved closer to the tunnel.

I stretched my arm over Tom's and Music Head's trunks and squeezed myself back toward the tunnel wall.

The shadows were small and chubby, just like Brave's. Probably, the two shadows were divos walking randomly into us.

The two shadows stopped, then were still for a while before disappearing again.

A mouse roamed around our feet, and I hoped it wouldn't jump on me because I wouldn't be able to keep still or quiet.

The mouse moved in circles around us, but kept coming back as if it had recognized me from earlier.

I moved my feet slowly to discourage it from getting closer, but the mouse didn't give up. Incredibly determined, it climbed up my leg.

I stood still for a moment, but then moved and tried to shake the mouse off me at the end.

Tom and Music Head tried to keep me silent. I did my best not to shout.

The mouse ran toward the opposite wall in the tunnel, and I could finally take a deep breath. Suddenly, the mouse returned and quickly got up my sleeve.

This time, I couldn't control myself. I moved, lost my balance, and fell to the ground facing the opening.

The sound of my fall echoed in the divo-space.

Brave had placed his hands on the back of two other divos and tried to move them away from us and the tunnel.

He turned his head and looked at me. Brave was trying to signal me to hide again.

The two divos almost turned toward me, but Brave did his best to distract them both.

One of the divos turned around quickly and ran my way.

Brave ran as fast as he could behind the divo, but it was too late.

The first divo looked at me with a frightened face.

The second also approached me, and he also looked shocked, frightened, and worried all at the same time.

Brave and the two other divos made some noise, but it sounded strange to my ears.

Of course! I couldn't hear them because divos spoke at a much lower volume than others.

Music Head took a few steps and left the tunnel.

"They are saying that the divos have looked everywhere for Brave and suspect he's hiding us. The night demons are angry with the divos since they helped us kill Dr. Herbert's black snake and escape. Some divos still work for the night demons as they're afraid of the consequences," Music Head said after listening to the three divos' conversation.

Music Head continued, "The divos are worried that the night demons will soon destroy the divo-space in the kitchen... they're asking Brave to turn us in."

Brave looked at both of them while he shook his head.

"They are talking about what they should do next. Brave doesn't want to give us away," Music Head said. I looked at Brave's anxious face.

He was really between a rock and a hard place.

What could he do about the situation? I knew Brave had got into trouble because of us, and we had to help him.

"What would you say about us trying to help the divos? Brave's helped us a lot, and all the divos are in trouble. They shouldn't have part of their home destroyed because of us," I said.

"The divos can give the night demons a fake emerald and pretend they've killed us," Music Head said.

I stopped for a moment to think about what Music Head had just said.

A fake emerald? How could the night demons find out that the emerald given to them is not real? The night demons wanted the emerald to leave the castle too.

"But they'll find out," I replied.

"How?" Music Head said.

"The instructions we have are from Willow Witch. The night demons don't know how to use the emerald to leave the castle," Tom said, and it was evident that he found Music Head's plan brilliant.

"One of us still needs to stay in the castle for another eighteen hours.

"We can tell them what to do on a piece of paper. We can lie and explain to them that they need to hold the emerald for a total of *twenty* hours. That way, we should have all left by the time they find out we've tricked them," Tom said.

"Remember what Willow Witch told us? We have to place the emerald in the Mirror Hall once we purify the castle. By the time the night demons realize the truth, they'd have already transformed into ghosts, unable to harm anyone. The divos can live in the castle in peace as they'll be safe when the night demons have become ghosts. Dr. Herbert won't be able to do any experiments in his laboratory, and Duke Lukas will be unable to release his bat," I said.

The three divos were still talking with one another. Judging by their faces, they were overly worried.

"Brave, we've found a solution," I said.

Brave ran a few meters to pick up his paper cone before running back, using it to speak.

"What plan do you have? The night demons are furious..." he said.

I had to interrupt. "Music Head heard you. He told us everything. We know how to help you with the night demons," I said, and Brave nodded in response.

"You and the two other divos can give a fake emerald to the night demons. A written instruction should follow the fake emerald. You should also pretend you've killed all three of us to get the emerald," I explained.

"But won't you need the written instruction yourself?" Brave asked and scratched his rough red hair.

"No, the written instruction is going to be made up. We were told exactly what to do by Willow Witch. This way, we'll all have hopefully escaped before the night demons find out they've been tricked," I said.

Brave turned to the two other divos and spoke to them. They both listened carefully and nodded. Eventually, all three jumped and clapped.

Brave placed the paper cone in front of his mouth and said, "We agree with your plan."

"That's great, but where do we find the fake emerald?" Tom asked.

I bent down, took up a rock, and said, "It's right here." A smile appeared on my lips.

The divos brought us sheets of sandpaper and green color solution in just a few minutes as if they had it already at hand somewhere in the divo-space.

"I can make the fake emerald," Music Head said and took the rock in his hand.

He used sandpaper to smoothen the rock's surface before he splashed a few dark green color drops on the rock and continued rubbing the color with the sandpaper.

It took us less than an hour to have a brand new, fake emerald!

Music Head took out the original emerald from his pocket and compared it with the fake one. He made some final adjustments before saying, "The emerald is ready for delivery to the night demons."

Tom and I were both surprised by how real the emerald looked. Besides, how did you tell if something was fake when you hadn't seen the real one?

"Are you sure you haven't mixed the emeralds?" Tom asked.

Music Head nodded confidently.

"We won't be able to leave the castle if you mistakenly switch the emeralds. Please hold onto the original one," I said, nervous over a possible mistake that could destroy our plans.

Music Head smiled as he threw up the fake emerald into the air before catching it in his fist.

"This is fun. The fake emerald looks so real," Tom said.

Chapter 16

THE NOTE

"A piece of paper and pen, please," Music Head said and sounded like a surgeon in an operation theater, about to start a complex operation.

The divos ran as fast as possible and brought a piece of paper. Music Head looked at them and said, "And a pen, please."

One of the divos ran and brought a pen in just a few minutes.

"How can they find everything so quickly?" I asked.

"I was thinking the same thing. It's remarkable," Tom said.

"This is how we, divos, operate when we're determined," Brave said with the paper cone directed at us.

I looked at Tom and said, "I guess we have to delay our food and sleep?"

Tom nodded.

"Hold the emerald in your hand for twenty hours? Does it sound good?" Music Head asked.

"Also add '*to be held by the smartest, bravest, and greatest of all*,'" Tom said with a laugh. "This will lead to a conflict between the night demons as they all have a great ego, from what I've observed. Their egos will destroy them." Tom sounded excited.

"I think we have to write, '*To be held in the hands of the person deserving freedom the most, for twenty hours,*'" I said.

"Night demons aren't people, are they? Maybe you should replace the word *person* with, *one*," Tom said.

"Let's write, '*To be held in the hands of the one deserving freedom the most, for twenty hours,*'" Music Head said.

Tom and I approved.

Music Head wrote the sentence on the piece of paper the divos had given him.

"Here you go," Music Head said as he wrapped the fake emerald rock in the piece of paper with the note and handed it over to one of the divos. The divos didn't move.

"Oh, we almost forgot. We have to also pretend that you've killed us," Tom said, took off his shoes, and started damaging them by rubbing them against the rough ground.

Tom accidentally injured his finger, and a few blood drops smudged on his shoe.

Seeing the drops made all three divos faint.

"What happened?" I asked, surprised.

"They fainted," Music Head said bluntly.

"The sight of blood made them faint," Tom said, and none of us understood how they could all faint so quickly and simultaneously.

"Poor divos. They defeated the monstrous black snake but can't stand the sight of a few drops of blood," I said. We all laughed.

The divos started slowly regaining consciousness and stood up one by one.

"That was scary!" Brave said as soon as he held his paper cone.

"Sorry," Tom said.

"Should we also give them some of our belongings?" I asked Music Head.

"No. That will look too suspicious," Music Head replied.

I looked at Tom's white shoes. They looked completely damaged and having the blood drops smeared on top of them made the lie more believable.

The divos were scared to touch Tom's bloody shoe.

"Take it!" Tom said and held his shoe in front of the divos, but none would touch it.

"How badly do you want the night demons to believe that you killed us?" Tom asked.

One of the divos slowly took the shoe in his hands and stared at it as if it was the scariest object he had ever seen.

"It's fine," I told the divo, but he gave it to the divo next to him.

He, in turn, gave it to Brave.

Brave looked at the two divos and then at us before shrugging. He talked to the other divos before putting down the shoe and picking up the paper cone.

"You have to wait for me. The best place to wait would be the opening of the tunnel," Brave said.

"Good luck, Brave," I said.

Music Head and Tom walked over to Brave.

Tom placed his hand on Brave's shoulder and said, "You got this! We'll be waiting for you." Brave smiled nervously. However, the smile on his face faded quickly.

"Where's the fake emerald?" Tom asked.

The divo standing next to Brave took it out of his pocket.

"I recognize you two from the kitchen," I said as soon as I remembered the two divos.

They looked at me and smiled before one of them took up the paper cone from the ground and replied, "Yes, we met in the kitchen."

The divos looked like Brave, but were slightly taller with broader faces. The other was a bit chubbier and had a small round face.

The third divo took the paper cone from the other divo and said, "Don't worry about us. We will be right back."

"Good luck all!" Tom said.

The three divos turned around and walked away.

Brave carried Tom's shoe. The other divo held the fake emerald wrapped in the piece of paper containing the instructions.

The third divo had the honor of carrying the paper cone, the most important tool.

They walked away on short, chubby, divo legs. I hoped everything would work out.

"We should wait inside the tunnel," Tom said and walked toward the tunnel.

"I really don't like it. There are mice in there. For some reason, mice seem to like coming near me," I said.

"Maybe you have food in your pocket?" Music Head said.

"I don't think so, but I'll check," I replied as I placed my hand in my pockets. I could feel a small object in one, and I took it out.

"It's a piece of dry… pumpkin!" I said as I looked at the pumpkin piece in my hand. Tom and Music Head came closer and looked at it in disbelief.

"Well, we now know we don't have to make recipes to have a special power," Tom said.

"Should we use the pumpkin?" I asked.

"Why?" Music Head asked. He was right. We didn't have any reason to use the pumpkin to gain magical power.

"Using the pumpkin may destroy our plans," Tom said, and I knew he was right.

"At least I know what the mouse was looking for," I said.

"Maybe I should throw it away. That way, mice won't come near me while we're waiting in the tunnel," I said.

"No. We could need it again later," Tom said.

"Yeah, you're probably right," I said and placed it back in my pocket.

We all walked inside the tunnel and sat down, leaning against the tunnel wall.

The same mouse I'd seen before ran toward me from nowhere and took the pumpkin in his mouth, running away before releasing it on the ground and eating it.

"Well, I guess the mouse wouldn't give up until he got the pumpkin," I said. The mouse flew up in the air as soon as it was done chewing the small pumpkin piece.

The mouse moved all its limbs in the air and flew around. We all laughed, never having seen a flying mouse before.

"It feels so good to be resting," I said and shut my eyes.

"I hadn't realized how tired I was until now," Tom said.

"What about you, Music Head?" I asked, noticing he was absolutely silent.

"I'm also tired," Music Head replied.

"We shouldn't sleep yet. If we do, we won't be able to stay asleep for a long time," I said.

"Yes, this is probably not the best place to be sleeping," Tom replied.

"We should just stay awake," Music Head replied.

"I'm already falling asleep," I said.

"Me too. I'm fighting to not fall asleep. It's hard to be tired in a cool, dark place like this tunnel and stay awake," Tom said.

"Should we do something to stay awake?" I asked.

"What can we do?" Tom asked.

"We can talk," Music Head replied.

"Great idea, we should keep on talking to each other. This way, we'll stay awake," I said. Everyone stayed quiet for a while since we didn't know what to say.

"What should we talk about?" Tom asked.

"Isn't it funny? It's more difficult to find something to talk about when it's forced," I said with a laugh.

"I wonder when Brave will be back?" Music Head said the most reasonable thing while we were all waiting for Brave to return.

"It's hard to say. I hope the night demons won't realize that the emerald is fake. That way, we'll win time," I said.

"When did Brave leave?" Tom asked.

"He left thirty-six minutes ago," Music Head replied.

"It feels like ages ago," Tom said.

"It's because we're waiting for him to come back. Waiting is always hard," I said.

"I just want to lie down on the big, soft lavender pile and sleep," Tom said with a sleepy voice and appeared to be imagining his lavender bed.

"Me too," Music Head said with a sleepy voice.

A thought came to my mind, that I couldn't shake it off, so I decided to talk about it instead.

"What if the elixir makes us immortal? Wouldn't that be awful? That would be kind of unfair, wouldn't it? Music Head and I would have been the only ones immortal since we had the elixir. Death and ageing may be the fairest thing in life.

"Mighty kings and queens throughout history have aged and died. The most powerful people in history have died. History's smartest, most beautiful, and most charming people have all been mortal, and most are already dead.

"Wouldn't we disrupt the fairest circle? The circle of life and death?" I asked.

"Yes," Music Head answered briefly.

Tom was quiet and didn't say anything.

Usually, I could easily read Tom's emotions by just looking at his face, but I couldn't in the dark.

The mouse floated in the air and tried eagerly to get back down on the ground.

It held onto the tunnel wall to stop flying but couldn't hold on after a few seconds and flew toward us. Poor thing had no idea that it would start flying when it first chewed on the small piece of dried pumpkin from the pumpkin farm. Thinking of it, neither did we!

"We can help the mouse stop flying by dropping water drops over it. I don't think the mouse enjoys flying as much as we do," I said.

"Where can we find water?" Tom asked.

"I will leave the tunnel to see if I can find some," I said.

"OK. We'll stay here," Tom replied. I got up and left the tunnel.

A few water drops ran down the wall on the right. I opened my palm and let a few drops collect in my palm. I then walked back to the tunnel and splashed the few water droplets onto the flying mouse. The mouse fell down on the ground and ran away as quickly as possible.

"Now the mouse can move around freely," I said. But I couldn't hear any replies. "Tom? Music Head?" I said. One of them started snoring. "We shouldn't sleep yet. Let's wait for Brave to come back and sleep when we're lying hypnotized on top of a pile of lavender."

"It's so comfortable to sleep in the tunnel. It's cool and dark," Tom said, yawning loudly.

"You two can sleep. I will be waiting for Brave. I don't want to fall asleep," I said and sat on the ground, leaning toward the tunnel wall.

I don't know how long it took, but Brave finally returned.

I could see from afar that he was waving his arms in the air, accompanied by the two other divos.

"Wake up! Brave is back! He looks... happy!" I said.

Tom and Music Head slowly woke up.

"The two other divos are also with him," I informed them and ran out toward the divos.

"Brave, how did it go?" I asked.

"It wasn't too bad. We handed the fake emerald to the night demons and the piece of paper with the message. We also showed them Tom's bloody shoe and told them that we killed you all. They ignored us and started fighting over the emerald immediately."

Tom and Music Head were now fully awake and walked out of the tunnel.

"I don't think the night demons will bother you or us. They each seem so determined to get their hands on the emerald," Brave said.

The three divos started jumping up and down, clapping their hands.

"That's great! Can we walk toward the Mirror Hall and sleep?" I asked.

"Yes," Brave replied.

"We need three piles of fresh lavender and a small pocket clock," Music Head said.

Brave turned to the two other divos and spoke to them before turning to us, saying, "We will bring you all the things you need once we reach the Mirror Hall divo-space. My friends can help too."

The three short divos walked behind the elevator, and we followed. They kept talking to each other, and it was apparent they were good friends.

"Brave is telling them about our plan," Music Head said after listening to the conversation between Brave and his two friends.

"That's good. The other two divos should know because they'll be helping us too," I said.

Tom appeared exhausted. He didn't speak and just followed the divos.

It didn't take long before we reached our destination: Mirror Hall divo-space.

The Mirror Hall divo-space was much wider than the other parts of the hidden network.

The ground also appeared less bumpy.

Brave turned to us and said, "This is a good location to sleep, even for days." I nodded in response. Tom looked happier as soon as we finally could sleep.

"We will bring the lavender piles and find a pocket clock. Wait for us here. It's not going to take much time," Brave said and walked away with the two other divos before we could say anything.

"Finally, we get to sleep!" I said.

"I don't need a lavender pile or to be hypnotized with a pocket clock to fall asleep. I can even sleep for days!" Tom said.

"Shhh..." I said as soon as I heard the night demons speaking behind the walls.

"If you give me the emerald, I'll give you the elixir in return, I promise." That was Dr. Herbert's voice.

"You keep saying that, but I have started to doubt the elixir even exists," Duke Lukas replied. We were all completely quiet and tried hard to hear what they were saying, but it was hard to listen to their words through the castle's thick walls as they moved further away.

I turned to Music Head to ask him to listen to the conversation between Dr. Herbert and Duke Lukas, but he was fast asleep.

I was about to ask Tom if he could hear the conversation between Duke Lukas and Dr. Herbert when a sound echoed in the divo-space.

The noise woke Music Head up from his sleep.

It was a sound of friction, a strong smell of lavender accompanying the noise. The pleasant and calming scent made us sleepier than before.

Everyone turned toward the sound and saw a massive pile of lavender moving toward us.

"Brave?" I said, but it looked as if I spoke to the lavender pile.

Suddenly, I noticed Brave's tiny feet sticking out from under the pile. His bright red hair appeared in the center before he came out fully.

"We got you three lavender piles and a pocket clock," Brave said with a big smile.

"That was quick," Tom said. Brave laughed and pulled the pile he was carrying to the center of the divo-space, jumping on the lavender until it became flat and resembled a bed.

The two other divos also carried a lavender pile each and placed their piles next to the first lavender bed. They followed Brave's example, jumping on the lavender, creating two other lavender beds.

Brave picked up the paper cone from a corner and said, "I forgot! We haven't brought you any food!"

My stomach made a rumbling sound as soon as Brave mentioned the word *food*.

"Can you please bring us food?" Tom asked.

I could tell he was at least as hungry as I was. Brave scratched his bright red hair, turning to his friends as he started discussing something with them. They spoke for a while, and one of Brave's friends picked up the paper cone for the first time.

"We are...." He started saying but stopped almost immediately.

He took some time to examine the paper cone as he'd never used it before.

We giggled as he continued talking, "We are... going... to... bring you... food... Why is... this thing... making me... shout?" He turned to Brave and shrugged.

He looked at the paper cone again and scratched his head. His expression gave away that he wasn't used to talking via the paper cone yet.

Brave took the cone from his friend and said, "You need to use the cone to speak because humans can't hear us when we don't. Don't worry, it's great to be heard by everyone... it's like having wings to fly! It's like having a chocolate cake on a rainy day! It's the ultimate freedom!" Brave had a dreamy look, as if seeing a unicorn for the first time in his life.

The third divo with the round face ran toward Brave with outstretched arms and wanted to take the paper cone from him.

Brave smiled and gave it to him with his small, blue hands.

The third divo took the paper cone and observed it for a few seconds before speaking and climbing on top of one of the lavender beds.

"Hello," he said and waved at us as if it was the first time he had met us. We all looked at each other and waved back at him, replying, "Hello."

"It's a great honor being here today. I'm done with my speech," the divo said, giving himself a round of applause. He jumped down from the lavender bed and returned the cone to Brave. The three divos started jumping up and down, raising their hands in the air. Looking at the divos made me envy how they could celebrate and appreciate even the smallest things.

Brave said, "We're going to the kitchen to bring you food. Don't go anywhere. We will try and be as quick as possible."

Tom jumped on the first bed and said, "This is amazing! It smells heavenly. It's working as I'm sleepier than before." He then stretched out his arms and legs as he shut his eyes.

Music Head also lay on top of one of the lavender beds.

"I'm not going to lie down yet. I'm afraid of falling asleep before the divos bring us food," I said as I fought to keep my eyes open.

"Wake me up when the food has arrived," Tom said and rolled onto his stomach.

Music Head was determined to stay awake and kept tapping his fingers on the ground, making sounds with his fingers.

"Have you always liked playing music?" I asked.

"Yes, as far as I can remember," Music Head replied and became silent.

He didn't even look at me when I spoke to him.

Why is it always so difficult having a conversation with him? I thought.

"How old were you when you started playing music?" I asked.

"Maybe two," Music Head said as he kept looking down.

"Wow! That's very good. Where are your parents?" I asked, but somehow, I knew I shouldn't have asked that question.

Music Head's black hat covered his face almost entirely when he looked down even further. He stopped playing music and appeared quieter than usual.

"They abandoned me," Music Head replied, and I didn't know what to say.

"I'm sorry." I decided not to ask him any further questions. I walked over to the third lavender bed, sat down, and locked my hands together. I felt sorry for Music Head, but didn't know what to say or do, so decided to be quiet. Silence filled the divo-space.

The faint breathing sound and heartbeat were the only sounds in my ears. When was the last time I'd been in such a quiet environment? I couldn't remember, but the silence ended when Brave and his friends returned with three trays full of food.

"Oh... so much food!" I said.

The three divos held one tray each and had brought us everything from cheese, oranges, grapes, and bread to different soups and baked potatoes.

"Tom, wake up! The food has arrived!" I cried.

Tom got up faster than I thought. He must have been very, very hungry. "It smells wonderful!" he said.

The divos placed the trays on the ground.

We all sat around eating our final meal before going to sleep.

"Do you want some?" I asked the divos.

They were standing there just looking at us.

"Come and have food. There's more than enough," Tom said, and the three divos sat down and joined us in having food.

Brave took up the paper cone and said, "The night demons never allow us to eat with them. We weren't sure if you would."

"Food tastes better when it's shared," I replied.

The tallest of the divos took the paper cone from Brave and said, "Brave told us that you gave him a name. Are you able to name us too?"

All three divos stopped eating and looked at me.

"Hm... yes... sure," I said, but I wasn't ready for their request.

"What name will you give me?" the tallest asked.

I thought of a proper name for him for a moment before saying, "Which of you found the clock so quickly?"

The small chubby divo pointed to himself. "We can name you *Quick* if you like?"

The small chubby divo started smiling wide, nodded, and rolled on the ground from happiness.

I looked at the taller divo. "Did you give the fake emerald to the night demons?"

He nodded.

"We can name you Clever?" I asked to see if he liked his new name or not.

Clever also started smiling and nodding before picking up the paper cone.

"Thank you, Lily, for our names! We have been nameless for centuries," Clever said.

I smiled and replied, "You're welcome! You helped us, all three of you. We'd never have managed to escape the night demons if it weren't for you—Brave, Quick, and Clever!"

Tom stopped eating and added. "I agree with Lily! You now have nice suitable names."

The three divos started clapping their hands.

I rushed to stop them, afraid that the night demons would hear us.

"Shhh," I whispered.

"Did you hear that?" a soft female voice said from behind the wall.

I identified it as Isabel's voice.

"What?" another voice asked. It sounded like Dr. Herbert.

"I heard several people talking and clapping their hands. It seemed to be coming from the wall," Isabel said.

I couldn't breathe from worry. I'd assumed that we had reached the end of our time in the castle, but started doubting my judgment.

Chapter 17

THE RAY OF SUNSHINE

"A sound of clapping came from the wall? It doesn't make any sense," Dr. Herbert replied.

"Yes, it came from the wall. I'm sure of that," Isabel confirmed.

"Well, we should check the other side of the wall," Dr. Herbert said with a faint voice. He was perhaps whispering as he prowled to the other side of the wall.

Maybe he was trying to walk behind the wall and catch us.

They were silent. We couldn't hear the conversation anymore.

We all stopped moving.

No one dared move an inch, and Brave started shaking from fear.

We waited patiently for a few minutes, prepared to run if detected by the night demons.

They spoke again. This time, their voice came from the other side of the wall.

"No one's here. You may have just imagined hearing the sounds. Like some sort of auditory hallucination," Dr. Herbert said.

"No, I know I'm right," Isabel said with a lot of determination.

"What if the children are alive and they are in the... wall?" Isabel whispered with a mysterious voice from the other side of the wall.

Nothing could be heard after that.

Everyone was absolutely frozen. We all looked at one another, scared. Our eyes were the only body parts we weren't afraid to move.

What were the night demons planning? Would Dr. Herbert believe Isabel? And would they tear down the walls? It was hard to know as Isabel and Dr. Herbert had stopped talking. Not even Music Head could hear them anymore.

A chilling sensation spread among everyone in the divo-space. It seemed unrelated to the voices behind the wall.

Someone had joined us. Once again, Betty had arrived.

Betty floated in through the Mirror Hall wall and looked at us in a calm, entertained way as if she knew what was going on. She looked at the trays of food and the three lavender beds. She knew she should remain silent.

A loud smashing sound shook the walls! It didn't take long before the next hit.

We all rolled away as far as we could from the walls.

Luckily, the lavender beds cushioned us from hitting them and injuring ourselves.

Intense fear cast a shadow on everyone's face.

Betty was the only one remaining untouched by the event.

She stared at me. My heart skipped a beat.

The last time she appeared, I got lost. What trouble will she get us into this time?

Betty illuminated in her white dress despite the darkness in the divo-space. The wall hits became more intense, and cracks appeared at the bottom of the old castle walls.

Betty faced the wall slowly, started singing, and walked through the wall.

"What is going on, Isabel?" Betty asked once she had stopped singing.

"I think the children are alive and hiding in the wall," Isabel replied. The hits resumed soon after.

"I told her that she just imagined hearing hand-clapping sounds, but Isabel is sure that she heard clapping coming from the walls," Dr. Herbert said.

"Clapping?" Betty asked, surprised. Her reaction was so natural that she surely could win whatever acting prize was available in that place and century.

"Where did you hear the clapping from again, Isabel?" Betty asked softly, in a way that even I questioned whether we actually were inside the wall.

"Hmm... I could be wrong. Maybe I heard something else, or maybe I just imagined it, like Dr. Herbert suggested," Isabel said.

"No, you said you heard hand clapping coming from the wall. I have been going back through the wall, and haven't heard any clapping. I can check again to reassure you," Betty said and walked straight through the wall before going back again.

"I checked, and no one is inside the wall, clapping or otherwise," Betty said in a way that sounded as if ridiculing Isabel. She sounded like a parent who wanted to show their child that there were no monsters in the dark by turning on the lights.

"Isabel, it would probably be more useful if you used your time to figure out what to do with the emerald that the three stupid divos gave you. Stop destroying the castle walls because of your vivid imagination," Betty said.

Brave, Quick and Clever looked at each other as soon as they heard Betty use the word 'stupid' to describe them.

Isabel was utterly silent.

We all looked at each other. No one dared to say a word.

Betty walked through the wall several times as she kept singing and ignored us.

We all understood that we shouldn't move or whisper until Betty acknowledged us. Finally, after a long while, Betty passed one last time through the corridor wall and stopped in the divo-space.

"They are gone now," she said quietly and turned to the three divos.

"You should stop making so much noise. You'll get into a lot of trouble if they find you," Betty said.

The three frightened divos nodded vigorously and looked regretful.

Betty turned to me and said, "You better follow the plan you have and go to sleep. I will come and take you to the forest one by one when the time comes. We made a deal and, therefore, I will help you leave the castle. Remember, I'm going to follow you to the house."

We all nodded as no one dared to say a word.

Betty turned to the divos again and said, "You should return to the kitchen before you cause more trouble."

The three divos nodded again.

Betty walked away, and we could all finally take a deep breath.

"That was close," Tom whispered and shut his eyes.

"We better go to sleep," Music Head whispered.

I didn't want to take any risk of being heard by the night demons again, so I just nodded and signaled to Tom and Music Head to lie down on their lavender beds.

I lay down and closed my eyes.

Suddenly, something very rough shook my arm. I opened my eyes and saw Brave's face.

He held up a pocket clock. I knew what he meant: someone had to show him how to hypnotize first before he could do it himself.

I looked at Brave and at the pocket watch. I had no idea how to hypnotize, but Music Head had told us he knew.

I turned toward Music Head and pointed to the pocket clock in Brave's hand.

Music Head got up from his lavender bed, walked over to Brave, and took the clock.

He turned to Quick and started moving the clock in front of his face horizontally as he kept whispering something to him.

It didn't take long before Quick fell backward and started snoring.

Music Head then walked over to Tom and did the exact same thing.

Tom was also hypnotized to sleep.

Brave stood by Music Head's side, observing and learning how to hypnotize so that he could hypnotize Music Head when it was his turn. Music Head held the small metal pocket clock in front of my face and started rocking it horizontally as he said, "You know you're tired and can sleep for a long time. Breathe in the smell of lavender. Relax." I couldn't understand what he was saying after that. I'd already fallen asleep.

"Lily, it's time for me to leave now," a soft voice whispered. I slowly opened my eyes and saw Music Head standing next to my lavender bed.

"Do you want to hold the emerald next?" he asked. I rubbed my eyes.

I couldn't fully understand what was going on.

Have five hours already passed? I thought. It felt like a few minutes. I looked around and saw that Tom also was awake.

"Give it to Tom. I wouldn't mind sleeping some more. Good luck," I said before sinking in my soft, comfortable, warm lavender bed again. Music Head then walked over to Tom.

Betty was waiting for him a short distance away. This time, I wasn't scared of Betty.

I just wanted to sleep. The last thing I saw was Music Head and Betty walking away, and I shut my eyes, and fell into a deep sleep.

***

I was awoken with a gentle tap on my arm, bringing me out of my sleep.

"I have placed the emerald in your pocket, Lily. It's time for me to leave too. See you in a few hours," Tom said. I slowly opened my eyes. I didn't leave my bed or sit up.

"See you soon, Tom," I said and took a deep breath.

Tom followed Betty, and I fell asleep once more.

***

An intense light woke me up by shining on my face.

Ladybirds flew around the divo-space. I could hear the familiar laughter of Willow Witch. Her face became visible as the light started vanishing.

"Hello! It's nice to see you again, Lily," she said.

It was nice seeing Willow Witch again too. I had to gather myself as I'd just woken up from an almost eighteen-hour-long sleep.

"Hello," I replied with a sleepy voice.

"I see you have been doing well despite being in the castle for a total of eighteen hours. Congratulations! You're now free to leave," Willow Witch said.

"Thank you! It wouldn't have been possible without the help of Brave, Quick, and Clever," I said and sat up on my lavender bed.

Had I really been sleeping for eighteen hours already?

"I'm here because I have to tell you a secret about the emerald," Willow Witch said and walked closer to me.

"You have a choice. Suppose you decide to place the emerald in the center of the Mirror Hall before leaving the castle. Sunlight will shine through the emerald, reflect in all the mirrors and purify the castle from all the cruelty.

"As a result, the night demons will transform into ghosts."

Willow Witch took a few steps before continuing, "On the other hand, if you decide to throw out the emerald into the forest from the window, the night demons will be destroyed forever. The choice is yours, Lily. What do you choose to do?"

I had to think about it hard as it was a great responsibility deciding on the night demons' eternal destiny.

"I think I know the answer, but will ask to be sure. Will the night demons be able to harm others if they are ghosts?"

She looked at me and replied, "They'd be much less harmful."

"In that case, I choose to place the emerald in the Mirror Hall," I said.

Willow Witch looked at me and nodded gently.

"One last thing, why will you choose to not destroy the night demons?" she asked.

"Because we should never stop being good because of those who are bad."

Willow Witch smiled and disappeared before I had the chance to say anything else.

That was it! It had gone twenty-one hours since we'd got the emerald, and I was the last one completing my seven hours holding it!

What will Charlotte and Poppy say about us going missing for such a long time?

They'll never let me visit them again!

I was still in the castle. Unless I successfully left the emerald in the center of the Mirror Hall and got back to the forest, there was always a chance I'd get stuck in the castle forever.

There were still a lot of things that could go wrong.

How can I get out to the Mirror Hall? I forgot to ask Brave. Where is he? How could I forget something so important? I thought.

I'm alone in the castle and have to figure everything out myself.

It didn't take long before I got up and did what I'd seen Brave do so many times before, which was to examine the wall and find an opening.

The Mirror Hall was just behind the wall. The problem was partly solved. I only had to find the exit in the divo-space.

I walked along and tapped the wall with my hands.

The wall covered a long stretch, and it took a long time for me to search the whole wall. But I couldn't find the exit.

After completing the wall search once, I sat down to rest from exhaustion.

How could Brave always find the openings so quickly with his tiny hands?

I sat down on one of the lavender beds and looked around.

There was no sign of an opening.

Slowly, I got up and walked in the same direction we'd walked with Brave earlier.

Probably, the only option I had was to look for another opening somewhere else, exit the divo-space and walk to the Mirror Hall.

What if the night demons saw me? It wasn't too difficult for them to harm me if they chose to do so. Holding the emerald for seven hours enabled me to leave, but it couldn't stop the night demons from harming me.

It was cold in the divo-space, and I had to hug myself with my arms to keep slightly warm. "Brave?" I whispered and hoped he'd reply or walk toward me.

But there was no sign of him.

I continued walking when suddenly, something fell from my pocket and made a sound. I turned around and looked to see what it was.

It was the emerald falling from my pocket before hitting the wall.

How could I drop the emerald? I needed to be careful because everything could be ruined if I lost it.

Suddenly, a green light brightened up the divo-space; the source was the emerald! I walked to it and picked it up.

The light was immediately gone. How was that possible? The divo-space was dark again. The emerald shone just before I picked it up.

Next to the wall, I placed the emerald down on the same spot.

A bright light started shining again! I lifted up the emerald, and it became dark.

I saw a pattern! I bent down and ran the emerald horizontally along the wall.

The emerald was shining for a few inches before it stopped. Again, I ran the emerald along the wall in the opposite direction until it stopped glowing.

"Yes!" I said quietly to myself as I had just found the small opening leading to the Mirror Hall! The emerald had emphasized the small fracture of light shining into the divo-space from the edges of the door.

The smooth emerald could easily fall. I held it tightly in my fist to avoid losing it. The small door leading to the Mirror Hall was in front of me.

A few more steps, in addition to the thousands I'd taken in the castle, and the night demons would be defeated. My hands were icy, my nail beds blue as a result.

"One... two... three!" I counted and pushed the small door, firmly but cautiously.

It didn't take long before the door was wide open.

Daylight shone through the large castle windows and blinded me for a short moment.

Having multiple mirrors in the hall made the light even more intense.

The light didn't stop me from proceeding. Two steps, and I was in the Mirror Hall.

My eyes were so used to the darkness, it took a moment for me to overcome the overwhelmingly bright light.

A startling sound echoed.

Isabel entered the hall from the same side from which the sound was coming, followed by Dr. Herbert.

Duke Lukas entered the opposite end, and Danielle followed behind.

All night demons were dressed in black from head to toe.

They wore long black cape coats. Sharp black high-heeled shoes.

Long black hats. They all looked almost identical.

"There you are! You little brat! I knew you weren't dead! Those useless divos can't even kill an ant. How could they possibly kill three clever children? The emerald you asked the stupid divos to give us was also fake, and we knew it!" Isabel said in a taut voice. She took out the fake emerald from her sleeve and threw it at me.

Her evil laughter filled the space.

I bent down quickly. The small rock missed me by just a few inches, but I stood up straight again and continued walking toward the center of the Mirror Hall.

This time, I wasn't scared of the night demons. I wasn't afraid of Isabel, Duke Lukas, Danielle, or even Dr. Herbert. I walked with a straight back, head held high.

Nothing could hurt me.

The night demons walked toward me firmly. They appeared alert, controlled, and powerful. All had a vile smile on deep red lips.

The cold, dry emerald touched my increasingly warm moist skin. I clenched my fist even harder. The emerald was in my hand, ready to purify the castle from all cruelty.

The night demons were prowling around me in circles, but I didn't take a step back, and just continued walking.

Up on the ceiling, a massive crystal chandelier was hanging.

My instinct urged me to walk and stand under it.

The extensive castle windows framed the sky beautifully in a way that made it impossible for me to turn my eyes away. It must have been dawn since the sun appeared on the horizon, changed the sky, gently ending the long dark night.

The black and white shiny floor reflected light and all the mirrors hanging from all four walls of the hall. The four night demons resembled a king, a queen, a rook, and a knight against the chessboard-like floor.

I was the white queen of the chessboard, the force for good, calling the shots with the help of the emerald in my hand. Or so I wanted to believe.

"Isabel," I said and looked at her. I was just a few steps from the center of the hall.

"Yes?" she replied with a powerful voice. The night demons made strange movements as if in a ritual. They kept going rhythmically, sideways, and stopping for a moment, jumping high up in the air in a way I'd never seen anyone be able to do before.

They paused in the air and looked at me from high above before landing again.

I moved carefully forward as I was afraid that they'd suddenly attack.

The night demons jumped up again simultaneously and made a horrifying noise.

The sound reminded me of something.

Sure enough, they suddenly transformed into four colossal, black crows and dropped their hats on the ground. The crows flew around me, making cawing sounds. The four crows swiftly attacked with their beaks, aiming mainly at my fist and the emerald.

"Ouch! Stop it!" I shouted and looked up at the crystal chandelier. A few more steps forward and I'd be in the center of the Mirror Hall.

My legs couldn't take the final steps. The demons prevented me from continuing as they kept striking with their beaks.

I held on to the emerald firmly, knowing crows would quickly spot and fetch shiny objects in their sharp beaks.

The night demons transformed back into their human shape, their laughter echoing in the castle, shaking the ancient building like a minor earthquake.

"That was fun! Let's do it again!" Dr. Herbert said.

This time, the four fearsome demons jumped up in the air and landed on the ground with an even greater force. Everything shook, and this time, all the mirrors in the Mirror Hall fell to the ground and broke into thousands of pieces.

"This is extremely amusing! We should do it more often," Duke Lukas shouted loudly.

My ears were hurting from the noise, but I knew I shouldn't hold them. I could lose the emerald if I did. I clenched my fist hard and continued toward the hall's center.

The problem wasn't getting to the center of the Mirror Hall. The problem was that the night demons stopped me from moving from the spot I was standing on.

They kept changing between their human and crow forms.

It was horrifying, but fear was missing from my mind, and I became immune to the creepiness of the situation.

The night demons continued their ritual dance whenever they went back into human shape. "We are going to get the emerald from you! You're going to be trapped in the castle forever! You're going to be here alone without your friends!"

They sang it over and over.

The previously clear sky was suddenly covered in dark, gray clouds, and it started raining heavily, so heavily, it was as if someone high above had decided to water the forest.

How can the weather change so quickly? I started doubting that I could complete the mission of placing the emerald in the center of the Mirror Hall and finally leave the castle.

The night demons' laughing, ritual dancing, and singing to the music in the background made my fear worse. The night demons were four, and I was on my own.

They had broken all the mirrors in the Mirror Hall.

Even the weather seemed on their side, no sunshine in the dark gray sky.

The light in the castle can't possibly be enough to shine through the emerald and purify the castle, I thought.

"Did you believe that we knew nothing about the emerald after looking for it for centuries?" Duke Lukas barked.

"You also used the elixir! You have to pay back!" Dr. Herbert said with a superficially calm voice.

The night demons transformed back into crows, using their beaks to attack me again. One of them targeted my clenched fist as it tried to get the emerald. This time, it was even more painful. I made sure to cover my face, afraid the crows would pull my eyes from the sockets.

"No!" I shouted aloud and fought the crow with my clenched fists.

I had to stop the night demons from distracting me, and I had to realize that the power that I had inside me was much greater than the castle and all the night demons.

I looked up at the ceiling and saw I was standing almost under the crystal chandelier.

"Isabel?" I said calmly, and the night demons transformed back into their human shape.

She looked at me, now so close I could see the pulsing vessels in her pallid neck.

She stretched out her hand. She was wearing black mesh gloves.

"Yes?" Isabel appeared prepared for me to place the emerald right in her hand.

All four night demons were now all ears, and stood completely still as if frozen in place.

No one made a sound.

A small patch appeared in the thick, dark gray clouds.

A ray of sunshine broke through and reached the castle, the Mirror Hall, and one of the small crystals in the chandelier.

"Do you know why divos can't even kill an ant?" I asked Isabel.

Isabel almost dropped her jaw, but she stood still.

She stared deep into my eyes, waiting restlessly for my words long before they were shaped in my mouth.

"Judging from your look, I can tell that you don't know the answer to the question. It's because the divos are small, but they have great beautiful minds!"

I rapidly threw the emerald up in the air, aiming at the chandelier.

"Noooooooo!" Isabel screamed.

All the night demons made a very high-pitched noise. This time, I had to lie down on the floor, holding my ears from the extreme pain.

My eardrums kept vibrating long after the noise had stopped.

I opened my eyes slowly and saw that a deep green light was shining up the castle and, perhaps, beyond. One single ray of sunshine had passed through a tiny crystal in the chandelier. The crystal had spread the ray of light in a few different directions, and one had passed through the emerald.

The emerald had, in turn, spread the light in hundreds of different directions.

The hundreds of rays of light spread by the emerald shone through the many crystals of the chandelier.

The lights from the crystals reached the hundreds of broken pieces of the mirrors.

The hundreds of broken mirror pieces reflected the bright green light further to many other pieces of broken mirror.

In the end, millions of deep green lights lit the entire castle!

Everything had started from... one single ray of sunshine in the cloudy sky.

"Isn't it beautiful? All this started with a small ray of sunshine breaking free from dark gray clouds," a voice said.

I knew immediately it was the voice of Willow Witch.

"It's mesmerizing," I replied calmly and felt at peace.

My tears blurred the mystical scene.

"In life, every small act of kindness resembles the small ray of sunshine. The ray of sunshine succeeded in lighting up the castle and ending a centuries-long curse," Willow Witch said with a soft voice. I looked around, but she was nowhere to be seen.

The night demons had also disappeared from my sight.

The only things remaining were four black capes and four black hats.

Chapter 18

MIRRORS

The deep green light in the Mirror Hall converted it into a light hall.

I stood up, but it was hard for me to leave the castle since I was captivated by all the beauty reflected through the emerald.

The emerald wasn't behind the magic but was the small ray of sun shining through it.

"I wish Tom, Music Head, and the three divos could see this," I said aloud to myself and danced in circles despite the pieces of mirror underneath my shoes.

I had to leave. Tom, Music Head, and Brave waited for me outside the castle.

They must have been overly worried, having no idea that I'd successfully defeated all the night demons.

Slowly, I moved toward one of the Mirror Hall entrance doors.

Several small blue divo heads appeared in every corner, too scared to come out yet as they weren't sure the night demons were no longer there.

"You're all safe. The night demons don't exist anymore as they are ghosts. You're freer than you have ever been!" I happily told the divos.

The small divos then carefully entered the Mirror Hall.

Several shadows went through the walls, and I suspected it was the ghosts of the night demons running away, or maybe they were confused about what had happened to them.

The divos looked around for a while to ensure there was no sign of the night demons. Once they knew I was telling the truth and didn't spot any, they celebrated by jumping up and down and clapping their hands divo-style.

"Have fun and make sure you take good care of the castle!" I told the divos as I left the Mirror Hall. "It belongs to you now!"

Before taking my final step out of the Mirror Hall, I turned to have a good look at the shining hall one last time.

All the divos had now entered and celebrated the destruction of the night demons, laughing, smiling, dancing, and of course, clapping and jumping with joy and jubilation.

A shadow floated smoothly past me.

Initially, I suspected that it was Betty, but it turned out to be another ghost: Isabel!

Isabel didn't speak to me, and walking through wall after wall as if just getting used to being a ghost. Being a ghost had its benefits, after all.

The atmosphere in the castle had changed, and it was evident that the emerald had made a miracle. It was a far happier place.

The corridor outside shone brightly from all the reflections.

The red carpet covering the stairs no longer appeared red but dark green. I walked down and reached the ground floor.

I saw Dr. Herbert's ghost going through the walls of the laboratory, shouting. "Oh no! I will never be able to do experiments in my laboratory again! What is going to happen to all my great experiments!" He kept shouting as he ran in and out of his laboratory.

"Dr. Herbert's ghost has gone mad," I said, knowing he was unable to harm me now.

I walked through the corridor and entered another room.

Duke Lukas' ghost stood at the entrance, staring at me with great anger.

"I wish Betty had never brought you to the castle! You have destroyed everything!" he said bitterly.

I ignored him and continued walking.

How can I leave the castle? I thought and looked for a way out.

The castle seemed like a different place. I enjoyed walking around and looking at the castle properly for the first time, now being untouchable.

Fortunately, I reached the dining room and saw that the deep green light had found its way even into the previously dark dining room.

"Let's leave," I heard a familiar female voice say from the other side of the dining room.

I turned toward the voice and saw Betty with her usual emotionless expression.

She stood next to a door.

"Of course!" I replied and walked toward Betty with a smile.

"I see that you completed the task," she said and didn't bat an eyelid.

"Yes! I'm ready to return home!"

"Follow me." She went through the door.

It looked familiar, and I suddenly recognized it was the same door that Betty had taken us through when entering the castle!

I opened the door and followed Betty, unable to pass through things like Betty and other ghosts. We continued down the stairs and got to the dark, stony corridor that led out of the castle. The corridor was no longer dark as the deep green light shone through the keyhole.

It felt unreal that I could finally leave.

"You can't get away!" a voice said behind me.

I turned around and saw Isabel's ghost.

"Do you think I'm going to accept losing? I won't, and I will find a way to get back to you and destroy you!" Isabel said.

"Goodbye, Isabel. I'm leaving. I'm sure that the divos will take good care of the castle from now on."

Betty looked at Isabel and shrugged before turning around and continuing toward the secret exit.

"Betty! You're a big traitor! You knew they were alive and hiding inside the wall, but you lied to me!" Isabel shouted.

Betty continued walking as she replied with a calm voice, "You have yourself to blame, Isabel. You were the one who believed my lie."

Isabel screamed uncontrollably behind us.

It didn't take long before we reached the final barrier between us and the world outside the castle: the last door. Betty went straight through it, and it hit me for the first time: *How come we didn't realize Betty was a ghost when she first brought us to the castle?*

I placed my hand on the door handle and hoped from the bottom of my heart that it would be open and nothing else was going to stop me from leaving.

I pulled down the handle but the door didn't open.

Was it locked? I held my breath and tried again. The door didn't open! I tried for the third time, pulled down the door handle, and pushed the door with great force.

Luckily, the door opened on the third try.

The green forest trees appeared in front of me. Betty was standing behind the door, waiting. A big smile appeared on my face, and I took a deep breath of fresh air.

Betty turned around again and walked in the direction she had found us.

"Betty, how come you could touch the handles when you first took us to the castle?" I asked.

"It's because ghosts can touch certain objects for a short period," she replied.

I swallowed hard as I knew Betty would return to the house with us!

Suddenly, taking her along with us was the worst idea. Ever.

However, it was too late to stop her. We had already made a deal. She was on her way back with us.

I thought of what Charlotte and Poppy would say.

Betty was going to stay in their home after all.

I'd go back to my own home, far away from the house on the pumpkin farm! I didn't want to think about it as there was no way I could undo our deal with Betty.

We walked around the castle's outer walls. I could see Tom, Music Head, and Brave standing on the same spot on which we had appeared!

"Look! Lily made it! She has left the castle!" Tom shouted as soon as he saw me.

I waved at them. Music Head waved back with a smile on his lips.

"Yes! We made it!" I said as soon as I approached them.

"A lot of noise came from the castle, and we were considering returning to the castle to help you. We didn't as we saw a bright green light radiating out of the castle and knew you had made it. How was it?" Tom asked.

"It's a long story, but the night demons are ghosts now, and the divos are in charge from now on," I replied.

"I'm glad you made it," Music Head said.

Brave jumped on me and gave me a big hug before clapping. He ran, took up the paper cone, and started speaking. "Lily, you made it! I was so worried about you because I forgot to show you how to get to the Mirror Hall from the divo-space."

"It's OK, Brave. I found the opening somehow," I replied.

Quick and Clever walked toward us from the forest. The divos were both carrying a basket full of apples and berries. I looked at Tom, and he read my mind.

"They wanted to come with us too," Tom explained.

Quick and Clever smiled as they both gave me a hug the same way Brave had.

Brave picked up the paper cone and started speaking. "Quick, Clever, and I would like to go to the house on the pumpkin farm with the rest of you. Is it OK?"

I looked at all three divos standing in front of me, waiting nervously on my response.

"The house on the pumpkin farm is not my home. I don't decide if anyone will be allowed to stay or not," I said, and the divos looked immediately sad and looked down. "But you can come with us. We can ask Poppy and Charlotte if you can stay. Poppy and Charlotte are my second cousins, and both very nice. You can come back to the castle if they say no," I added.

Brave, Quick and Clever looked happy again and started celebrating. Betty was standing still, without saying anything. *What if Poppy and Charlotte don't want Betty in the house?* I thought and knew we didn't have any other choice.

Betty glanced at me as if reading my mind.

"Ready? We have to stand on the spot together, Willow Witch said," Tom stated.

"We appeared on that spot," I said and pointed to where Tom and I had first appeared earlier. We all walked to the site and stood next to each other, but nothing happened.

"I know... I know. We were facing the castle!" Tom said.

Tom, Music Head, Betty, the three divos, and I turned to the castle, but nothing happened. We looked at each other in doubt, worried about not following correct instructions.

"Maybe we need to face the forest," I suggested. Once again, we all faced the forest, but still, nothing happened. We felt lost and confused.

Tom turned to me and said, "I don't know..." and we all fell to the ground.

I opened my eyes and saw we were back in the library, in the house on the pumpkin farm, on the exact same spot where we'd disappeared when the scarecrows chased us!

Knowing that I'd returned made me happier than ever!

I could finally get to see everyone again! Mom, Dad, Kate, Charlotte, and Poppy!

There were luckily no scarecrows around.

What should I tell them if they asked where I'd been all this time? I had to explain as they'd never believe me if I told them the truth.

Mr. T was on one of the shelves, placing back the book he had dropped on us.

He made his usual hamster sounds. I suspected that he didn't like what he saw: a ghost, three little monsters, and a stranger alongside Tom and me.

I looked around and saw Tom, Music Head, Betty, and the three divos, all on the floor close to me. They all slowly recovered from the fall and stood up.

Betty soon disappeared as she walked through the library wall, and I guessed that she, unfortunately, already wanted to explore the house.

"Oh... I just wish I could tell Poppy and Charlotte about Betty before she started roaming around the house," I said, worried.

Brave looked around, and his jaw dropped, but I didn't know the reason. He picked up the paper cone and said, "Wow! There are so many books here!"

"This is the library," I explained.

Music Head walked over to one of the bookshelves and looked at the books.

Tom was at least as happy as me to be back.

"Who is Betty, and what's going on here?"

We all turned around and saw Poppy standing at the library's entrance.

"Where have you been?" she asked. "Who are all these people?" There were fewer than three seconds between all her questions.

"Hi Poppy," I said and could see that she was waiting for my explanation.

Should I just tell her the truth? Will she believe me?

Twelve pairs of eyes stared at me.

"You won't believe what happened…" I started saying.

But Charlotte walked in and interrupted. "What happened was that I did my best and told them to go to bed, but they didn't. Instead, they experimented with the pumpkins from the farm, found the pumpkin recipe book, and got into trouble when they called on the scarecrows accidentally. They were chased by the scarecrows, and Mr. T helped them by hiding them in a book," Charlotte filled in. "Isn't that right?"

Charlotte walked toward me with crossed arms and a disappointed face.

I could tell that she was upset.

"How did you know?" I asked before thinking.

"It's because we have both lived here our entire life," Poppy answered instead.

"Luckily, you're both fine, but there was no guarantee that you would survive in the story and get back here safely," Charlotte said.

"Survive in the story?" I asked as I was processing everything.

"You'll enter any book that falls on you from any bookshelf. Depending on the book you're in and the events in the story, you may or may not return to the library. Once inside the book, you don't have any control over leaving the story. The only way to return to the library is if someone places the book back on the bookshelf again.

"In addition, you have to stand on the same spot as you first appeared in the story. If you die in a book, you'll be gone without any trace," Charlotte explained.

I finally understood what Willow Witch meant when she said we'd know how we could return later.

"Mr. T was trying to place the book back in the bookshelf the whole night. He finally reached the bookshelf a while ago. Look at him. He looks so exhausted! He did it to help bring you home. That's why you got back," Poppy said.

Mr. T is the real hero! I thought.

I wanted to run and hug his small, furry hamster body and thank him.

Somehow, Poppy and Charlotte knew everything, so we didn't have to convince them about our experiences.

"Did you come from the book?" Charlotte asked while looking over at Music Head.

Poppy gave her a stern look before smiling at Music Head and saying, "Welcome! It's nice to meet you. My name's Poppy, and I'm Lily's second cousin. Charlotte is my sister. We live in this house."

"I'm Music Head because I enjoy playing music. Yes, I came from the book," Music Head replied bluntly.

"Are you OK, Tom?" Poppy asked and looked over at Tom.

"I just have a headache, but I'm fine," Tom replied.

I looked for Brave, Quick, and Clever, but they were gone. A small blue hand could be seen on Tom's leg. The three divos were hiding behind him!

"Poppy... Charlotte, Music Head is not the only one who came back with us from the book," I said nervously.

"Did you bring another person?" Charlotte asked, surprised. Tom looked at me and saw that I didn't know how to explain.

"It's actually not a person," Tom explained.

"What is it then?" Poppy asked, and they were both patiently waiting for a response.

"We brought back divos," I replied quickly before I could stop myself.

"What is divos?" Charlotte asked. They knew almost everything but about the divos... and Betty perhaps.

"It's the plural form of divo," Tom so nicely helped me to explain again.

"Are you trying to say that there's more than one?" Poppy asked with a serious look.

"Yes, there are... three of them," I said.

Brave, Quick and Clever all fell abruptly to the ground since they had been standing on each other's shoulders, hiding behind Tom for a long while.

Poppy and Charlotte looked at the three blue divos in the middle of the library, and they then looked at each other.

Brave was the first one getting up, and he quickly picked up his paper cone and said, "We're very sorry that we came to your house. We will return immediately!"

Brave turned around with his back toward the rest of us, attempting to return to the castle. It was a rather funny scene, and we all had to fight hard not to laugh.

"Why are you using a paper cone to speak?" Poppy asked. "Wait a minute," Poppy said and couldn't stop herself from laughing any longer.

"It's because this is the only way you will be able to hear me," Brave answered with his distinctive gruff, divo voice.

Poppy and Charlotte both smiled as they were already charmed by Brave.

"Brave, what are the names of your two friends?" Charlotte asked.

"The taller one is called Clever, and the other divo over there is Quick," Brave answered.

"Let's go to the kitchen. We'll make you something to eat and drink," Poppy said.

Brave and the two other divos immediately walked behind Poppy and Charlotte. It seemed as if they already enjoyed being in the house on the pumpkin farm.

Tom, Music Head, and I followed behind.

"At least they aren't angry," Tom whispered.

"They still don't know about Betty, remember?" I whispered back.

"That may be a problem," Music Head said as we all walked down the corridor.

"What may be a problem?" Charlotte stopped walking and turned toward us.

"Nothing... there is no problem," I said and laughed nervously.

Charlotte appeared suspicious, but she didn't say anything further and headed toward the kitchen.

The divos were dazzled by Poppy, and kept taking turns using the cone to speak to her.

"Welcome to our kitchen! This is arguably the most important part of the house!" Charlotte said.

"Not the library?" Music Head replied cleverly, and it was kind of true.

Poppy and Charlotte looked at one another and said, "Maybe," simultaneously.

Music Head helped the divos sit up on the kitchen chairs as they were too short to take a seat independently.

"Lily and Tom, I'm glad you have both returned to the house," Charlotte said while she placed a big tray full of bread with a particular spread on the table.

"It's good to be back," I said but with a hint of nervousness, hoping to never go back to the castle ever again.

"What is the orange-colored spread?" Music Head asked.

"It's pumpkin seed bread with smashed, cooked pumpkin and sea salt. This is our traditional Halloween meal. After dinner, everyone in the house has to help make a bonfire on the farm. It's great to spend time in nature and celebrate Halloween by having hot drinks.

"We follow the same Halloween tradition every year on the 1st of November and have done so as far back as I can remember!" Charlotte explained proudly.

"Is it the 1st of November?" Tom and I cried out as we still couldn't process that we had been gone for less than a day.

"As I said before, you were gone overnight. You'll go back home tomorrow morning," Poppy replied.

"It's great there are so many of us celebrating Halloween here this year," Charlotte said.

Tom was still trying to recover from all the recent events. He looked around before holding his head in his hands.

"Which book did you enter, by the way?" Charlotte asked as she took a bite of her pumpkin seed bread.

"I don't know. But we were in a castle in the middle of a forest," I said.

"Oh my. Hope it wasn't too bad? I don't know which book that is as we have thousands of books in the library," Poppy said.

"It was... OK," Tom said, untruthfully and with hesitation.

The three divos, Music Head and I looked at him and nodded in disbelief as we knew all too well what he meant by 'OK.'

Tom looked down and stopped eating.

"What is wrong?" Charlotte asked.

"We found an elixir that could heal all sorts of diseases. I wanted to bring it back and give it to my mother," Tom said.

"Wonderful!" Charlotte answered impatiently.

"But... we used it as Lily and Music Head were injured and needed the elixir," Tom said.

Everyone at the table was silent for a while.

I took out the small empty elixir bottle from my pocket, placed it on the kitchen table, and said, "This is just the bottle."

Poppy took the bottle in her hand and observed it for a while before opening the wooden top and smelling it.

"I may be able to recreate the same elixir," Poppy said and got up instantly from her seat and rushed upstairs.

Tom and I rushed behind her.

"There's a hint of several plants and herbs that I have in the greenhouse," Poppy said and swiftly made her way outside to the garden.

She walked between the plants and herbs, smelling her way to the different plants before making her final selection. Additionally, she picked several exotic flowers.

She turned to us with a smile as she said, "Let's see what I can do."

Poppy, Tom, and I made our way to the greenhouse's exit. Poppy walked out before promptly stopping. "I almost forgot." She then turned around and took a pinch of mud in her hand. "Come," she said and continued down the corridor, away from the greenhouse.

Tom and I followed Poppy silently, afraid to disrupt her train of thoughts about the elixir. She walked inside the same lab we'd been in when we tried escaping from the scarecrows.

Poppy's laboratory appeared much less scary compared to Dr. Herbert's.

It was much smaller, and there was no awful smell of dead animals.

The floor was covered in a dark carpet. One could easily mistake it for a perfume-making station due to the floral scent and elegant glass bottles on the shelves.

I looked at a spot on the wall where we had witnessed the explosion but couldn't see any damage to the wall or the floor.

Poppy placed several empty glass bottles on the empty desk in front of the window.

She cut and then mixed the ingredients with a small amount of water.

She kept smelling the original elixir bottle I'd given her and used the smell as guidance to make the same. It took some time for Poppy to cut, mix, cook, cool and finally check it.

Tom and I observed Poppy restlessly as the moment we had waited for had finally arrived: Poppy smelled her final mixture and focused.

Without saying a word, she took up the original elixir bottle again and sniffed it.

"Hmm... not good," Poppy said and placed down the bottle on one side of the table, and a feeling of disappointment filled us.

Poppy then took up the dark blue, empty elixir bottle, sniffed it, and mixed ingredients.

"Still not good," she said as she sniffed the second solution.

She placed the second bottle next to the first.

Poppy kept trying repeatedly, but was never satisfied with the elixir she had created.

The cycle went on for a long while.

"No, not good," Poppy said again and placed the eleventh glass bottle next to the rest of the failed experimental elixir solutions.

Tom and I were sitting on the floor, leaning against the wall. We were losing hope.

"How is it going?" Charlotte asked as she entered the laboratory.

"I have tried over ten times, but can't get it right," Poppy said and took a deep breath.

Charlotte picked up the original elixir bottle and sniffed it. Once she had smelled the bottle, she walked to the end of the desk with the collection of all the failed elixirs.

She picked up a bottle, inhaling it before saying, "This one is missing at least two ingredients, cedarwood and pink flower."

Charlotte then took up another bottle, smelled it, and said, "This solution misses at least three ingredients." She took up the third bottle, smelled, and said, "This solution misses just one ingredient, but the mixing sequence seems to have been faulty. What I also noticed is that the same key ingredient is missing from all of these mixtures."

Poppy had observed her with great attention and smiled as soon as she heard Charlotte's final comment. "Let's create the elixir together, Charlotte," she suggested.

"I think we'll succeed if we work together as mixed solutions are very difficult to perfect," Charlotte said before adding. "Follow me. We have to go down to the farm."

Tom and I followed Charlotte through the house toward the pumpkin farm.

Music Head and the three divos were still sitting at the table, enjoying their food.

"Any luck with the elixir?" Music Head asked as we walked by.

"No," Tom replied without stopping to talk.

The air was fresh, the sky was clear, and the calming sound of the wind spread in the air.

Charlotte went between pumpkins, knocking on them as if knowing exactly what she was looking for. She finally announced, "Here it is. The pumpkin that we need for our elixir."

Charlotte picked up the pumpkin, and we all rushed back upstairs again to the laboratory where Poppy was waiting for us.

"I think we're good now," Charlotte said as soon as she entered. "Here you go,"

She placed the pumpkin on the desk.

Poppy looked at the pumpkin and replied, "We better start over again."

Chapter 19

HALLOWEEN TRADITION

Poppy took up the original elixir bottle and smelled it for perhaps the hundredth time.

She continuously smelled the empty elixir bottle as she looked at the ingredients on the desk. She handed it to Charlotte.

Charlotte selected an exotic leaf, placed it on the lab table, and walked back again. She stood there with her eyes shut for a moment before picking up another ingredient.

She kept repeating the cycle by selecting one element at a time.

No one said a word. We just looked at the process.

Poppy helped by bringing a clean glass bottle and cutting the ingredients into small pieces. She placed the elements back in the same sequence Charlotte had placed them.

Charlotte eventually took a deep breath, and with her eyes still shut, she said, "I think we have everything we need!"

She opened her eyes, turned to Poppy, and walked to the table with the cut ingredients.

Poppy continued by adding the finely cut ingredients to the empty glass bottle.

From the bottom of my heart, I was hoping they'd triumph this time. Creating the elixir wasn't a simple task after all. It had taken Dr. Herbert centuries and great effort to make it.

He knew how scarce the elixir was, so was very protective of it.

"Oh, we almost forgot," Charlotte said and placed the pumpkin on the table, cutting a small slice before putting it last in a line of a long row of ingredients on the desk.

Mixing, heating, and cooling the solution took less time with Charlotte's help.

Poppy and Charlotte had together identified and organized everything that was possibly needed to create the elixir that Tom's mother needed.

Together, Poppy and Charlotte smelled the original, empty elixir bottle one last time and placed it down.

"Ready?" Charlotte asked with a serious face. Poppy nodded confidently in response.

At last, they both smelled the final solution.

"We have it! We have the elixir!" Poppy said aloud with excitement.

"Yes!" Tom shouted and raised his fist up in the air. I had never seen Tom so happy.

Charlotte took a deep breath and smiled as she said, "I'm glad we managed to create the elixir. However, we won't be sure unless someone has it and proves it works."

Tom and I looked at her and nodded as we knew she was right.

I remembered having doubts about the elixir when I first took it in the castle.

"We have to cover it with a wooden top," Poppy said and looked inside a box on the other side of the room and came back with a wooden top. "Here you go, Tom!"

She handed the elixir bottle to Tom.

Tom couldn't take his eyes off the elixir bottle and handled it so gently as if it was a thin, fragile crystal bowl about to break any moment.

He looked up at Poppy and said, "Thank you!"

"You are welcome! Let's hope for the best. I'm almost certain we made the right elixir."

"Let's now join the rest downstairs. We've been gone for hours," Charlotte said and Poppy, Tom, and I followed her out of the laboratory.

Tom was happy, but didn't speak much. He was lost in his own thoughts. He was walking on clouds, so close to us but yet so far away.

"Your uncle is coming to pick you up tomorrow, late in the evening," Poppy said as we all walked toward the kitchen.

"Late in the evening? That's a long time from now. I won't be able to visit my mother tomorrow then. The visiting hours will be over," Tom said.

"I'm sorry, Tom. Your uncle is busy tomorrow, and that's the only time he can come," Poppy replied.

I looked at Tom, and could clearly see that he was upset about not being able to see his mother sooner. He had the elixir she needed to recover from her illness after all.

Maybe he thought that waiting for two more days would be just... too late.

"Don't worry," I whispered. Tom nodded but avoided my gaze. We walked down the stairs and discovered that the three divos had eaten all the food and fallen asleep on the table.

Music Head looked at us and said, "Good that you're back. Is it done?"

"Yes! We have a new elixir," Tom said and held up the bottle for Music Head to see.

Music Head responded to Tom's comment with a satisfied smile.

Brave, Quick, and Clever started moving their bodies and woke up slowly from their sleep, roused by the sound of Tom's voice.

"It's time now! We should make the bonfire," Charlotte said.

We all started chatting as we walked out in the cold, dark farm with a clear sky.

The divos were mesmerized by the farm as they had never seen one in their centuries-long life. They ran around freely, dancing and clapping their hands.

"Look at the divos! They're really enjoying themselves," Poppy said, looking at them with a smile. "I'm glad to have them here. Well done, Lily, for bringing them from the book."

"Does it mean that they can stay?" I asked.

Charlotte and Poppy looked at each other, turned to me, and nodded with a smile.

"Brave! Quick! Clever! Poppy and Charlotte will allow you to stay with them," Tom shouted as the three divos were too far away to hear the conversation.

Hearing what Tom had just said made the three divos even more excited.

They all ran toward Poppy and Charlotte, jumped, and gave them a hug before running around the farm again. They couldn't express their gratitude in words as they had left the paper cone in the kitchen.

Music Head was sitting down and looked out over the pumpkin farm.

"You're also welcome to stay, Music Head," Poppy said.

Music Head turned toward Poppy and replied, "Are you sure?"

"Yes, I'm more than certain," Poppy said.

"Thank you. I like it here. I've never been to anyplace like this before," Music Head said.

"You don't need to thank us," Charlotte said.

Music Head continued looking over the pumpkin farm. I felt deep in my heart that he had found the home that he truly deserved. The stars seemed to be shining brighter than ever. The moon was also shining bright, adding an extra layer of shimmer to everything under the sky.

"I can help bring wood for the bonfire," Tom said and got up.

"That's great. I was just about to ask for help," Charlotte said.

"I can also help," I said and got up from the slightly moist ground.

"Me too," Music Head said and followed us.

"It's not going to be hard. We already have wood piled up next to the house," Poppy explained and showed us the way.

The three divos also joined without knowing what we were about to do. We picked up wood from a pile and placed it where we wanted to make the bonfire.

Brave tried to help us bring wood, but fell backward and hit his head.

"Careful, Brave. It's too heavy and twice your size," I said and helped him stand again. He looked at me and gestured that he was OK by nodding before running around the farm.

Poppy brought a matchstick and lit the bonfire.

The fire was initially small, but it didn't take long before we had a proper bonfire that kept everyone warm on the year's first November night.

We all sat down around the bonfire, trying to absorb some of the radiating heat.

I observed the faces around the bonfire one by one. Everyone seemed happy.

"Let's now have hot chocolate," Charlotte said and headed toward the house.

I kept following Charlotte with my eyes when I suddenly noticed a familiar, bright aura standing behind the kitchen window staring at me. I had goosebumps before I knew it.

Poppy and Charlotte still don't know about Betty, the ghost we brought back to their house! I thought and looked at Poppy. She responded with a smile. I also managed to press a nervous smile back, but Betty was all I kept thinking about.

"Tom, they still don't have an idea about Betty," I whispered.

Tom looked at me and said, "I'm sure they'll find out soon."

I looked at the house again and could feel my heart beating fast. Betty was still staring at me from the kitchen window.

Oh no! Charlotte's going inside the house! I thought and ran as fast as I could toward Charlotte. I couldn't let her face Betty alone, in the dark kitchen.

Everyone looked at me as they didn't know why I'd suddenly started running toward the house without any apparent reason.

"Lily? Where are you going?" Poppy asked, surprised.

"I have to pee," I replied before I could stop myself.

I blushed, and everyone around the bonfire laughed.

There's always a secret behind every embarrassing, funny, or unusual reply, I thought as I kept running.

I was completely breathless by the time I'd reached the kitchen. Charlotte turned around and asked. "What is it, Lily? Why did you run?"

I bent forward to catch my breath as I couldn't speak. Finally, I gathered myself and looked up, but couldn't see Betty. She was gone.

Charlotte looked at me, concerned.

"I... I just... wanted to come in and help you carry the hot chocolate drinks," I replied.

"Don't worry. I don't need any help," Charlotte replied.

"Oh, OK." I felt embarrassed as my behavior was weird.

I joined the rest around the bonfire again.

Everyone continued chatting and ignored my comment.

"What happened?" Tom whispered, noticing something was wrong.

"Betty appeared in the kitchen when Charlotte walked inside the house."

"So, what happened next?" Tom asked impatiently.

"Nothing. Betty was gone by the time I entered the house. I wanted to be there when they met, but Betty disappeared again," I replied.

Charlotte came back and handed everyone a cup of hot chocolate.

"It's getting very late. We should go to bed soon," Poppy said.

"Good idea," Charlotte replied and took a sip from her hot chocolate.

"I want to see my mother soon. Waiting until Monday feels like ages," Tom whispered.

"That's a long time from now," Music Head replied.

"I have an idea! You can visit her tonight!" I whispered.

"Tonight? How?" Tom asked.

"We have to find a way," I replied.

It didn't take long before we were inside the house, ready for bed.

Music Head had his bedroom close to mine. The divos were also given a bedroom, but I could see them tapping on the walls.

I knew their intention: to build a new divo-space for themselves in the house!

"Good night, everyone," I said loud enough for Poppy and Charlotte to hear so that they wouldn't suspect anything about what Tom, Music Head, and I were about to do.

Our plan was to meet up in the kitchen once everyone else had gone to sleep.

All three of us sat in the kitchen an hour later.

"We should go to the hospital tonight and give your mother the elixir," I said as soon as we sat down.

"But how?" Tom asked. Good question. Probably, Tom's mother wouldn't be happy to see him there late at night, but she needed to get the elixir as soon as possible.

"I don't know. We have to figure it out," I said.

Music Head walked toward the window and looked out. "There are two bicycles on the farm. We can cycle to the hospital," he said.

"Really? That's good! Should we maybe put the elixir in some food?" I asked.

"Yeah, Mother will get suspicious if she gets a small bottle like this. I know her," Tom said.

"What food should we put it in?" I asked.

"Maybe pumpkin pie? She loves it," Tom replied.

I walked over to the kitchen and looked inside the fridge.

"Hmm... I think there's some leftover pumpkin pie in the fridge," I said, but couldn't see any pumpkin pies.

"Let's bake," I said.

"No, last time it didn't go well," Tom replied, horrified.

"This time may be different," I said.

"Maybe..." Tom said.

"I don't know, but we can't let our fear stop us from baking."

I started looking for flour, eggs, cinnamon, ginger, milk, sugar, vanilla extract, and pumpkin. It took less than an hour for us to bake the pumpkin pie.

"Tom, give me the elixir," I said.

Tom was a bit hesitant to hand it over and said, "Are you sure it works that way?"

"Why not? It should still work," I replied.

"OK," Tom said and handed me the elixir. I carefully removed the brown wooden top and slowly poured the elixir on top of the pie.

Tom and Music Head looked at the process carefully, and I felt anxious.

What if I drop the bottle? I thought until the very last drop fell on top of the pumpkin pie.

"Let's leave before Charlotte and Poppy come and check up on us," I said.

Luckily, the two bicycles were unchained and we could take them without any difficulty.

"I'm holding onto the pie," I said.

"Maybe sit on the bicycle carrier, Lily? I can ride the bicycle," Music Head whispered.

I nodded and sat on the carrier as soon as Music Head was ready to cycle away.

Tom took the other bicycle.

The cold autumn wind blew as we cycled through the dark forest toward the hospital.

The dark forest reminded me of Willow Witch's house.

The hospital was much nearer than I'd anticipated, and it took us less than fifteen minutes to get there.

"Here you go, Tom," I said and gave him the pumpkin pie.

Tom held on to the pie as hard as he could. He seemed anxious, happy and excited simultaneously. He then walked in through the hospital's main entrance.

Music Head and I watched him from behind.

The glass doors closed behind him, but we could see Tom walking all the way down to the main reception before turning right and disappearing from our sight. Music Head and I looked at each other and smiled, happy for Tom.

Tom walked back after a few minutes and said, "She got it."

"Did you really see her? Was she angry with you?" I asked.

"Yeah, I saw her, and no, she wasn't angry. I was going to give it to the nurse, but she agreed to sneak me in despite the visitor restrictions," Tom said.

"Good," Music Head replied.

Tom looked up and waved at his mother. She was standing behind her hospital bedroom window. Music Head and I also waved at her. She was smiling as well.

We cycled back to the house on the pumpkin farm in less than ten minutes, and went straight to bed. Fortunately, there was no one looking for us in the house.

***

On Sunday morning, Charlotte and Poppy made breakfast for us.

We were all very talkative as we knew we'd have to separate soon.

"It will certainly take time for me to get used to not seeing the two of you," I said.

"Same here," Tom said.

"We'll meet again," Music Head answered.

"Of course. I live nearby," commented Tom.

"I live far away." I made a sad face.

"Maybe ask to come back?" Tom suggested.

I nodded. But then I remembered Betty and replied, "Depends, let's see how our friend in the house will... appear." I swallowed hard and then coughed, since I was referring to Betty. Poppy and Charlotte still did not know about her.

"Here you go. Have some fresh bread. Help yourselves," Poppy said as she placed a small wooden basket on the table.

"Thank you," Tom replied before taking a slice of bread.

"When are my parents coming?" I asked.

"They should be here any minute," Poppy replied.

"Where are the divos?" Tom asked.

"Probably, they're next to a wall, trying to create a divo-space in the house," I whispered, and we both burst into laughter.

"What are you laughing about?" Poppy asked.

"Nothing," I replied quickly.

Although it was sad to leave the house on the pumpkin farm and my new friends, I was looking forward to seeing my parents and returning home.

Surprisingly, I also missed all my classmates, even Alice. I wasn't mad at her for not inviting me to her Halloween party anymore. I'd had a far bigger adventure!

Someone knocked. I saw my mother and father standing at the door a minute later!

"Hello, everyone. Hope you're all well. It's time to go, Lily," my mother said.

"Hi! How are you? It's nice to see you," Charlotte said and got up from her seat to give my parents a hug. Poppy also walked toward the entrance and greeted them.

"Do you want to join us for a coffee?" Poppy asked.

"Thank you, but we have to leave now as we need to be somewhere later today," my father replied.

I got up and gave my parents a hug. I'd missed them!

"Thank you, Poppy and Charlotte," I said and hoped that my parents wouldn't find out the truth about my weekend.

"You're welcome, Lily. It was great having you," Charlotte replied.

"These are my friends, Tom and Music Head," I said.

"It's nice to meet you," Music Head said.

"Hi," Tom said and didn't say anything else as his mouth was full.

"Hi Tom and... Music Head. Nice to meet you both," my father said, and I could tell that Music Head's name had surprised and bemused him.

"Do you have your bag ready?" my mother asked.

"Yes, it's next to the door," I said.

"What happened to your shoes?" she asked as soon as she looked down.

"I damaged them on the farm," I replied and hoped they'd believe me. Poppy and Charlotte looked at each other and laughed secretly as they knew I was lying.

"Say goodbye to your friends," my mother said.

I got up from my seat and gave everyone a hug. "Goodbye! See you all soon!"

We left the house, and I was glad that I was finally sitting in my mother's car.

I couldn't wait to go to school the next day.

I was even missing my strict, grumpy schoolteacher, Miss Eze.

"It looks like you had a fun weekend," my mother said. She turned around and looked at me from the driver's seat.

"Yes, and I made new friends," I said and smiled.

Nothing can surprise or scare me after this weekend, I thought as I looked out of the window. I turned around and looked at the house on the pumpkin farm. A white figure was standing there, looking at the car. I looked closer; it was Betty!

I quickly moved down in the backseat, hoping that she wouldn't follow us home for some strange reason. I had goosebumps until we got home.

***

The following day, my mother dropped me off at school.

I got out of the car and waved at Kate from a distance.

"Lily, have you forgiven Alice for not inviting you to her party?" my mother asked.

"Sometimes, we have to be the people we want others to be. Only then will we see a change," I replied, smiled, and got out of the car.

My mother smiled before driving away.

Kate joined me, and we walked toward the school building.

Alice, Juan, and Ben walked ahead of us.

"Hi, Lily!" Kate said with her usual serious face.

"Hi!" I replied and realized how happy I was at seeing her.

"I heard Alice's Halloween party was fun. Apparently, Juan dressed up as a zombie and scared everyone!" Kate said and rolled her eyes.

"It was AMAZING! Such a scary Halloween!" Alice said aloud while laughing just a few steps in front of us.

"How was your Halloween?" I asked Kate and ignored Alice and the rest.

"It was OK. I watched some horror movies," Kate said before asking, "And yours? How was the farm?"

"You have no idea, Kate, you have no idea," I replied, honestly.

"Maybe I can come next time?" Kate asked.

"Not sure I'll get invited again," I said and genuinely meant it.

We laughed, walking inside the school building cheerfully, ready for Miss Eze's class.

Printed in Poland
by Amazon Fulfillment
Poland Sp. z o.o., Wrocław

24838186R00183